"Storyhood As We Know It"
and Other Tales

JOHNS HOPKINS: *Poetry and Fiction*
John T. Irwin, General Editor

"Storyhood As We Know It"

 and Other Tales

Jack Matthews

THE JOHNS HOPKINS
UNIVERSITY PRESS

Baltimore and London

Stories in this collection have appeared in the following periodicals, to which the author and the publisher extend their thanks: *Georgia Review* ("Lovely Things That Should Not Pass Away"), *Iowa Review* ("The Thunder and the Grass"), *Kenyon Review* ("Isaac Trimble's Tale"), *Mid-American Review* ("The King Solomon of the Market District"), *Mississippi Valley Review* ("Poison"), *North American Review* ("A Slightly Different World," "Inviolate on Shawnee Street," and "In the Dark," which was originally published as "In the Neighborhood of the Dark"), *Oxford Magazine* ("Storyhood As We Know It"), *Shenandoah* ("Medicinal Enchantments"), and *Western Humanities Review* ("The Ascension of the *Belasco*").

This book has been brought to publication with the generous assistance of the G. Harry Pouder Fund.

The Johns Hopkins University Press
2715 North Charles Street
Baltimore, Maryland 21218-4319
The Johns Hopkins Press Ltd., London

Library of Congress Cataloging-in-Publication Data

Matthews, Jack.
    Storyhood as we know it and other tales / Jack Matthews.
        p.   cm. — (Johns Hopkins, poetry and fiction)
    ISBN 0-8018-4622-6 (acid-free paper). — ISBN 0-8018-4623-4 (pbk.
    acid-free paper)
    I. Title.   II. Series.
PS3563.A85S76   1993
813'.54 — dc20   92-42477

A catalog record for this book is available from the British Library.

Contents

"Storyhood As We Know It"

and Other Tales

A Slightly Different World

I CAME ACROSS an old photograph the other day and I was surprised to get a glimpse of myself as I was thirty years ago. It's not that I had forgotten about that brief time at the Occam Springs camp when I was one of Al Cory's sparring partners. Those days still seem right in back of me; something I've just emerged from, and haven't had time to figure out yet, completely.

It was the spirit of the picture . . . the look of surprised indignation on my seventeen-year-old face, the wrinkled smile of Al Cory as he looked into the sun (it was an old camera, I remember, with a milky lens, and it wouldn't take pictures in anything but blinding sunlight). In addition, it was the shock of seeing us standing there in a row looking so old-fashioned. Had we really dressed like that? In the picture, I am wearing a large, Scotch golfing cap slanted across my forehead and a turtleneck sweater. Al's wearing a white shirt, open at the neck. I had forgotten so much.

In the middle there is fat Moxie Fisher, Al's manager, dressed in a suit with his vest buttoned and wearing a sailor straw hat that looks clean in the photograph. There is Booboo Haines, the black sparring partner, in a dark turtleneck and light, satiny pegged pants. There is Phil Poldek, another sparring partner, and Herman Weeb, the trainer. All standing there squinting into the sun like men from another, slightly screwy world. As I guess we were, in a way. Thirty years can seem as far away as Sirius or Betelgeuse.

If you were a boxing fan in those days, you would have known about Al Cory. Al had been welterweight champ for exactly eight months when I was twelve years old. He was the first big-timer I had ever seen fight, and watching him that one time had affected my whole life. He was a fast, sharp, clean fighter. From ten rows back you could hear his jab snap a man's chin. When an opponent tried to hit him, he was all elbows and air. He was known as a

3

boxer's boxer, but he never became really famous. He narrowly lost the championship on points in Boston in fifteen rounds. He didn't get a return bout, and then he had manager trouble and finally dropped out of sight. Nobody seemed to care. He was a hard-luck fighter.

I had started fighting in the clubs at the age of fourteen. To me, it was a grand sport. At this time, I had never been badly hurt, and I hadn't knocked many boys out. I was a sharp puncher, but not a deadly one. If I dazed a man, my idea was to step back and let him come out of it. That's the way Al Cory fought, and in my opinion he was the best.

Nevertheless, I admired Gene Tunney greatly. The idea of a boxer being a gentleman and a scholar excited me. I had heard that Tunney read Plato, and one day I got *The Republic* from the city library and read it straight through. A man didn't have to be ignorant and uncouth just because he was a fighter. A man could be anything he wanted.

Those were great days to have heroes, and one of the secrets of having a hero is in having one all to yourself. For me, this was Al Cory. All the wise guys knew about him, said he was a good man, and that was that. But to me, he was an inspiration.

For there was something authentically heroic about Al. He never weighed over 142 pounds, and most of the welterweights he fought came in right at the limit, 147. Al was always gentle-manly in the ring . . . tough, deadly, poised, but gentlemanly. He seldom clinched, never butted, never hit low, never lost his temper. He didn't have to, for he always knew exactly what he was doing.

I didn't know whether he read Plato, or not, but in my deepest heart I felt that such a man as Al Cory had to possess nobility of mind. The qualities I didn't know about in this man I assumed were perfect.

By the time I finished high school, I had already fought five professional bouts in the local clubs and I had won four. One day I was reading the sports page of a newspaper and I saw a small article saying that Al Cory was in training at Occam Springs in his recent comeback. That was all I needed. I didn't have a job, so I hocked my watch for ten dollars and bought a train ticket the next morning. At Occam Springs Moxie told me they didn't need sparring partners, but I said I'd work for nothing except room and board.

Moxie was a thick little man who smoked cigarettes in a silver holder. The cuffs of his shirt were stained amber with dirt. He didn't seem impressed by my attitude, but he told me I could sleep on a cot in the kitchen. After dinner, he had me spar a couple of minutes with Phil Poldek, to see if I could handle myself. Poldek was a bald man with a sad old pugilist's face. I stood back and jabbed while he beat me severely on the shoulders and elbows. In a few minutes, he was wheezing, so he strolled over to the ropes.

"He's okay, Moxie," he said in his hoarse voice.

I felt pretty big by then.

I hadn't met Al Cory yet. Booboo Haines came out, smoking a cigar stub. He was a round-faced little black man with a knife scar at the corner of his mouth. It made half of his face appear to be grinning. Booboo claimed that he had two aortas, although he didn't use that word. He said that a doctor in Kansas City had told him that. Booboo said the doctor told him that was why he never got tired. Later on, though, Moxie told me that if I ever boxed Booboo I shouldn't hit him on the head or he'd go out.

"He ain't like other niggers," Moxie said philosophically, twirling his cigarette holder in his fingers. "He's got this here head injury and you just touch him and he goes cold as a goddamn dead catfish."

"Only . . ." Moxie frowned and spoke very slowly. "Only, don't tell nobody what I said about Booboo. You understand? Because Booboo's funny about his head and we've all agreed not to mention it . . . even to ourselves. We all just pretend his head ain't like that. Understand?"

I said I did.

Later, I found out that Booboo wasn't getting paid, either. I guess Booboo just didn't have anywhere else to go, or anything else to do.

Late that first night, Al Cory came in. I was sitting by the radio playing a game of gin rummy with Booboo. Phil Poldek and Moxie were sitting on the screened-in porch, talking about the old days and smoking.

I was just thinking what an odd training camp this had turned out to be. One of the sparring partners was old and bald and about as sharp as an old woman with a broom, and the other one, Booboo, had a head that was like a light switch . . . you touched it and turned him out.

I hadn't seen Herman Weeb, the trainer, yet. He and Al had gone to town for something.

The gin rummy game went slowly. Every time I laid down a card, Booboo went: "WhooEE!"

This disconcerted me for a while, until I realized it was simply part of Booboo's metabolism, like finger-snapping or clearing your throat.

Suddenly, I realized that Booboo hadn't played for a while. I'd been staring at the card table thinking of this afternoon. I looked up and Booboo was fast asleep, sitting there in the chair. I didn't know what to do, so I got up from the table and went out to the kitchen to my suitcase. There, I got a book out and went back into the front room to read.

A minute later, Moxie and Phil came in, and Moxie, seeing my book, said: "What the hell you got there in your hand?"

"A book," I said.

"Oh," Moxie said, apparently satisfied.

It was late when Al and Herman came in. I recognized Al from his pictures right away, of course. Moxie and Phil had put Booboo to bed, and now they were sitting in chairs reading newspapers.

When the other two walked in, Moxie talked to them for a few minutes, then he waved the back of his hand in my direction and said: "This here's your new sparring partner. Room and board."

Al Cory shook hands with me, and Herman just stared. Herman Weeb, the trainer, was in his mid-thirties, but he looked like an old man. The pale skin of his face was lined and loose. Fifty feet away, his complexion looked like a newspaper. His eyes were tired. He was smoking a strong, tan-colored cigarette.

After the introduction, Al went to bed. I sat there for a while listening to Herman and Moxie talk. Then I thought of Booboo lying up there in bed, asleep.

Earlier I had asked Phil about it.

"He does that all the time," Phil had said.

WE ALL HAD breakfast around the big kitchen table the next morning. Booboo and Al had run a couple of miles, and now they were busy shoveling in large forkfuls of fried eggs and sausage. Moxie wouldn't let Al eat any toast.

"Bread cuts your wind," he explained to me.

When Al left the table for a short nap, Moxie lighted a cigarette and said: "You know, Al's sharper now than he ever was."

"That's the truth," Phil said, shaking his head.

"Sho is," Booboo agreed.

They seemed to be trying awfully hard to convince one another.

At ten o'clock the sparring began. I climbed up in the ring and Herman put a headguard on me. I looked across the ring at Al.

He was standing there, looking at me calmly. There was a big buttonwood tree near the ring, and the bright sunlight shining through the leaves made dark, moving shadows on the canvas as the wind rustled the limbs.

"Okay," Moxie said.

I stepped out and moved to Al's left. He jabbed me a few times and I jabbed. We each countered another lead. Then, I saw Al's right glove drop when he jabbed. In that split second, I wondered if he was trying to kid me.

And yet my reflexes were already whipping my left around in a hard half-hook. It caught Al right on the side of the headgear and knocked him off balance two steps to the side.

When I thought about it later, I came to the conclusion that if he hadn't had the headgear on, Al would've been dazed by the punch sufficiently for a good right cross to put him away.

The realization whirled crazily around my head. I didn't know what to think. But one thing to me was certain: I *couldn't* be in the same class as Al Cory.

WHAT YOU TRYING to prove?" Moxie asked me later that day when we were alone on the porch.

"I wasn't trying to prove anything," I said. "He dropped his right."

Moxie was fastening a cigarette in his holder. I noticed it was one of the tan ones Herman had been smoking last night. The color matched Moxie's dirty cuffs.

"Al can handle himself all right, golden boy. Don't forget, he was champ once. And he's coming back. But get this straight: all you're supposed to do is make a nice moving target for him. It's his timing Al's got to work on."

Moxie walked away. I had wanted to ask him why Al had dropped his right, though. That didn't make any kind of sense.

Right then I heard Booboo call out: "WhooEE!" It sounded as if he was at the ring. I figured somebody must have told a joke, or done something crazy.

I went around the house, and Al and Booboo were hard at it against the ropes. Al must have belted him a good one in the stomach for him to yell out like that.

They didn't know I was nearby, although I'm not sure that made any difference. Anyway, Al suddenly stepped back and slammed a hard right to Booboo's head. Moxie certainly hadn't exaggerated.

Because Booboo turned around in a kind of dance, sparring at air for an instant, then he rolled over and fell on his back. I saw his head jump and his open gloves hit simultaneously at his side. I felt a catch in my throat at the sight. I had never seen a fighter fall so absolutely limp.

I went up to the ring, and Herman was working over him with the ammonia. Booboo came to in a little while and said: "WhooEE!"

Al helped him to his feet, and Phil Poldek put his arm around Booboo's shoulder. I thought I saw a glint in Phil's eye, but I wasn't sure. Nobody was paying any attention to me.

But I had seen too much, and I was sick at heart. I turned around and went into the house.

I BELIEVE IT WAS right after Booboo was knocked out that the picture was taken. It's no wonder I look bitter and that I'm standing as far away from Al Cory as I could get and still be there.

That evening I went to the room where Herman and Phil slept. Phil was in his undershirt, sitting on his bed.

"Where's Booboo?" I asked.

"He's gone to bed," Phil said.

"Is he all right?"

"Sure. Why not? He's been knocked out a thousand times. It just comes natural."

"Did Al know about his head?" I asked.

"Ask Al," Phil said. He reached under the bed and pulled out a newspaper, which he cracked open and started to read.

I went to the kitchen and lay down on my cot. I tried to read from a history book I had bought in a second-hand bookshop, but I couldn't concentrate. Finally, I put the book down and just stared past the sink and out the window. I could see a limb tip from the buttonwood that stood beside the outdoor ring. The leaves trembled silently in the breeze, and a fly buzzed in the space between the screen and the half-opened window.

"He probably saw Booboo open up," I finally said to myself, "and just automatically let the right go. He probably didn't mean to hurt Booboo."

THE NEXT MORNING they found Booboo dead. The two aortas, which he was so proud of, couldn't save him when a blood vessel burst in his brain.

We didn't work out that day. I remember Moxie sitting at the kitchen table, frowning and smoking as he tried to figure out the answers to the questions on the death certificate.

For Booboo's age, he put thirty-seven, although he had no way of knowing. For his hometown, he put St. Louis, but that was a guess, too. Herman sat at the table smoking his dust-colored cigarettes and Phil sat there shuffling a pack of Bicycle cards.

Moxie paused for a minute and stared at Herman. "I sure didn't expect nothing like this to happen, Herman," he said.

"Nobody could have figured on it," Herman said. "He'd been knocked out a thousand times before and nothing like this never happened."

Moxie stared at him a second, shook his head a couple of times and looked down again at the certificate.

The chief difficulty concerned Booboo's name. Nobody knew him by anything other than Booboo, and Herman thought his last name wasn't really Haines, but something like "Paine."

"Now look," Moxie said, frowning."This ain't nothing to joke about. Maybe Booboo wasn't much, but we got to have his right name on this death certificate. So I want you to think hard. As long as he hung around, one of us had to hear *something* about his real name."

Phil laid his cards down on the table and looked out the window, frowning. Herman scratched himself under one armpit and closed his eyes, trying to remember.

"Well?" Moxie said.

"Damned if I ever heard him called anything but 'Booboo,' " Herman said.

"Me neither," Phil said, picking up his cards. He didn't deal the cards; instead, he started looking at them, one by one, as if he'd never seen them before.

"Just write down 'Booboo,' " Herman finally said. That's what he was called, for Christ's sake."

Moxie sighed. "No," he said. "For something like this, there's got to be a better name . . . I mean, a . . ."

Moxie glanced at me questioningly, and I said, "A more formal name."

"That's right," Moxie said. "A more *formal* name. I mean, 'Booboo' was all right for everyday, but. . . ."

Moxie's voice ended like a turned-off radio. The kitchen seemed hot and stuffy. I heard a bird start to sing out at the edge of the woods, and I swear its two-note song reminded me of Booboo going, "WhooEEE!"

I glanced at the others, but apparently they didn't even notice the bird was singing.

Finally, Moxie said, "Well, maybe we should give him a name."

"That's crazy," Herman said.

Suddenly, Moxie got mad. "Goddamn it," he yelled. "You think I should just put down 'Booboo' on this goddamn paper and let him be buried that way? What the hell do you think this is anyway?"

"What'ya getting so mad for?" Herman said. "Jesus, it don't make no difference to Booboo, one way or the other."

"That doesn't have nothing to do with it," Moxie said.

"How about 'Walter,' " Phil said.

Moxie stared at him glumly for a minute, as if he didn't understand what he'd said.

"Or how about 'Robert,' " I suggested. "Maybe 'Booboo was kind of a takeoff on 'Bobby,' which is a nickname for Robert.' "

All of them turned and stared at me. Then Moxie nodded and said, "That sounds pretty good. How do you spell it?"

"Robert?"

Moxie looked at me and nodded. So I spelled it for him, and Moxie said, "That's the way I thought it was spelled, but I wanted to be sure for something like this." Under next of kin, Moxie wrote: "No body."

MOXIE PAID THE coroner's fee, but he refused to cover any of the funeral expenses. So the town of Occam Springs gave Booboo a charity burial, along with a service in a little colored chapel.

We were all there: Moxie, Herman, Phil, Al and myself. There were also newspaper reporters, and they took pictures of Al looking solemn with his sailor straw hat in his hands. I heard Moxie say that this was terrific publicity. The best you could get. "Everybody likes a killer," he said to Herman.

It was incredibly hot in the little chapel. The fat old preacher had a lisp and, straining conscientiously with each word, he sweat harder than anyone else. After the service, at the casket, he shook hands with us and thanked us for coming. Moxie slipped him a couple of dollars. Some women cried, and I found that touching, because Booboo had never come into town. And no one knew him . . . Moxie and the coroner had found that out when they tried to find someone to take responsibility for the body.

Afterward we all walked uptown to a bar. We sat around a table in wire-backed chairs, and Moxie ordered beers and then lighted a cigarette, which was stuck crookedly in the holder.

"Too bad about Booboo," Al said.

Moxie exhaled a powerful jet of smoke through his wide nostrils. "Al," he said, "it was a good clean punch."

Al nodded and sipped his beer.

B ACK AT THE CAMP the air was cooler. We loafed mostly the rest of the day.

Right after dinner I went outside to get some air. I walked down to an old barn and listened to the insects singing in the high grass and watched the hot, red sun sink behind the trees.

I heard a noise behind me and turned to see Phil standing there. His old boxer's face looked troubled. He looked at me a moment out of his folded-down eyes and said: "After this, they ought to draw a good crowd."

"Who do you think will win?" I asked.

"Are you kiddin'?"

I looked at him. "You mean Al's lost it?" I asked.

"Every bit of it," Phil said.

"What about Booboo?"

"What do you mean?" Phil asked.

"Al knew about his head, didn't he? Well, why did he belt him like that?"

Phil turned his head, and I stared at his battered, old pug profile. For a moment he was silent, then he said: "Al belted him, Pal, because he didn't know nothing about Booboo's head. It was Moxie's idea. He figures Al needs confidence and if he got a good head shot in on Booboo, he'd knock him out sure and then he'd figure he had all his old stuff back."

Phil stopped and shook his head back and forth, as if he had water in his ear. Then he thumbed his nose a couple of times and sniffed.

"Pal," he went on, "the old champ couldn't hit nobody, except somebody like Booboo. Hell, I could beat Al the way he is now. Look at the way you hooked him the other day. Anybody could take him. He's half blind, Al is."

I was too surprised at what Phil Poldek told me to say anything. I remember picking up some spikes of dry grass and skinning the seed off them, and staring at what I was doing as if it could clarify what I had just been told.

Phil kept on talking, meanwhile, and I remember that after a while I began to listen. I was a little irritated with Phil's habit of always calling me "Pal" . . . as if he didn't know my name at all. I was better than that, I kept thinking. And yet, Phil called everyone by that name, and poor dead Booboo hadn't really had a name at all. It was almost as if Booboo had been a dog, or a pet monkey.

Phil was talking about an old fighter he had once known who had started drinking shaving lotion.

I interrupted him. "How's come?" I asked. "About Al, I mean."

"About Al?"

"Yes. Why is he doing all this? What's the point of it all?"

"Pal, I'll never tell you. Except, that's all Al knows in this here life. He can't lay bricks, he can't build a house, he can't teach school, he can't be a lawyer. He can't do nothing. He's just like Booboo was, only maybe a little better off. I mean, him and Booboo was just alike under the skin."

"That's awful," I said. "By God, that's awful."

Phil looked at me. "I could tell you were pretty hot about Booboo," he said. "And I was too, until I started to think about it. I mean, pal, that was the right way for Booboo to go. What was left of Booboo, that is. Because most of Booboo had already went. Booboo wasn't no living human being. And Al isn't neither. You see, I had a wife, once, and I know what the difference is.

"This here's a different world, pal."

I SUPPOSE IF a second picture had been taken of the group at Occam Springs, Moxie and Phil and Herman and Al would have all looked the same. But I fancy there would be differences in the picture. There would be a tall, skinny white fighter there in place of Booboo, and on my face, I would like to think, would be the expression of a man, and not that of a boy . . . an older, wiser, sadder expression.

But a calmer one. When you're young, it's good to see your heroes fall, because then you can start creating others. And maybe they'll be better. They're always needed. Now, I take mine from the pages of history; nothing can break them down.

But a second picture of the Occam Springs camp might not have included me at all. For I had made up my mind that I no longer wanted to stay in the strange world of Booboo and Al and Phil.

Moxie, who was a kind of priest of this world, watched me closely when I told him I wasn't staying around anymore.

"Well," he said. "You might make a pretty good fighter someday. Only, you ain't as good now as you think you are. But if you ever decide to give it a try, look me up. They's always room at the top."

Al was knocked out in the third round. I had no reaction whatsoever. I heard some fellows talking about the fight a day or so later and they asked me my opinion. All I told them was that Al had been a great one in his day.

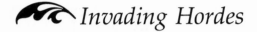 *Invading Hordes*

ON THE MORNING of Saturday, October 26, which was Granger College's Homecoming Weekend, Jerry Lefever awoke and went downstairs to eat breakfast with the other guests of the Bresch Halfway House. On this particular morning, the hosts, Sharon and Rudy Isinger, were serving waffles, Karo Syrup, orange juice, sausage patties, whole milk, McHappy's applesauce donuts, and coffee to the guests. Generally, the menus were prescribed by the terms of Edna Bresch's detailed bequest, as were the daily schedules and treatment, down to and including such considerations as the nomenclature of "hosts" and "guests."

Rudy Isinger came out of the kitchen, where he had fetched the coffeepot. He stood there with the fingers of his right hand slipped under his belt, as if palpating the appendix, holding the pot in his left hand, even though he was right-handed. Lately he had been working hard in an effort to train himself to be left-handed, which was causing him a great deal of trouble and inconvenience.

Now, surveying the six male guests gathered quietly around the large table in the dining room, he asked if they wanted coffee. When none of them answered, he cleared his throat and, holding the coffeepot at left-arm's length, asked about today's Homecoming Game. "Who's going to emerge victorious in this traditional annual rivalry between Granger and Mount Heber?" he asked. When, predictably, no one answered, he continued: "I will remind you that this is a ceremony descended by intricate and tortuous paths from the harvest rituals of yesteryear, complete with fertility goddesses. Is it any wonder that the local citizenry are up in legs?"

No one said anything, but several of the guests looked uneasy. Then, after a moment's silence, an old fellow named Ted Posner mumbled something, but no one bothered to listen, because he was a chronic cataphasic, and even the other guests realized that since he hardly ever said anything comprehensible it was too much work trying to pluck sense out of his word salads. It was almost as hard as having to listen to Rudy Isinger in one of his crazy, left-handed moods. Like this morning.

But with firm control, Rudy splashed coffee in two of their cups, then filled his own, saying, "Or did I misspeak myself, gentlemen? Was something awry? When I said, 'Up in legs,' was I confusing a traditional metaphor, verging upon idiom? Was I, in short, guilty of a solecism? Should I have said 'up in arms'? What *should* I have said? Which is it, gentlemen? I prithee help me, for I cry out to you in my ignorance?"

After saying all this, Rudy fell silent, staring bemusedly at the fingernails on his left hand, first, and then his right.

Posner was a fat old man, bald on top, but with long gray sideburns, dark fleshy lips, and heavy, sagging, bruised-looking wrinkles around his eyes. He always wore dark shirts open at the neck, and rolled his sleeves halfway up his plump, hairless forearms, and held his arms out at the side, as if thrust akimbo by massive shelves of *lattisimus dorsi,* and walked around with the expression of a man who has just finished accomplishing a difficult task involving considerable heavy manual labor, along with a certain *macho* savvy.

"Is the great metropolis of Granger," Rudy Islinger continued, taking his seat again at the head of the table, and pouring his third cup of coffee with a shaking left hand, "home of Granger College, an institution of higher learning serving some 3,123 young scholars, occasionally referred to by the older generation as 'students' . . . is the small city and/or college of Granger about to be invaded by its or their counterparts, the stalwart sons of Mount Heber College? In short, gentlemen, my question is this: Are the invading troops of Mount Heber, wearing the traditional Brown and Gold, about to triumph in their annual assault upon us, the citizens of Granger?"

"That's where we live," Billy Koontz pointed out. "In Granger. Granger is the name of the college, too."

"Thank you for that report, Billy," Rudy said. "Gentlemen, it gives me singular pleasure to inform you that Billy is 100 percent correct. Let's hear it for Billy."

"Today's the Homecoming Game," Jerry Lefever explained to the man next to him, who always ate frowning, with his eyes closed, as if he were moving his jaws in a troubled sleep. Jerry tried to think of his name, but he couldn't remember.

"Ah, the Homecoming Game!" Rudy repeated, nodding.

"I was explaining it to him," Jerry explained to Rudy.

At that instant, Sharon Isinger came into the dining room from the kitchen, put her hands in the pockets of her jeans beneath her white apron, a familiar gesture, and rocked back and forth on her feet as she asked if everybody had had enough breakfast.

"I think we are amply fulfilled," Rudy said judiciously, continuing to blink for a moment after he'd finished speaking.

"I wasn't asking you," Sharon said without looking at him.

"We have just found out the name of the place where we live," Rudy said, "and were discussing the forthcoming event that looms over us, town and gown." He carefully placed all of his silverware on his plate.

Seeing him do this, several of the guests took the cue and did the same; then looked up at him, first, and after that, at Sharon . . . who wasn't noticing, but was wiping her red hands on her apron. Jerry noticed that her eyes looked swollen and sleepy. Then, thinking of this, he looked at the man next to him, whose name he suddenly remembered. It was Ken Ralston. Ken Ralston was still chewing with his eyes closed, and Jerry realized that his eyes didn't really look sleepy because they were closed. Eyes can only look sleepy when they are open.

Sharon nodded and went back into the kitchen, whereupon Rudy stuck his right hand in his belt, lowered his voice, and said, "All right, men. I think you realize that we have our work cut out for us. Anybody catching a glimpse of the enemy's colors, which, I need not remind you, are Brown and Gold, should report to me. Stay alert, those of you who have walking privileges in town."

He stopped a moment, seeming to consider his words. "Upon receiving such reports," he went on, "I shall convey them to our local command posts, as prescribed. Everything according to the book. Any questions, men?"

Jerry thought a moment, then said, "Are these command posts nearby, Rudy?"

Rudy studied Jerry a moment, remembering that he was one of those with a history of pathological literal-mindedness. The only reason he was here, in fact, had to do with his inability to see through the brightness of words to a dark intent. Almost a year ago one of the college groundskeepers had seen Jerry walking by and, in a frolicsome mood, suggested that he put his hand under the apron of the idling lawnmower to see if the blades were moving. Then, before he could stop him, Jerry had amputated three fingers and was standing there saying, "Ouch!" and shaking his mutilated hand so hard he sprayed blood for twenty feet up and down the flower border.

"Never joke with a loony," an old hand at the hospital once told Rudy; and of course he'd been right. But Jerry wasn't a loony. He wasn't really even retarded. Or only marginally so. He had an I.Q. of 78. It was just that he didn't have any imagination, or was incapable of using it, which is pretty much the same thing. So now, Rudy studied the three stubs on Jerry's right hand, resting comfortably on the white tablecloth.

For almost a minute, Jerry sat awaiting an answer. Then he repeated his question. "Do they have any of these command posts nearby, Rudy?"

Rudy inhaled. "No, the command posts are not nearby, but we do have the telephone, remember."

Jerry nodded.

"In fact, Jerry, you have used our telephone upon occasion, if I mistake not."

"I know a lot of numbers," Jerry said.

"Commendable," Rudy said, nodding, "if not exactly command-*post*-able. Hah, hah."

"I know them all," Jerry said.

"The best way to know a lot of numbers," Rudy pointed out, blinking up at the photograph of Henry Bresch, the father of their benefactress, Edna, on the wall, "for the ones you know, if they're to be known at all. I think you should know all of what you know, even if the total of what you know is only a part. Don't you agree?"

Jerry took a sudden deep breath and held it.

"But let us not forget the ominous threat we are faced with today; let us not forget the profound and patriotic duty laid upon us, and the imminent invasion by the sinister battalions of the Brown and Gold."

Hearing Rudy speak this way excited Jerry. He remembered the Homecoming parades of past years; but he had never until this moment realized how much they meant. He had never realized how much was at stake. The thought excited him, and he gripped a spoon so hard, his crippled hand began to hurt.

"Only an hour ago," Rudy said in a low voice, "the Brown and Gold were reported within ten miles of Granger. Some of them are right at this moment entering town."

"Why do they call them the Brown and Gold?" Jerry asked Rudy.

"Nobody knows. It's a secret organization, filled with spies."

"Spies?"

Rudy closed his eyes and nodded.

"Brown and Gold, Brown and Gold," Jerry whispered several times, and Rudy blinked and said, yes, old Jerry had it right, for those were the very colors of the invading hordes of Mount Heber College, last reported within ten miles of Granger, and probably at this very instant infiltrating the outskirts. Rudy talked on and on about the Mount Heber team's invasion, while all of them listened with entranced expressions on their faces . . . although with the guests it was always hard to tell exactly what or how much was happening inside their heads.

Sharon came out of the kitchen, and Rudy fell silent, giving Jerry Lefever a big wink.

"Well, what are you all up to now?" Sharon asked.

"Up to doing our share in cleaning up after breakfast," Rudy said, winking at the butter dish. "Right, men?"

None of them answered, but they got up and accompanied him into the kitchen, where they cleaned their plates and put them into the dishwasher. Rudy watched them quietly, to see that everything went smoothly, while Sharon took her cup of coffee into the rec room so she could watch the morning news in peace. It was one of the few free moments of her busy day.

JERRY HAD FULL walking privileges, and when he went outside, he could feel the excitement in the air. The sunshine on his skin was hot, but in the deep shade of the maple trees it was so cool the air felt almost like stepping in water. White clouds were piled up high in the blue sky, and the breeze rippled the dead leaves that still clung to the trees, and the fallen leaves were blown scratching like thousands of little fingernails along the dark paved street and the red brick sidewalks.

He walked two blocks up Congress Street without seeing any Brown or Gold, then turned and headed down the hill toward the courthouse. A red fire truck passed by, but it didn't have its siren going. A skinny and bearded college boy walked past, wearing a yellow T-shirt and baggy pants. In front of the courthouse, two old men with dark rumpled faces were sitting on a bench, talking. They nodded at Jerry, and he nodded back. Then one of the old men leaned forward with his elbows on his knees and spit a slow gob of tobacco juice down past his clasped hands so that it landed splat on the sidewalk, halfway between his feet. On the other side of the street, there was a boy wearing a brown baseball cap. But Jerry couldn't see any Gold on him.

There were a lot of people on the street. They were walking all around, and a lot of them were college students, for he was getting near the campus. Everybody seemed to be happy and in a hurry. Some of them wore Brown, but none of those people who were wearing Brown also wore Gold. A few wore Gold, but Jerry did not see anything Brown on their clothing.

Why were there so many people, and yet none of them wearing Brown and Gold together? Surely, some of the Invading Hordes had to be around, somewhere. Jerry stopped in the middle of the sidewalk and thought about it; and then the answer came to him: they were hiding their colors, somehow, so nobody could tell who they were.

When this thought came to him, an awful darkness started to grow in his mind. The Brown and Gold might be everywhere, only they wore other colors, so you couldn't tell that they were Brown and Gold at all. It could be anyone, anything. There was no telling what was dangerous and what wasn't. The whole world was this way. The two old men in front of the courthouse didn't understand what was happening. The people walking along the street didn't know what was happening. And none of those college students were aware. They didn't understand anything.

Then, the instant he turned off Court Street onto Union, Jerry got a glimpse of Brown and Gold. It was just a quick flash of the colors in a crowd of people at the far corner. Whoever was wearing those colors had quickly turned the corner, and Jerry walked there as fast as he could without drawing attention to himself. Nevertheless, several people turned their heads and looked at him.

But he got to the corner too late, for whoever was wearing the Brown and Gold had disappeared. Jerry walked down the sidewalk and looked inside several stores, but he didn't see who it was, so he circled back.

Suddenly, a band started playing on the next street. The noise was so loud and unexpected, Jerry jumped. He had forgotten all about the Homecoming Parade. He had been thinking too hard about the Brown and Gold, and now he might miss the parade if he didn't hurry. He saw an old man wearing a gray sweater and cap. It was the kind of cap golfers in old-fashioned movies wear; and when the old man looked at him, Jerry asked him where the parade was, and the old fellow just stared at him a moment, then pointed toward the next street, which was called College Street.

Of course, that was where the sound was coming from. But Jerry was afraid that if he went down one street in the direction of the music on College Street, the band would march down another street and end up on Court Street, after he had left. He might miss the band entirely. If you went one way toward people who were moving, they might come back to where you had just been by a different street, and you would never see them.

But he had to take the risk. He walked swiftly toward the music. It got louder and louder. Ahead of him, on College Street, there was a crowd of people standing. He could see that they were all looking one way, watching the parade that was coming toward them. Then Jerry saw a huge white float moving slowly in his direction. There were pretty girls sitting on it, and they were smiling and waving at the crowd. Suddenly, the music stopped, so all he could hear was the sharp clicking of drumsticks and the pounding of marching feet. Ahead of the float there were a number of antique cars, and one of them honked a horn, going "Ooh-gah, Ooh-gah," at the people lining the street, who were applauding and calling out to the cars.

When Jerry reached the crowd, the float was turning the corner, and one of the girls looked right at him and waved. She was a pretty girl, with long blonde hair, and her eyes looked right at him for an instant before she looked at somebody else. The float looked like a big birthday cake as it glided slowly and silently away from them.

The band started playing again, louder than ever, because it was getting closer. There was another float, with Halloween witches on it, but Jerry didn't really look at this one, because right behind it, for the first time he saw the band marching quickly, with everyone in step and playing so loud it almost hurt his head . . . and every single person in the band was wearing Brown and Gold!

AFTER THAT, HE was terrified and wandered for hours. By the time he got home, the shadows were long and dark, and it was getting very cold out. Sharon wasn't in the house, but Rudy was. He was standing on a short stepladder in the kitchen hallway, putting a bulb into the socket.

Seeing Jerry, he said, "You know, she's been asking me to put a fresh bulb in here for about eight years, now, so I think it's time I got to it, don't you?"

Jerry nodded.

"Eight years is long enough. Right?"

Jerry nodded again.

"Strike while the iron is hot—that's my motto."

"I saw them," Jerry said.

"Ah," Rudy said, shaking the burnt-out bulb next to his head and listening to the tinkling sound it made. "You did, did you?"

"A whole bunch of them in the band. Every one of them."

Rudy climbed down off the stepladder and folded it up. Then Jerry followed him as he carried it into the pantry and hung it on a rusty spike on the wall. "So you saw the band playing. Well, thanks for the report, Jerry, but it's too late. We lost, 20 to 3. The evil invaders have triumphed over the forces of righteousness. Where've you been, anyway?"

"I couldn't help it," Jerry said.

"Really? Well, not to worry. That's the way it goes sometimes. I'm sure you did all you could."

"I did."

"It's been my observation that what's past is past. Moral philosophy begins with that axiom." Rudy closed one eye and scratched his head. "Or *ends* with that axiom. One of those. Or something."

Jerry frowned at the floor, then followed Rudy as he walked through the living room into the front hallway, where Billy Koontz was sweeping the floor. Rudy told Billy to be sure to remember to use the dustpan and pour the dust that he gathered in the dustpan into the garbage can in back.

"I saw them," Jerry said. "But I didn't know what to do."

Rudy stared at Jerry a moment, then offered him a stick of peppermint chewing gum. But Jerry didn't take it. Blinking, Rudy leaned backward with his hands under his belt. "Now, isn't that something," he said. "And here I was holding you solely responsible. I don't know what I'll tell the Command Posts."

"They all wore Brown and Gold," Jerry said, "every single one of them. And nobody else even noticed."

Rudy nodded seriously. "Do you know something? That's the way it always happens."

"I was going to call here, but do you know what happened?"

"No, what?"

"All of a sudden I couldn't remember the number."

Rudy frowned. "But you've called here before. I remember the time you called and talked to Sharon, asking if she wanted anything at the store."

"That's when I was at Becker's Carry-Out."

"Yes, I remember well."

"But today I forgot. And they just marched right on by. But I don't think they saw me."

"Well, that's good. But, hey, Jerry, don't worry too much— because those people you saw weren't the team."

Jerry looked at him, but he wasn't sure he could believe what Rudy had just told him. Suddenly everything had gotten very strange once more, and it was hard to know exactly what was happening.

ALL OF THEM watched television that evening, just as if it had been any other night. Sharon came in and sat with them, watching several of the shows with them, while Rudy sat there talking in a low voice, saying things that didn't make any sense at all. It was hard to tell what he was saying, and who he was talking to, exactly. Jerry had noticed that sometimes they hardly paid any more attention to Rudy than they did to Ted Posner.

When it was almost ten-thirty, which was bedtime, the television set was turned off, and Jerry went out to the kitchen and got a glass of water. Sharon called out, saying there was apple juice out there in the refrigerator if he wanted a glass, but he said he was just thirsty for water.

He drank half a glass, and then started back through the dining room toward the front room. Someone had left the light on, and just before he reached the front room, where they were all seated around the television set, Jerry looked up and noticed Henry Bresch's framed photograph on the wall. He had often noticed this photograph, because there was one just like it in all the rooms, and even in the front hallway. The photographs showed an old man, with a big angry pale face and wet-looking dark hairs combed sideways in stripes across his bald head.

While he was standing there, Rudy came in and said, "Well, Jerry, I see you are studying the face of the man responsible for all this. Along with the necessary intermediation of his daughter, of course."

"That's Edna Bresch's father," Jerry said.

Rudy narrowed his eyes and looked at the picture. "The very man to whom I was referring. Do you understand how he's responsible for our being here?"

Jerry shook his head no.

"Well," Rudy said, rubbing his hand through his hair and blinking, "one dark night or perhaps gloomy day, he sired Edna Bresch and when she grew up, he died and left her a bagful of money so that she could live a long and frugal existence and eventually instruct the courts by means of her will that her accumulated wealth should go into the purchase and remodeling and subsequent upkeep of the Bresch Halfway House, where you and I are now living . . . a place named for her father, whose image is at this very moment before us, gazing back in silent speculation upon what . . . well, never mind. Suffice it to say, here we are."

Jerry nodded. "He's dead."

"Yes, and I predict he will remain dead for a long time."

"Now you're teasing me."

"Well put," Rudy said, clapping Jerry on the shoulder. "But what do you think old Henry Bresch would say if he were alive and knew that. . . ." Rudy stopped and leaned to the side, so that he could see into the front room, where Sharon and the rest of the guests were sitting and watching television. Then Rudy continued, whispering, "What do you think he would say if he knew that the Brown and Gold had finally infiltrated our community?"

"What?"

"Shhhh!" Rudy said. "We'll talk more about it later."

At that instant, Sharon appeared in the entranceway and said, "What are you two up to?"

"We're up to no good," Rudy said, and Sharon said that was just what she was afraid of. Then she went into the kitchen.

"Do you know what they used to call Henry Bresch?" Rudy asked, still keeping his voice low.

"No, what?" Jerry said.

"*Colonel* Bresch. That's what they called him."

"Was he a colonel?" Jerry asked.

"Why do you think," Rudy said slowly, blinking heavily, "they would call him 'Colonel Bresch' if he wasn't a colonel?"

"I don't know," Jerry said.

"I thought you knew he was a colonel, Jerry."

"I did," Jerry said nodding.

Then Sharon came back into the dining room from the kitchen, carrying a little brown ceramic tray with three matching brown ceramic mugs of apple juice on it; and she gave them both a suspicious look as she walked past, heading for the living room, where the television set had been turned up too loud by Ted Posner, who not only couldn't speak very well, but couldn't hear very well, either.

Later, Jerry heard her ask Rudy, "Why were you two looking at her daddy's photograph?"

"We were just looking," Rudy said.

"Yes, but what were you talking about?"

"We were talking about lymphoma."

"He didn't die of lymphoma; he died of a heart attack."

"*Everyone* dies of a heart attack, if you think about it."

"I don't want to think about it," Sharon Isinger said, "and I think you're absolutely, pathologically, terminally nuts."

"An interesting thought," Rudy said. "Or thoughts."

All the time they were talking, Jerry imagined that Rudy was blinking.

At that moment, it came to him: Rudy was one of the guests, too. He was just pretending to be Sharon's husband. Because Rudy was one of them.

And yet, Rudy knew something terribly important. He was always trying to tell Jerry, personally, about it. He had a message to give him. It was something that Sharon didn't know, even if she was a host and one you could depend upon a lot more than upon Rudy, who was hard to understand most of the time. Lately, it was getting harder and harder to figure out what he was trying to tell you.

But Rudy knew something. It was obvious he had a message of some kind, and it was very important. Jerry was certain of the fact.

THE NEXT MORNING after breakfast, Jerry came into the kitchen and saw Rudy leaning against the counter and drinking a glass of water. Rudy's eyes were red, and he was staring at Jerry as if he couldn't quite recognize him. This made him uncomfortable, because Rudy didn't speak, but simply stood there staring at him. Then his lips started moving silently as if they were whispering. The glass of water he was holding had ice cubes in it, and a lemon. Nobody else was there. Rudy had just finished the breakfast dishes, with Billy's help, since it was Billy's turn today.

Jerry had come out to get a glass of water, but now he wasn't so sure he wanted one. Because something was wrong; there was something different about Rudy.

After staring at him a moment, Rudy took another sip from his glass, and said, "Are you thirsty, Jerry?"

Jerry shook his head no. He wanted to leave the kitchen, but the way Rudy was acting made him feel funny, and he didn't know how to leave without causing trouble or maybe hurting somebody's feelings. It was almost as if Rudy wanted to speak with him, but didn't know what to say.

"Have you noticed," Rudy said finally, smacking his lips and blinking at the same time, "that there is no framed photograph of Colonel Henry Bresch on any of the kitchen walls?"

"What?" Jerry asked.

"I refer," Rudy said, pausing to belch, "to the fact that. . . ."

He stopped and walked quietly to the door to the pantry, and then to the door to the dining room. "Where's Sharon?" he asked.

"I think she's upstairs seeing that the beds are all made right and that everybody's cleaning up their rooms."

"Cleaning up their rooms," Rudy repeated, nodding.

It was then that Jerry noticed something strange. Rudy wasn't blinking when he talked.

"I feel I am at the beginning," Rudy said, "of the creation of a myth. You mustn't ever tell Sharon, though. Do you promise?"

Jerry nodded.

Rudy clapped him on the shoulder. "I knew I could depend on you, Jerry, my friend. You and I share something in common. We are both geniuses, each in our, which is to say *his*, own way. Do you follow? No, of course you don't. But you did awfully well the other day, my friend. I am speaking of the Brown and Gold. The marching band of the enemy."

"What about them?" Jerry asked.

"Do you remember what I told you about Henry Bresch?" Rudy asked.

"He was a colonel."

Rudy nodded and belched again. Then he drank from his glass. "Jerry, I am going to a place that is called Bonkers. Not Yonkers, which is in New York State, but Bonkers. I wanted you to be the first to know. Sharon will be one of the last to know, because she has so many problems of her own, poor sweet woman, that she can't notice what's happening right under her nose. Assuming, that is, that I am capable of happening under her nose, even though I am five inches taller than Sharon is."

"What?"

"What I am speaking of, my friend, is *insidious infiltration!* You don't know what insidious infiltration is, do you, Jerry?"

Jerry shook his head no.

"Well, among other things, it is hard to say. Try it some time. 'Insidious infiltration. Insidious infiltration.' But never mind that. Because, the fact is, you *do* know what it is, Jerry. You have within the past two days become one of the world's greatest experts on the subject. I speak of the little world, of course, rather than any of the larger ones. All theoretical, of course. Do you follow? Of course not. Nor would I respect you if you did. But the point is this, my friend. I have something to confide in you. Would you like to know what it is?"

"Yes."

"Jerry, I am distressed to inform you that the Brown and Gold have triumphed. I am not speaking of the game alone; I am speaking of a final and negotiated peace, with closely articulated terms of surrender. I am speaking of Appomattox, Jerry old chap. Edna Bresch's old daddy would understand what I'm saying. It takes a certain mentality, you understand. Or do you? But never mind that. Jerry, I am concerned about you. Do you know why?"

"Why?"

"Because I know you are still troubled about the other day. You feel that you let the Brown and Gold slip through your fingers. You feel responsible for their victory. Rather, you feel responsible for the terrible loss suffered by Granger College. Please don't interrupt, for I have much more to tell you, but I shall make it brief. *Multum in parvo,* old buddy."

In the far distance, a siren sounded. Rudy and Jerry paused to listen for a moment.

Then Rudy inhaled and began talking again. "Anyway, the essence of my message is as follows: the Brown and Gold have taken over. They have triumphed. How do we know? Can you answer that, Jerry?"

Slowly, Jerry shook his head no.

"That's the question: How can we be sure? How can we know? Well, the way we can know is this, my friend: we know because, *wherever you look, you cannot see any sign of the Brown and Gold.* This is the surest indication, old friend. We know they have triumphed because they don't reveal themselves. When something is not evident, it is most powerful. Do you realize how monstrous it all is? *Nothing's changed!"*

At that moment, Sharon came downstairs and walked into the kitchen, looking at both of them. She breathed quietly at them for a moment, then said, "Jerry, you haven't made your bed."

"We are aware," Rudy said slowly, "but we have been talking. If I had not had something to discuss with my old friend Jerry, here, he would have been upstairs making his bed."

She stared for a moment at the glass in his hand. "For God's sake, Rudy, vodka at *this* hour?"

"Colonel Bresch would understand."

"Whoever he is."

"His photograph surrounds us. That is to say, copies thereof. He was the father of the woman who established our little microcosm. He was the eponym of our establishment."

"Why don't you quiet down and sober up."

"Down and up, is it?"

"Whichever direction you take to get sober."

"I am as far sober as any sober man would ever wish to be."

"Sure."

"All is in order. Nothing is amiss. Take my word for it, my dear."

"I'll take your word for it!" she uttered bitterly, then went striding into the dining room.

"Jerry," Rudy said, rattling the ice cubes in his glass, "you have learned a great and subtle human lesson, and I congratulate you. Do you know what you have learned? Answer me: Do you?"

"No."

"Good. But for Christ's sake, whatever you do, don't ever mention it to Sharon, because she is a woman, and no woman could ever understand. But I will say this, Jerry, and don't ever forget it for as long as you live: it is they who have made us what we are, for better or for worse. Why, compared to them, the Brown and the Gold are as nothing. Do you understand?"

Jerry nodded.

"Ah," Rudy said, sipping from his glass. "I feared as much. God bless us, every one!"

The King Solomon of the Market District

O F ALL THE torments Gordon suffered, the worst was the mystery of Goldfarb's success as a cut-rate shoe tycoon. He often complained of it to Meyer Leftus and me, and we had to listen. Gordon was the manager of Goldfarb's home store, located in an ex-brewery made out of pink brick in the old Market District. A produce warehouse stood on one side of the store, and a noodle factory on the other.

This was during the 1930s, and I had been hired part-time over Gordon's bald-headed nephew. Gordon claimed that Goldfarb had made the decision because I was a college student, majoring in Greek. To Goldfarb this meant I was a scholar, and I deserved the job, even though I was a goy and Gordon's bald nephew was a miserable son of a bitch who needed experience.

"But who doesn't need experience?" Gordon asked, shrugging and lifting his hands in a parody of what he expected me to expect. Gordon liked to argue my side of the case, even though it made him miserable. Gordon was a complicated human being, and his life wasn't easy.

He was the store manager and understood duplicity as well as how to throw his weight around. He asked questions constantly; his world trembled in complicated balances. He was a gambler and often asked us personally why he didn't give it up. "Gamblers are suckers," he muttered darkly. "Statistics prove it."

Once he said this to me between sales, and when I didn't respond in any way, he drifted off. But a few minutes later, I heard him back in the shoe racks, throwing odd pairs of remaindered carpet slippers around. Nobody was back there with him, but he distinctly said, "Still, you got to do something to climb outside the box you're in!" Maybe he was still talking to me. It was hard to know.

Gordon's face showed it. He had large bulbous wet eyes, socketed in dark pouches of flesh. Often his popped-out eyes were bloodshot, and I once suggested to Meyer Leftus that Gordon might be a drinker; but Meyer swore this wasn't the case. He said Gordon was too dedicated to his misery to seek such a cheap out as booze. Since Meyer was a distant cousin, I figured he might be right. Meyer was also a college student, majoring in psychology. Old Goldfarb liked for his shoe clerks to be educated, even scholarly, and during the 1930s this wasn't too much to ask.

Mr. Goldfarb had four stores, but the Market District Store was the original one, and the old man had a natural fondness for it. He spent as much time there as at all the other stores together. This was another burden for Gordon.

It wasn't that Goldfarb was difficult or nasty in any way. He wasn't. He was a tiny old man who always dressed immaculately. An old-world dandy. A natty, erect little Jew with Continental manners and a formidable accent. He wore gray spats and carried a rosewood cane with silver inlays. Since his feet required a boy's-size shoe, he had his pointed-toe oxblood cordovans specially made and shipped in. Sometimes he would pass out cigars to Meyer and me, saying, "Enjoyment is mit people, not the other way with makes enjoyment."

The first time I heard this, I thought I'd heard it wrong. The little old man's expression was that of shrewd benignity. I stood there holding the cigar while Goldfarb eased away, tapping his cane along the carpet runners of the middle aisle.

"You see what I mean?" Gordon asked in a low voice, surprising me because I hadn't known he was that near.

"What's that?" I said.

Gordon nodded. "You got it," he said.

"Got what?"

"You got 'What's that?'; that's what."

I pounded the side of my head with the heel of my hand, the way you do when you have water in your ear. "I don't know what you're talking about," I said.

Gordon sighed. "What you mean is, you don't know what *he's* talking about. I ask you honestly—you're a college student and studying the classics and all that—did what he said just now make anything like sense to you?"

"I figured I didn't quite hear it right."

"No, that's what everybody figures. They figure it's *their* fault, but it isn't. You heard right. It's the old man."

"Pretty strange," I said.

"Strange doesn't do it," Gordon said, closing one eye. "Strange doesn't come close. The old bird is 100 percent crazy, and he's been that way all his life. Now you tell me something."

"What?"

"You tell me how that old son of a bitch got to own this little cut-rate store empire when he can't speak a straight sentence in the English language."

"Beats the hell out of me."

"Beats the hell out of anybody who pauses for a moment to think about it," Gordon said, darkly.

"He's sure a funny little old duck, though."

"Funny I don't see. Grotesque and impossible, yes. But funny, never."

"That's sort of what I meant."

"You listen to him for ten years, and you won't hear two sentences that add up to anything. How does he do it? Tell me. How *did* he do it? Not two sentences in a row that make sense. Once that old bird gets beyond hello and good-by, he's in trouble with the English language. But what does he do? He builds this little goddamn cut-rate shoe empire. Four stores, no less, and he couldn't tell a stranger in straight English what he does for a living."

Gordon's first name was Frantz, but I never heard anybody call him that. Meyer Leftus called him "Gord"; otherwise, he was just "Gordon" to people, including his wife, who dropped in one evening to complain in a loud coloratura about their furnace. Her hair was dyed red, and she'd plucked all her eyebrows out to emphasize her resemblance to the movie actress Miriam Hopkins.

Gordon had severe headaches worthy of his exophthalmic glare, and no wonder. He took everything to heart, especially the contrast between Goldfarb's success in business and his inability to communicate. "It's not just accent," he mumbled; "it's deeper than accent. Accent don't hurt you in this business in this neighborhood. Accent is accepted. But with the old bird, there's something else at work. It's deeper."

It was too bad Gordon didn't have a sense of humor, Meyer Leftus often said to me; and I agreed, saying that Gordon was the only Jew I'd ever seen who didn't have even the beginnings of a sense of humor.

Meyer nodded and said, "It's too bad for him, is all I got to say. A sense of humor would help in this business. Goldfarb's not such a mystery if you think about him with a sense of humor."

That was a little ambiguous, but I kind of saw what Meyer meant and agreed with him.

A few days later, the old man came up to us and patted our shoulders. He said, "What's it mit here how it's doing?"

Meyer had been waiting for him and shot back: "Plenty of what, like it goes."

Mr. Goldfarb's smile unfocused a moment, but then he nodded and walked on, carrying his cane like a rifle over his shoulder.

After the old man was out of sight behind a rack of Ladies' Specials, I told Meyer that it had been pretty risky for him to answer like that.

Meyer shook his head. "The way I figure it is, if that's an honest way for the old man to talk, he's crazy and wouldn't know the difference how I answered. But if he's putting us on, he might enjoy the joke being turned back on him."

"Anyway," I said, "that was a nervy thing to do."

"It's a language Gordon ought to learn," Meyer said.

THE HOME STORE in the Market District stayed open until nine o'clock at night. I had worked there all summer and into the autumn. The fall quarter was halfway gone when Meyer Leftus phoned in to ask Gordon if he could have the night off. He said he had to study.

Gordon was surprised, but gave his consent. As luck would have it, there were hardly any customers. It was a cold and bitter evening for that time of year. Gordon seemed miserable; I think he would have preferred enough business so that Meyer's absence would have hurt us.

To make matters worse, Goldfarb was prowling the aisles. Along about seven-thirty, Gordon came up to me and said, "Christ, what a night! Not one customer and here we are standing around like a lot of goddamn turnip trees!"

"Turnips don't grow on trees," I said.

Gordon straightened his tie angrily. "That's why Goldfarb hired you? You know about Greek and Latin and whether turnips grow on trees? Let me ask you a confidential question: who gives a shit?"

I shrugged. "I just thought I'd let you know."

"I was happier not knowing," Gordon said lugubriously. "For all I care, turnips grow in the air, or come down the chimney like Santa Claus. Who cares about turnips?"

These complaints were devoid of both malice and point, so I

only half listened. But then Gordon's voice changed, and he spoke more softly. "And what makes it worse is the old man. I can't stand it when the old bird roosts in here and there isn't any business!"

He drifted off, then, and I sat down on a fitting stool and began to fiddle with two shoehorns. I was figuring that if you filled a white sock with clay and stuck two shoehorns in the right places, the result would be a rabbit's head with shoehorns for ears.

I was wondering what Gordon would have done if I'd mentioned this to him.

Finally, I got up and walked down an aisle of summer specials we hadn't gotten around to storing yet, and stood before the plate glass window in front. The street was virtually deserted. It had gotten colder and the wind had picked up. Bits of newspaper, dead leaves and flecks of sawdust from the warehouse blew down the sidewalk past our lighted window. I could smell the hot metallic odor from the radiators.

I stared at the old gutters in front, dotted with bits of cabbage leaf, an empty Camel's pack smashed into the brick, and the stiffened, blackened corpse of an old cloth glove. Somewhere in the ladies' shoes I heard Goldfarb say, "It's not the habit, but think where you go might help possibilities." At least, that's what it sounded like. God knows what the reference might have been. There was a Mrs. Ruby who worked over there, and I supposed he was talking to her, although I couldn't hear her say anything. But what could she have answered to something like that, anyway?

I was young in those days, and interested in all the variety that life afforded. I read a great deal beyond the required work for my college courses, and I yearned for deep conversation. Dos Passos and Sherwood Anderson were proletarian saints in my view. The filth of the Market District impressed me aesthetically: if it was dirty, it was not sterile; if it was sordid, it was vital and real.

All about me I fancied I could feel the pulse beat of the life of our time, filled with authentic men and women. I was drunk with the idea of plenitude, not to mention Reality; and I thanked God for the Jews, Negroes, Italians, Hungarians and hillbillies whose feet I measured tirelessly. I was inspired by a sense of obscure significance beneath the drab configurations of despair and ignorance all about me. I read omnivorously, passionately, far into the night, sometimes getting only three or four hours sleep. I was seriously considering the principles of Technocracy, which seemed to me the most rational form of government ever conceived.

O N THIS PARTICULAR evening, as I stood at the window watching discarded bits of the city's reality blow past, I was suddenly intrigued, not to say astonished, to see two one-legged men approach. They were arguing violently. Their crutches moved in step with choreographic precision. One, a short, brawny man dressed in a shabby navy blue suit coat, was looking straight ahead. The tall skinny one swung his head in circles and blinked his eyes spasmodically behind steel-rimmed glasses.

They stopped in front of Goldfarb's door, still arguing. I couldn't hear them, but in pantomime, their talk seemed corrosive.

Finally, they reached some kind of stern agreement and entered. I glanced back at Gordon and saw that he was gazing at the two men in a spasm of meditative surprise. Gordon habitually saw people in terms of sales, and these two men presented an obvious problem.

But even then, I think, he'd taken in one important fact: these two fellows had different legs missing. Between them, they had the feet for one pair of shoes.

The short, stocky one had his leg off at the knee, and I'd noticed he worked the stump up and down when he moved, as if he hadn't been able to break it of its walking habit. Beneath his tawdry blue suit coat, he wore wrinkled and grimy trousers of sailcloth gray. His face was ruddy and masked in black whiskers approximately a quarter of an inch long. His eyes were black and feverishly alert. His skin was red and raw-looking, as if it had been sand-papered by wind and grit.

The taller, delicate-looking fellow had no left leg at all. It had been carved off right up next to his groin. He was a sallow man, and his skin looked dirty. He wore a cheap, double-breasted suit, and his thin, straw-like hair was combed nearly back over a balding head. His eyes behind thick glasses looked bleary, disturbed and suspicious. The short, swarthy man called him Walt.

"Walt," he said as they swung around into seats side by side, "I'll tell you what: just let me handle it."

Walt breathed audibly through his nose as he glared at me. He had the look of a sick and angry boy.

"May I help you, gentlemen?" I asked.

"Show us a pair of brown oxfords for about a dollar," the swarthy one said. "Or maybe less."

"Yes, sir. What size do you wear?"

"Ten B," Walt said.

"Nine and a half E," the swarthy one said.

"That's too damned short and wide," Walt said. "That's more like a horseshoe than a shoe fit for a man!"

The swarthy one pounded his crutch against the floor and growled, "Dammit, C's too narrow!"

"Do you gentlemen both intend to wear this one pair of shoes?" I asked.

"Naturally," Walt said.

Somewhere in the back room, Mr. Goldfarb said, "No more what they don't make in this size we're full of."

I was beginning to get into the spirit of things. I liked the way these two fellows handled their problems, so I decided to treat them right. I gestured widely with a shoehorn and said, "Would you both mind taking off your shoes?"

Their present shoes were a pair, I could see that, even though they were in sorry shape. They scarcely had enough substance to hold them together. You could tell that these fellows had been friends for a long time.

When they removed their shoes, I saw that their dirty socks were also pairs, down even to the holes through which their dirty toenails shone like soiled pearls. The stink was palpable, but I reminded myself that this was part of life, part of reality. The whole package.

I examined both shoes, trying to find out what size they were.

"What's the matter?" the one named Walt said. "Something wrong?"

"He's just trying to find out what size they are," the short, swarthy one said. "Ain'tcha?"

I looked at him a moment and nodded. Then I went back to a desk in the back room, where we kept inventory records. Gordon had followed me. "What's up?" he asked. "What's the problem?"

"I can't make out the size in those shoes," I said.

"What difference does it make?" Gordon whispered, opening his eyes so wide he looked terrified.

"They don't agree on the size," I told him.

Gordon turned around and leaned far to the side so that he could see the two fellows. When he turned back, he said, "You know something? Twenty-five years in this business, and so help me, this is a first. A million to one shot. Maybe more!"

"There's a first for everything, they say."

Gordon clapped his hand over the back of his neck and closed his eyes, saying, "Listen to the philosopher." Then he leaned over again and peered out at the two one-legged fellows, as if he could hardly believe they were really there.

"This is one for the books," he finally said with a conclusive air. "Go back out there and sell them their one pair of shoes. If I had a camera, I'd take a picture. Nobody will ever believe this. Would you, if you hadn't seen it?"

I thought a moment and then shook my head.

"Well," Gordon said, "what's the delay? Get back out there and take care of them."

"I can't find the magnifying glass," I said, shuffling the drawers.

"What's the magnifying glass for? To see the size of a lousy pair of shoes?"

"They're customers, aren't they?"

"Use the shoe sizer, for Christ's sake!"

"You wouldn't say that if you'd seen their feet!"

That stopped him, so Gordon got busy, and before long he found the magnifying glass in a cream leather woman's slipper that somebody had put on a shelf.

"Now you tell me how this magnifying glass got in there!" he said, but I was too busy to answer, because I wanted to get back out onto the showroom and make this sale. I didn't want to hear Gordon quote odds on a magnifying glass ending up in a woman's cream leather slipper. If I made this sale I would do something Gordon had never seen done.

I picked up the shoes one by one, but still couldn't quite make out the figures on the instep. Then the obvious solution came to me: I took one of them over to a box and lifted out a pair of tens, which seemed a little short, and then I got a pair of ten and a halfs, which seemed just the right length.

Gordon and I had been too excited to think straight.

I went back to the two fellows and said, "These shoes you've been wearing are ten and a halfs. Probably B width. Were they all right?"

"Too long," the swarthy one said.

"Them's tens," Walt pointed out sullenly.

"Nine and a half!"

"Them's tens," Walt said.

"They're too goddamn long and narry," the swarthy one said.

I turned toward Gordon and raised my eyebrows. He was swinging his key chain, using all his will power to keep from interfering in a clerk's sale. This was one of Goldfarb's rules, and the old man was somewhere on the premises, maybe watching us.

"Well, I'll see what I can do," I said.

I went to the miscellaneous table and got a pair of ten C oxfords which cost ninety-eight cents.

"How do these look?" I asked, holding them up.

"Let's try 'em on," Walt said.

"What size are they?" the swarthy one said.

"Ten C."

The man pounded his crutch on the floor. "Too goddamn long and narry," he said.

"They'll fit fine," I said.

"No they won't!"

The two of them started arguing again, so I stood back and waited.

"Does there seem to be some trouble here?" Gordon finally asked in a loud, official voice, approaching me.

I explained the situation, just as if he hadn't known all about it. He stood there looking thoughtful.

"Well, all I can see is that we give them what they want," Gordon said. "Goldfarb's aims to please. That's our motto, and we live up to it about fifty to one. Let's create a pair especially for these two fellows. Ten C for this gentleman, and nine and a half E for this other gentleman here."

"But what will we do with the odd shoes left over?" I asked.

"Why, we'll just keep them on hand in case we have another situation like this. Might be that some day there'll be two other gentlemen who need a ten C and a nine and a half E, just like these gentlemen here. Only on the other feet. In fact, if we give these two gentlemen good service, it'll be good advertising. Excellent advertising, in fact. And maybe they'll return when they need another pair."

I stood there scratching my head over this nonsense, while the two one-legged customers stared at Gordon in considerable fascination.

"Just come with me," Gordon said, tugging at my sleeve.

When we got back into the stacks, Gordon handed me the pair of ten C's I had just shown them.

"Here. Tell them one of these is a ten C and the other's nine and a half E. They won't know the difference. Seven to five says the dumb schmucks can't read, either one of them."

I nodded and went back to them.

I sat down on my stool and was about to fit the shoes on their feet, when I looked up and saw Mr. Goldfarb standing there looking at us. He was small enough that he might have been standing unnoticed behind a tennis shoe display, picking up on everything that had gone on.

I think it was right then I realized this was going to be a remarkable evening. As if fitting two one-legged men with one pair of shoes wasn't enough, here was Mr. Goldfarb watching the whole business out of a very thoughtful if inscrutable expression. I half dreaded seeing him at any time, because I couldn't figure out what he was saying, and I didn't know what to answer when he asked a question.

Now he was intent upon the two one-legged customers. He held his hands clasped behind his back as he came forward, staring at the new pair of shoes I was trying to fit on the two men. His cane was under his arm.

Finally, in a soft voice, he said something like, "A shoe sprit with color sometimes, nu?"

"Yes sir," I said.

The two one-legged fellows frowned at me.

"Mit style in de way, what?"

"What?" Walt said, turning his head around.

Politely, Mr. Goldfarb gestured his cane in my direction, indicating that he had been addressing me.

"What?" I said.

"Left dere is two pairs, like mit customers?"

"I guess so," I said earnestly.

Apparently that was the right answer, because Mr. Goldfarb smiled, tapped me on the shoulder with his cane, and went away.

"What was he saying?" Walt asked in a low voice, frowning down into my face.

"It was a foreign language," I said.

"Hell, I *know* that. But what language was it?"

"Russian," I said. "Or maybe Turkish."

That seemed to ease his spirit a little, so he went back to the shoe, which he said fit pretty well.

"It ought to," I said, "considering the trouble we went to."

After the two of them paid and left, Gordon came up and stood beside me. We both stared out into the darkness.

"An episode I will never forget," Gordon said.

"Was Mr. Goldfarb pleased?"

Gordon turned to me. "What's that you say?"

"Mr. Goldfarb. Was he pleased with how we handled it?"

Gordon shook his head. "Hard to say what the old bird thinks. I'd guess he's pleased. But whatever is is a constant mystery."

"You mean you don't *ever* understand what he says?" I asked.

Gordon raised his eyebrows. "What's to understand? It's a language limited to one person. What use is a language like that? You're a scholar, studying languages and things like that. You explain it to me, will you?"

NATURALLY I DIDN'T try to explain it, but I thought about it often. And what I thought about mostly was not the two one-legged men, but Goldfarb himself. I kept coming back to his mysterious role in the whole business. And Gordon's tacit admission that he didn't understand Goldfarb either.

It took a little time, and some close attention to the old man's strategies as he paced about the store, gazing upon his merchandise and employees . . . speaking seldom, but when he did speak, uttering things that seemed oracular in the way of some dark, barely conceivable significance.

Once, in a moment of enthusiasm, I considered the possibility that Herakleitos had talked like this.

It was much later that I solved the matter to my own satisfaction. I concluded that the old man intended it all this way. Everything. It was a grand strategy. Maybe at one time he'd been lucid enough to make things work, but then he'd outgrown such devices.

Let the accountants communicate; Goldfarb would rule! Assume a position of authority, along with an innocent air of being one ahead of others, and you will, I concluded, be able to manipulate the world, providing you don't give things away by speaking clear sense to people who really, when you stop to think about it, want so much more than that.

If Gordon had been around when I came to this conclusion, I would have enjoyed telling him about it. I might even have said something about our being two one-legged men forced to wear the same pair of shoes the cunning old bird was selling.

But this might have been too fancy.

Not only that, Gordon died in his sleep of a coronary that winter; and soon after that, I got a better-paying job working in a chemical lab.

By the time I graduated from college, I'd heard that old Mr. Goldfarb had been shipped off to an expensive Rest Home in New Jersey.

I like to picture him there, sitting with a plaid blanket tucked high under his armpits, a derby hat tilted rakishly on his head. In my fantasy, his eyes are only half-open, and his tiny feet are fit snugly into tan-and-white oxfords with pointed toes. When a nurse comes up and asks how he's feeling, I can almost hear him saying, "Enough to be sometimes like this, if you ask me."

I figure that within a matter of weeks, the old man ruled all of them—doctors, nurses, technicians, administrators. Everybody. Whatever in this world could have prevented him?

 *Poison*

CHUCK RILEY WAS sitting in the manager's box next to the check-out lines, verifying an invoice for detergent sponges that Tod Unger, in kitchenware, had said was short, when Iona Hupp came over to him with a whispering look on her face. He knew that look too well and braced himself, prepared for the worst, wheeling his chair halfway around so he could face her.

With cold intimacy, Iona blew her bubblegum breath on his face, as she said, "Chuck, she's at it again."

Chuck Riley sighed and leaned back in his chair. His eyes were tired, his back ached, and the store was losing money this quarter. "All right, where is she?"

Iona raised her thick dark eyebrows in surprise and gestured with her thumb. "Why, she's right there on number three! Where the Sam Hill *else* would she be? Number three is where she always checks out. That's where you always put her!"

Iona was short and wide. She had a long upper lip and a pale face with dark eyeshadow so thick that, from a distance, her eyes looked like blue holes punched in soft white skin. Her hair was frizzled and the color of dried blood. Her lipstick was a brighter red, almost matching the shiny Dellmart apron all clerks were required to wear.

Chuck Riley, who, when he'd become manager not long ago, had asked all the clerks at Dellmart to call him by his first name, leaned forward and looked down the line of check-out counters. Iona was right; she was standing there at the third register, and she wasn't checking anybody out. He leaned back in the other direction, and saw that the other four open registers had two and three people lined up, waiting. It really was strange, you had to admit.

"I tell you," Iona whispered, "that bitch is nothing but *poison!*

Just look at that! Customers walk up and right away they can *see* she's poison. People just don't want nothing to do with her, Chuck. They just don't want to be checked out by a woman who looks the way she does. You might as well face it."

Chuck wiped his hand through his hair and gazed back down at the inventory sheet in his lap. He could hear Iona's hard breathing as she waited for him to say something. He sensed that whenever he didn't answer right away, it bothered Iona. But after all, he was the manager, and he often reminded himself that if he went off like a pistol every time Iona pulled the trigger, the Dellmart would sound like Dodge City at High Noon.

"Poison!" Iona whispered again. But this time her voice was muted and barely audible, for she was faced away from him, stretching back and to the side, staring down at the third register.

Chuck leaned forward and followed her gaze in time to see two boys, ten or eleven years old, come into the number three lane. One of them laid a cheap $9.98 Kid's Special fishing kit, wrapped in clear plastic, on the check-out counter in front of her. They weren't even looking at who was taking care of them. Kids that age were evidently immune to her sort of poison; or just didn't care. Chuck was going to point this out and mention that she had customers now; but Iona had seen them, too. And two kids with a $9.98 Special didn't change the basic, unavoidable truth of what Iona was telling him.

"Okay," he finally said, exhaling. "I guess I could put her back in kitchen supplies, pricing and stacking."

"If you ask me, this Band-Aid approach to the problem has gone on long enough."

Chuck shook his head. "Kitchen needs help. Maybe I'll ask Tod if he can use some help. Kitchen's been backed up too long. We can't have those aisles cluttered like that."

"If you ask me," Iona said, "you ought to just go ahead and fire her. What the Sam Hill, the way I see it, she was bad news from the word go. You're just going to have to face it, Chuck; it was a mistake to hire her."

Still seated, Chuck Riley half closed his eyes and looked up at Iona. She was five years older than he, and had been at Dellmart two years longer than he had. It was inconceivable that she did not resent him; probably she thought he'd been promoted because he was a man. Maybe that really was the reason; but whether it was or not, he could be certain that she criticized him behind his back, because nobody else escaped her disapproval, so why should he be an exception? And, being the manager, as well as younger than most of the clerks, he had to be a better target than most. Iona had a gift for resentment, and she cut a wide swathe. Still, her disapproval was all pretty much a matter of degree, he supposed. She was a hard and constant grader, and chronically shared her judgments with whoever would listen, not to mention a few who wouldn't.

"I've never known anybody like her in my whole life," Iona said. There was something almost devout in the way she said it. How diminished Iona's life would have been without her! Chuck thought about this and cleared his throat.

Now, still waiting, Iona lifted her chin and stared down upon him, waiting for him to speak. It occurred to him that someone of her stature didn't often have the opportunity to look down on others—men especially—and for him to stay seated was doing her a kind of favor. At least, it gave her an unfamiliar advantage.

But maybe that wasn't fair. Iona probably wasn't all that bad. And what she was saying was beyond any doubt essentially true. Nobody could pretend otherwise.

"I just thought you'd want to know," she said resentfully. "You know, about *her*."

"I'll take care of it."

"Now?"

Chuck Riley looked up at her. "Iona, will you please go on back to work? You've made your point. I said I'd take care of it, didn't I?"

"I know exactly what you said."

"Well, what else do you want?"

"What the Sam Hill, I was only trying to help!"

"I said I'd take care of it."

"You know, Chuck, it isn't fair to the rest of us here who do a day's work. It isn't fair to the rest of us who work so hard."

"Will you for Christ's sweet sake get your ass moving, Iona?"

"Listen here, Chuck, don't you ever, ever curse me!"

He stood up with his fists clenched, and Iona's eyes opened wide inside their blue circles, then she quick-stepped away, flapping the wooden door of the manager's box open, so that it whipped shut, and gliding back to her register. Her erect and chunky little body tilted slightly to the left as she tacked around register three, headed for her station at number five. Naturally, she didn't look to the side as she passed.

Chuck Riley tried to concentrate on the sponge mop invoice

again, but it was no use. Iona had a way of upsetting him, and he didn't know what to do about it. If he could have fired two people outright, Iona would be the second. Then, the way he felt right now, maybe Tod Unger would be third.

He sighed and stood up, stretching his back. He peered around at the third register and saw that she was checking an old man and woman out. The old couple weren't even looking at her; they probably hadn't even noticed the expression on her face, which was supposed to be enough to scare customers away. They both wore thick glasses; maybe their eyesight was too poor to see her diabolically outraged expression or exactly what it was that others presumbly saw. Chuck had to admit that she was strange looking, all right; and her mannerisms could be unsettling. But he couldn't help thinking that a busier and happier group of employees would have tolerated her and given her a place among them.

Two registers down, Iona was also busy. She was checking out what looked like a dozen half-pint specials of touch-up paint, banging them one by one on the counter. Loud enough for him to hear. He could only see the back of her head, but he knew that her lips must be compressed; and it was doubtful if she was crooning small talk at the customers checking out, as she liked to do when she was in a good mood.

Chuck stepped out of the manager's box, letting the spring door flap shut, and rubbed the small of his back as he ambled back in the direction of Kitchen Wares. Kitchen had always been one of his problems, and part of that problem had to be Tod Unger. Squatting in a clutter that almost entirely blocked the aisle by the pot and pan display, stripping tape off a box, was the man himself: a fierce-looking little bantam with thick wiry blond eyebrows, hair, and mustache. His red Dellmart apron was always wrinkled.

He glanced up. "I see Iona's talked to you."

Chuck nodded. "Yeah. She just now gave me her report."

Tod snorted angrily. "I guess you know better than to take it at face value."

"You don't agree with her?"

"Shit, no," Tod said, stuffing strips of tape into a cardboard shipping box he'd put aside for trash.

"You mean, *she* doesn't bother you the way she seems to bother everybody else?"

Tod frowned and caressed his mustache. "I wouldn't say that, Chuck. No, I wouldn't say that at all. What I mean is, Iona's got it all wrong. Iona thinks that the problem with *her* is, she alienates the customers—you know, by that expression on her face and the way she acts and makes up her face, like every day is Halloween, man . . . but that's not the problem as *I* see it. Forget about the customers. The customers take care of themselves, because they don't have to stay here. They buy what they want and then leave. Period. No, the problem as I see it has to do with the rest of us who have to work with her; let me tell you something, if you want my opinion, she's eating away the goddamn morale of this place."

Chuck nodded. "You think she really bothers the clerks that much? All of you?"

"Absolutely, Chuckie Boy. All of us. I'll tell you something: if I walked by that number three register right now, I could feel a chill clear into my bones. You know what I mean?"

"I suppose."

"You better believe it."

Chuck thought a moment. "I was thinking maybe I'd have her come back and help you stack and mark inventory."

"No fucking way. Not in my department, Chuckie Boy."

Chuck felt a flare of anger in his head; he was about to say that if Tod called him "Chuckie Boy" one goddamn more time, he'd. . . .

But just then, a large fat young woman, carrying a baby and wearing a short denim skirt and a yellow bandanna tied around her head, came up and asked where the frying pans were. Without rising from his squat, Tod gestured grandly to the side and said, "Right here, lady"; and the woman said, "Oh."

Chuck walked away, feeling rusty gears shifting deep down in his guts. Then, before he'd gotten as far as stationery, he heard the loudspeaker growl, and in a crackly voice Linda called politely for Mr. Riley to please come to register number two, so he headed back. It was a price check for boys' socks that were not marked.

But in walking by number three, he glanced in past the gum and candy racks, and saw that a young man and woman were being waited on by her. Two boys' shirts were piled on the counter, along with a thirty-inch roll of gift wrapping paper. Slowly, methodically, her hands separated the shirts. He did not look at her face.

But he did glance at the couple she was waiting on. The two of them didn't look very happy, Chuck noticed. But then, how great an expression of happiness did one have a right to expect on the faces of a couple checking out through a Dellmart line?

After a quick cheeseburger and coffee for dinner, he'd taken two aspirin and closed himself in his back office. Both his head and back were aching now, and he needed to get away from the floor for a while. He felt rotten, but he knew it was more than physical; he was sick of the whole business. Maybe he would quit his job, throw it over and go someplace else. Maybe he would get a job digging ditches, and work some of the fat off his belly. But this would be quitting. He could hear his old dad's scornful voice spitting out the word: "Quitting." His parents were living in Florida, enjoying the fruits of their years of labor. In fact, they joked about it, saying that the fruits of their labors were mostly citrus. They'd been there for eight years, now.

Every morning while driving to the Dellmart, Chuck would pass joggers and wonder how they could find the time and energy to exercise regularly. He envied them a little, because they seemed so free of worry—just working their bodies good and hard, sweating and bouncing along with their eyes glazed and cloth bands tied around their heads. Some of the men wore beards. Chuck had no interest in growing a beard; but the simple fact that beards were against Dellmark policy seemed to diminish the possibility in his life, somehow. It was the idea of the thing, he told himself.

When he drove into the carport of their little ranch house, it was almost ten o'clock. Normally, the kids would be in bed, and Traci would be waiting for him with questions; but yesterday, Traci and the kids had gone to stay for a few days with her sister in Cleveland. Her sister was having another baby, and Traci wanted to help out.

He missed having her there waiting for him. She was a comfort to him after a bad day. Sometimes, if she had a headache, she might complain about the kids; or about how confining and boring her life was; or what a nobody she was becoming. But usually she was just fine, and he was as glad to see her as it seemed she was to see him. The television would be turned on low; and she would have just made coffee. He always phoned to let her know when he was leaving, so she could put a pot of coffee on.

But this evening, the house was empty. He opened a beer and drank it from the bottle, then ate three sugar doughnuts. He had stopped at a McDonald's on the way home, where he'd eaten an Oriental salad with chicken.

If Traci had been home, by now she would have had the kids

bathed and put to bed; and she would have taken one of her long bubble baths, so she'd be waiting for him when he walked in. Nice and sexy and clean and cozy, waiting to hear all about his day. "You've had a rough day, I can tell," she would have said. Those would have been her first words. "You want to tell me about it, Hon?" She would have poured coffee in his mug and handed it to him.

Thinking about it, he sighed and opened another beer, then went into the front room and turned on the television. He thought of their conversation only last Tuesday or Wednesday, when he'd come home dead tired. The problem had been with him for several weeks, and he'd already discussed it with her several times.

When she'd asked him if he wanted to talk about it, he said, "There's nothing to tell. It's the same old thing."

"You haven't talked to her yet?"

Chuck shook his head no and sipped his coffee.

"Why not? The time isn't right?"

He shrugged. "I don't know what I can say. Do I just go up to her and say, 'You're fired'? And then when she asks me why she's being fired, do I just say because all the other clerks agree that she's got an expression on her face like some kind of monster and looks like there's something wrong with her . . . like she's sold her soul to the Devil and is angry as hell at the world and turns customers away and makes her fellow workers uneasy? All because of just some kind of *expression* she's got on her face?"

Traci sniffed the aroma of her coffee and thought. "Maybe you could just, you know, have sort of a private talk with her and be sympathetic and ask her if something's bothering her or something."

"God, I wish Bennett had never hired her."

"Well, you were off then, and they needed help."

"I know, I know."

"But what do you think? Couldn't you talk to her?"

"Listen, I'm not a psychiatrist. And she's about ten years *older* than I am. What business do I have asking her personal questions? What if she told me? What advice could I give her? I suppose there is something that's gone wrong in her life. I wouldn't be surprised. It happens all the time, doesn't it? But, Jesus, I can't go around and fix up everybody's private life, can I? Just because they work at Dellmart! I'm only the manager of the goddamn place, not their daddy or God Almighty or something!"

"I know," Traci said, sipping her coffee. "It's a terrible problem, Honey. I only wish I could help. I truly do."

"I know you do," Chuck said, patting her hand.

Remembering how they'd talked, he suddenly realized how upset his stomach was. No wonder. Who ever heard of sugar doughnuts with beer, for God's sake?

If Traci had been home this evening, she would have wondered out loud if he was doing the right thing, eating all those doughnuts along with the beer; and he would have come awake to what he was doing, and taken the hint.

He thought about phoning her, but decided not to, because there was nothing he would have felt right saying over the phone. So he took a hot shower and went to bed, where he spent a miserable, bilious night, streaked with nightmares and nausea and occasional episodes of thin, brittle dozing. He missed Traci. If her sister hadn't gotten pregnant, and she'd stayed home, he could have complained to her practically the whole night through.

DELLMART'S HOURS WERE eleven to eight, weekdays. Chuck Riley usually arrived at ten, a half hour before his employees reported, to get things ready. But with Traci gone, and having had a sleepless night, he decided to go in early and arrived fourteen minutes after nine.

There was a lot of work he could get caught up on, he told himself. It was really a good idea to get to work this early. In fact, he realized how much he loved the store when he was here all by himself early in the morning. He loved the long quiet vistas of the aisles, bordered by shelves filled with things that people wanted to buy. He loved the way the morning light shone against the windows, and how warm and pleasantly dark it was inside the little city of aisles before all the fluorescent lights were turned on and the store was filled with noise, and bustling ignorant greedy ill-humored customers.

He went into his office in back, closed the venetian blinds, got his coffeemaker and took it to the men's room, where he filled it with water. Then, returning to his office, he shoveled four heaping teaspoonfuls into the inverted paper cone, and plugged his coffeemaker in. He turned on the local radio station, which was playing a country and western piece he didn't know. He turned it down low. Soon, he could smell the delicious fragrance of the coffee brewing. Settling down at his desk with the latest run of invoices, he realized even more fully than he'd ever thought possible, and with a sudden surprising rush of emotion, how much he loved the store early in the mornings before it was invaded by customers!

He worked steadily for over an hour, typing out some forms that should arrive at the main office by next Tuesday, and catching up on a dozen things that he'd had to let slide. Occasionally, he paused to sip his coffee and listen to the music playing faintly in the corner. He was studying the conditions that accompanied some price-increase vouchers from hardware marketing, when he heard a tap at his window.

He got up, walked over to it, pulled the venetian blind cord, and was astonished to see *her* standing there. She was still holding the key that she'd used to tap on the windowpane, and simply remained there staring at him, until he nodded and motioned toward the front door, wondering what in the hell she was doing here so early.

The instant he let her in, she headed straight back toward his office, walking firmly and purposefully, as if what she had to say to him could not be discussed out in the store proper, where the ghosts of thousands of customers might overhear. The way she was walking suggested that she had more right in the store than he did. And thinking this, he realized that she had no doubt been in his office before he had even worked at Dellmart. Still, as he often had to remind himself with sickening futility, he was the manager.

When they reached his office, she went straight in and sat down in the only chair that faced his desk, then watched him as he took his seat behind it. He had never seen her eyes so focused as at this instant, watching him.

"Well," he said, "you're certainly early enough."

"Are you implying I'm ever late?"

He shook his head. "No, for God's sake, I wasn't implying anything!"

"Mr. Riley," she said, "Chuck."

"Yes?"

"I think this business has been going on far too long!"

"What business?"

"And I've had it up to here and I'm not about to take any more."

"Any more what?"

She narrowed her eyes. "Please don't play dumb with me. You

know very well what I'm talking about, Chuck. And I'm not going
to pussy-foot around any more. I've had it up to here."

Because she said so little to anyone else, he had forgotten how
soft her voice was. Behind the glare of her expression, it was almost a whisper. He could feel a sudden, terrible hollowness in his
stomach. "There's no way to stop people talking, you know."

"That's not what I'm talking about, and you know it."

He rubbed his hand back through his hair. For a moment, he
thought of offering her a cup of coffee, but it would have seemed
a ridiculous thing to do, like tossing a match into a roaring fire.

"In fact," she said, "it's just the opposite."

"What is?"

"What's *wrong*, that's what!" She looked at him as if he were
insufferably dense. "And that's why I'm giving notice."

"Giving what?"

"And I wish you'd stop repeating everything I'm telling you.
I just plain flat-out *quit*, that's what!"

"You what?"

"Jesus!"

He passed both his hands back through his hair.

"I think you heard what I said."

"You *quit?*"

"Absolutely, and don't try to talk me out of it, because I've
made up my mind. I'm quitting as of today. Right now. I've never
liked working here, and I've never liked those creeps I have to
work with. Although, I'll have to admit, *you're* not so bad. I could
get along with you all right, but not them. No sir! Never! Let
me ask you something: where did you ever get such a bunch of
misfits?"

"Oh, usually they're not so bad. I mean, you have to adjust,
you know."

"Yes they are, but you just can't see it."

"No, I can see it, all right."

"What?"

"Never mind."

"I thought you'd see it my way. Listen, I've worked hard all
my life, but I've got to tell you, enough is enough. Do you know
how long it's been since a single one of them has spoken a civil
word to me? Do you?"

"No, can't say I've noticed."

"But don't think for a minute I haven't seen Iona pouring poison into your ears!"

"Listen, whoever talks to me, I have to listen, and you know it! It's part of my job, after all."

But she didn't hear. "Why should I keep on, at my age?"

He stared at her a moment. "I honestly don't know."

She nodded. "I didn't think you would. Because there's no answering a question like that, and you know it."

Then she turned and, to Chuck Riley's astonishment, walked out of the Dellmart—apparently, from what she'd just said— forever.

L ATER THAT MORNING, he was sitting in the manager's box, read- ing a unit wholesale price reduction notice from the home office. Business was very light, and only two check-out stations were open. The invoice was for running shoes, spelling out four different special sale options. Once, halfway down the second page, Chuck paused a moment and reflected that at this very mo- ment he was experiencing Dellmart's version of human freedom.

The light changed subtly, and he looked up to see Iona Hupp and Tod Unger standing just beyond the counter. Iona swung the door open, and when she came in, he saw that she was holding her wrist in a sling. "What happened to you?" Chuck asked.

"I sprained it yesterday evening when I was pushing my niece in a swing. I took her up to the park, because it was so warm out. I couldn't believe how warm it had gotten. I didn't go to the doc- tor, but it's a sprain, all right. I won't be able to work the register, Chuck, the way I usually do, but I can work cosmetics. I've got inventory to catch up with."

Chuck stood up and stretched to ease the stiffness in his sore back, looking around the store. It was almost empty.

"Practically no customers, man," Tod said. "You ought to clear the stations. Iona and I was all caught up, so, hey, we come to pay you a visit. You know, taking ourself a little unofficial break, Chuckie Boy."

Iona sat down in the other chair, holding her wrist shoulder- high. "So what they say's true, she's really gone, huh?"

Chuck nodded. "That's the way it looks."

"When did you fire her? Was it right before we come in? Like I said to Tod, it must have been right before we come in."

"I didn't fire her. She quit."

Awkwardly, Iona lifted her elbow onto the high counter beside her. "Oh, sure. I've heard *that* one before! I wasn't born yesterday, Chuck, and don't treat me like I was."

"Well, I can't help it, that's what happened."

"I'll bet it was. Listen, I'll bet after you got through with her, she was *glad* to quit."

Chuck narrowed his eyes. "No, that's not exactly the way it was."

Iona snorted.

"I'll say one thing," Tod said, "when you act, Chuckie Boy, you don't fuck around."

"How did she take it?" Iona asked.

Chuck blinked. "Take what?"

"What the Sam Hill: *you* know what! How did she take it when you *fired* her!"

Chuck frowned and looked down at the home office notice in his hands.

Tod snapped his fingers. "You just told her to haul ass, and she hauled ass. Is that the way it was, Chuck? Shit, you can level with us, man!"

"Did she cry?" Iona asked.

Chuck looked thoughtful. "No, she didn't cry."

Iona nodded. "I'm not surprised, because I'll tell you something, I couldn't imagine *her* crying in a hundred years."

"How did it go, Chuckie Boy? Did you just give it to her straight? Like: 'Here's your fucking running shoes, Baby, now let's see you fucking *run!*'"

"Speaking of running shoes, Chuck said, "we're going to be having a special."

"Any specials in cosmetics?" Iona asked.

"Nothing yet."

"Never mind that," Tod said, leaning back in his chair. "Give us the dope, man."

"I'll bet she was shocked," Iona said, "but do you know something?"

"What?"

"I'll bet that frozen expression on her face didn't change one bit. I'll bet she didn't bat an eyelash. Did she?"

"No, she didn't."

Tod laughed. "So you just told her if she didn't quit, you'd have her ass in the frying pan. Right?"

For a moment, Chuck paused. Then he said, "Well, maybe something like that."

"Well, if you ask me, it was about time," Iona said. "If you'd like to know, I would have done it long before this."

Chuck looked at her. "Exactly when would you have done it?"

Something small changed in her gaze. "Long before this," she repeated, not quite as loud.

Tod laughed. "Listen to the man! When Chuckie Boy fires your ass, let me tell you something: *he fires your ass!*"

Chuck looked back down at the paper on his lap. "Okay," he muttered, "have it your way. I guess you've made your point. Now get back to work." He paused and took a breath. "And that means both of you—Iona and Toddy Boy both."

He forced himself to finish reading the paragraph. He took in the words, but they meant nothing. He knew he would have to read it again, and then maybe a third time.

After a long moment's silence, he heard the door swish open and flap shut, but he knew it was possible that they were still waiting just outside the manager's box.

He forced himself to think about the registers. They would be two short, today. Maybe he would put Tod on the third register. Tod hated working the registers, and once or twice announced that he simply fucking wasn't going to do it any more; but that was just the kind of noise Tod made. It didn't mean anything, now, because . . . well, hadn't he just seen how easily Chuck could fire somebody?

He nodded half to himself and decided that maybe he could get Dale Ketchum from plumbing, or Suzie Ottum from stationery, if they needed to open the extra register. Dellmart wouldn't really be short of help either today or tomorrow. Chuck took a deep breath and held it. Then he exhaled.

When he looked up, he saw that Tod and Iona had both disappeared, and for a brief moment he was surprised by the notion that there was nobody around, nobody at all in his store, for there wasn't a single person within sight. Not a single customer; not even a clerk. But this sense of isolation was only momentary and fanciful, of course, for the store was open and all the aisles were lighted. And he knew that the clerks and customers were hidden from his view by stacks of merchandise, only waiting to come forth, dragging the world with them. Which is to say, ignorance, selfishness, childishness, envy, resentment, stupidity, and the singular conviction that at every instant, every single one of them knew exactly how everybody else should behave, always and without exception.

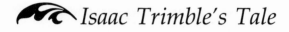

CAPTAIN SHACKFORD LIVED here most thirty years, and nobody knew him better than I did. I saw him come down the Ohio River and land here at Portsmouth two years after the century turned. He was already an old man of sixty-six. He bought lot seventeen from Henry Massie. I also saw him shortly before he died at ninety-three, an old man's woolen shawl hunched over his shoulders.

They named our town in his honor, being he came from Portsmouth, New Hampshire, all those years before, where he'd been captain of a frigate. He'd earned the title of Captain, and nobody grudged to give it in his hearing.

Never any doubt about one thing, though; Captain Shackford was peculiar and announced the fact louder than drum and bugles could have done, or a brass cannon. First thing he did was hire carpenters and tell them exactly how his dwelling should be. Build her straight up, two stories, he said. Windows all around and a board porch to reach from ear to ear. Plenty of room, and do not spare the black walnut.

Only thing was, he said, no stairway. No ladder, even. Nothing. The carpenters near to swallowed their faces. Just a hatch in the ceiling, right there. He drew up the plans, straight and true as mathematics could make them. Pointed to one spot and drew a square. Put a hatch there.

When the carpenters just looked at him like he'd spoken Dutch or Italian, he got disgusted. In case you don't know what a hatch is, he told them, it's a hole in the ceiling. A square hole, with a lid that falls plunk, nice and tight like an inlay.

How you going to get through that hole? they asked him.

He said, I am a seafaring man, you bumpkins, and I will fix me a rope ladder and drop her down every morning when I open the store. And climb up her at eve, like a jack-tar, and pull her after me.

So the carpenters threw their ladders up and built it exactly the way he told them, because he had plenty of money and would not tolerate argumentation.

The store part was the first floor, where he sold staples and harness, axes and powder, and such like. The second story was his dwelling place. And after the last carpenter came down, there wasn't a human being who ever once set eyes on that second story until they had to crawl up and fetch his corpse the morning after he died, in 1829.

What they found, it was all furnished, polished and fine as a ship cabin, and neat and clean as a surveyor's case. He'd fixed a pulley on one of the eaves and had the window made big enough so he could pull up whatever he needed, when he needed it. He lived alone in that big room, sure as an eagle builds his nest high off the ground.

Crazy as sin, people said, but Captain Shackford knew his mind and didn't care for talk. He was shrewd and judicious, with money in the till, and before long had the village in his hand, so that they even named it in his honor, as I have said.

Crazy is as crazy does, the saying goes, but you wouldn't guess the thing that was more peculiar yet, which was that Captain Shackford never once let a female set foot inside that store from the day he first pulled up that rope ladder of his until he died. Not even a little girl nor a female cat.

What was the reason behind all this? Everybody wondered, but nobody learned. Captain Shackford spoke not a word as to his reasons. We talked about it many a time, but ended our inquiries as dark as we'd started. The mystery of Captain Shackford's ways abided.

But did the women hold it against him? Not in the least, they didn't. Strange as it may be, they catered to the old man like he was a preacher or a foreign prince. If he took sick, they'd stand outside that big window with the pulley and call out to him until he'd lower a rope so they could tie a basket of pies or pork and biscuits for him to eat and get well. My wife was among them.

What it was, these women were all abuzz about him, and kept that way for most of thirty years. They could never get it out of their heads that Captain Shackford had been mortally hurt by a maiden who'd spurned him. No man could pry this notion out of them.

As for the men themselves, they accepted the old captain's peculiar ways and let him thrive. He was smart and polite, except for the way he treated females. Live and let live, the men figured, and that's the way it happened.

His first name was Josiah.

O NLY ONE TIME in memory was the old eagle shaken in his nest, and that was when the greatest preacher on that part of the Ohio River came down from Marietta in a steamboat, seeking him out.

I speak of Isaac Trimble, a man who once held forth with Parson Weems himself, the author of *The Life of Washington* and a famous pamphleteer, not to mention preacher and bookseller. Except for Peter Cartwright, there hadn't been a greater man than Isaac Trimble to visit Portsmouth since Lafayette come through in 1825. Isaac Trimble had drunk deep of Parson Weem's doctrine and could quote him like Scripture itself.

Why had he traveled all this way downriver? People naturally asked the question, but unlike other questions you could point to, this one was answered with emphasis and spirit. I have come to get that old man married, Reverend Trimble said, rubbing his hands together like he was about to pick up an axe and chop down a lofty oak tree.

Josiah Shackford's fame has traveled far and wide, he said, lifting his hand palm outward to thwart interruption. Your Captain Shackford here is known all up and down the river, famous for his ways and renowned in misogyny.

Captain Shackford had his silences, but Isaac Trimble was a talker. He was an orator and exhorter, not only a preacher. And he had his ideas about right and wrong that were clear as a flag. Captain Shackford, for all the good he did, was something of a cunning man. You couldn't help but notice it, given his peculiarities and silences upon a certain topic. My wife admitted as much.

But Isaac Trimble was as bright and merry as the sunshine in June. He was hearty and full of good stories, and if he had an idea, he told you what it was. In fact, you'd have had trouble escaping. They say Parson Weems was the same way.

People had trouble believing Trimble though. It was hard to swallow. Who could accept a reason like this? Who could believe that a man like that would travel all this distance just to get an old bachelor married?

The question didn't live long, because Trimble himself attacked it almost before it was asked. What he did was pull out one of Weems's famous pamphlets and show it around. Not only that, he read from it in a loud voice, practically striking sparks in the air with his oratorical ways. But his explanation was so direct and peculiar, nobody believed him.

What it seemed to add up to was: Parsons Weems and Trimble both were all for marriage, 100 percent. There was no other way, because marriage was *it*. Get married and raise up little Christians to praise the Almighty! Trimble shouted it, and even the dogs sleeping under the porch would wake up and look uneasy.

It was a matter of health and wholesomeness, he said. A man risks being splenetic when he commits himself to infidelity toward God and a life of unnatural bachelorhood. Man was not meant to be without woman. Without her by his side, he weakens and wanders derelict into the darkness of Sin and Atheism.

People laughed at him, ready for a jest even if it was from a preacher. They couldn't believe he was serious. Isaac Trimble didn't mind a bit. He said what he had to say, and it was up to those around him to catch his drift. He went on and on, like he couldn't let go of a good joke. And people went along with him, convinced he had something deeper and more subtle up his sleeve.

Along about this time, there was considerable trouble from river pirates and such. People were murdered in their beds, and whiskey fizzled and fired like gunpowder up and down the river, which wound like a snake through the wilderness. Trimble pointed all this out to those who'd listen, and then he'd elaborate until he had them in his power and could have marched them all into the mighty current of the Ohio, like the Pied Piper.

Instead, he resorted to Christianity and Argumentation. He pointed out that practically all thieves, cutthroats, drunkards, profaners, arsonists, assassins, and traveling mountebanks were bachelors, which was a fact I had never thought of before. But it was true, and the minute Isaac Trimble said it, everybody else saw it was true, also.

So you come all this way just to convert one old bachelor? they asked him, and Reverend Trimble nodded his head and said, Yep, that was it.

But Captain Shackford is an upright man, they told him. Everybody says so.

Trimble just shook his head. If, as you claim, he's the most powerful man on this part of the river, he has no right to set an example of bachelorhood to others.

But he's almost ninety years old, they answered, which was the truth.

Isaac Trimble just shook his head again, smiling a little, and said, In Captain Shackford's case I am not speaking of consummation or of siring a litter of babes; I speak only of the holy state of matrimony.

Then, fixing his eyes on the distant wooded hills, he swept his hand out and said, Thousands have died from the yellow fever in the cities back east, and out here in the west, there is only a scattering of human settlements. The Almighty means for us to settle this land.

What do you mean by that? people asked him.

But all Isaac Trimble said was, Let us pray, which everybody did, being no more able to resist the power of his words than water can fail to flow downstream.

Even if they still didn't believe that was the real reason he'd come here.

ABOUT A MONTH before Trimble come, Peter Cartwright had visited Portsmouth, and they'd built a platform for him back of the graveyard. There must have been a thousand people come to hear him and pray and fall down with illumination. Cartwright was assisted by twelve preachers, and let me tell you, there was thunder day and night until they pulled up stakes and went on downriver to Cincinnati and Louisville.

What they did was leave that platform standing in memory of the camp meeting, but Isaac Trimble decided to put it to another use. He didn't have twelve preachers, but he had a nephew to assist him and a voice that could flush the pigeons from a tree like a pistol shot. He made up his mind to hold forth on the same platform Peter Cartwright had stood on only a few weeks before.

Most of the populace was preached out, but a few people showed up anyway, because of Trimble's reputation and his way of talking. His nephew passed out announcements, along with that pamphlet by Parson Weems I mentioned earlier. It was called *Hymen's Recruiting Sergeant, or The New Matrimonial Tat-too for Old Bachelors.* My wife was there and got one.

People didn't see the connection right away when he started in. He circled. They didn't get the drift. They just couldn't believe him when he'd told them why he'd come to Portsmouth. They still suspected a deeper cause.

There was a crowd of maybe five score present, and it wasn't long before Reverend Trimble had them opening their eyes a little wider. Then he changed his tune a little, and all of a sudden alighted upon the main theme, and they began to sweat. By the time he'd finished, there wasn't any doubt about it. Isaac Trimble hadn't just come to Portsmouth to preach the Gospel and tell us what awful sinners we were, but had come for the reason he'd told us right at the start: to instruct, defy and change the marital status of the richest and most powerful man in town, Captain Shackford himself.

All afternoon Isaac Trimble stood and shouted the heavens down. He shook the hills with his trumpeting and made the leaves fall from the trees. And no matter how far he might seem to drift, maybe a half hour here and there on such topics as Original Sin, Hellfire, and Infant Damnation, he always returned to his main theme, which was the iniquity of bachelorhood.

Did that old man who was the object of his righteous wrath step forth to listen? He did not. But no doubt he heard everything, if not from the Reverend Trimble's spiritual cannonading, then from the reports of various and sundry who'd wandered into range long enough to get his drift and left.

W HEN EVENING COME, Trimble got up and left the platform. By then, he'd collected over two hundred admirers, who were just there for the excitement. Unlike other preachers, Trimble was more than just loud and eloquent. He was a scholar, in his way, and full of classical quotations.

If the mountain won't come to Muhammad, Muhammad will go to the mountain. This is what Trimble said, and people got the idea, even though nobody had much of an idea who Muhammad was. But Isaac Trimble didn't wait to enjoy the effect any more than he would have listened to caution. He took off right there, headed for Captain Shackford's store with men, women, and children trailing behind.

The females all stopped at the door, but the men trooped in and stood there.

Trimble said, I'm the Reverend Isaac Trimble.

Captain Shackford said, I'm Josiah Shackford.

That's exactly the way it started, both men wary and quiet as they sized each other up. Captain Shackford looked old enough to advise the dead, but Trimble was getting there, too, and afterward some said he should have been old enough to know better.

There is a Law, Trimble said, pointing upward with his finger, which contains a number of little laws.

He's a lawyer, too, a man name of Fenninger whispered, but somebody shushed him quiet.

And if you feel no guilt in your heart, Trimble went on, pointing his finger at Captain Shackford's face, you will consent to be tried.

The old man just stared at Trimble for a minute, and then he said, Tried for what?

For celibacy, Trimble thundered, and all the sins thereof.

I have no time for your games, the old man told him.

Nor would a guilty spirit! The Law I speak of is figurative, and a conviction won't put you in jail in this world, or cost you a penny from your store of wealth.

My life is my own, Sir, Captain Shackford mumbled, squinting through his glasses at an account book before him. Case dismissed.

Isaac Trimble closed his eyes and thought. Then he prayed. By the time he got through praying, there was an awful spirit of trial in the room. Everybody there was ready, you could tell. A man name of Oakes said these were the two greatest men to meet head-on west of Pittsburgh since he couldn't name when. People were excited, and they wanted to know who would come out on top.

Isaac Trimble knew more than Latin and Greek; he knew crowds as well. So he went ahead and set up the trial, right then and there. Never mind that it was all in fun, because if Trimble won his case, Captain Shackford would be publicly disgraced and his power would slacken and he might not even have enough strength left to crawl up his rope ladder into his dark retreat. Bachelorhood itself was on trial, and every man there was set upon finding out how it would all end.

Right away Trimble set about appointing a man name of Babcock for defense counsel. Then he pointed at an old fellow name of Urdang and said he was judge. After that, he counted off the jury, one through twelve, right in a line, the way you shoot green apples off a fence rail.

Everybody was excited by this time. The spirit of play had gotten to them, and yet they knew there was something serious behind it, even if they couldn't exactly name it. It was more than Trimble versus Shackford, and it was more than bachelorhood. There was something else there, too, which was like the air you breathe, only you can't speak it in a word.

Trimble fixed them in place all up by the counter, so that before long it looked like a real courtroom. And by the time he lined the jurors up and appointed a bailiff, a man name of Poldi, there was not a sound in the whole room, except for the sound of maybe thirty or forty men breathing in and out.

Nobody could say Isaac Trimble had come unprepared. He took out a sheet of foolscap that he'd written on and read as follows: the defendant, Captain Josiah Shackford, being the most prominent and influential man between Gallipolis and Cincinnati, as well as being one of the wealthiest and therefore one of the most powerful, is hereby charged with pursuing a way of life that is known to be pernicious to the common good, according to law and Scripture. Said way of life is bachelorhood, which as maintained by a man of his standing in the community constitutes a potent example of unnatural and irresponsible license that amounts to shiftlessness in the eyes of God and man. Said way of life is in itself, by mere fact of being, an implicit denial of the merits, fruits, and joys of marital bliss, which, since God made Eve for Adam's comfort, pleasure, and support, is the right true state of man.

These are the exact words Isaac Trimble read, for he gave me the sheet later on and I copied it to the last syllable. Only I have just given the start of the charge, for Trimble's handwriting was neat and small, and he'd managed to crowd practically a whole sermon on both sides of that one big sheet of foolscap.

It was impressive, you'd have to admit. By the time he'd finished, Isaac Trimble had every bachelor in that room ready to go out and find a maiden so's he could tie the knot. His delivery was as good as Peter Cartwright's ever was, maybe better. And you could tell he *believed* the things he was saying, because his face got red and he ended up sweating. It didn't look like poor old Captain Shackford had much of a chance.

Silas Urdang had caught the spirit all right, and after Isaac Trimble finished, he banged the butt of his horse pistol on the counter, pretending it was a gavel and he was a real-life judge instead of the man Trimble had just picked out to play the part on the spur of the moment.

And how does the defendant plead? Silas Urdang said, looking at the old man.

Right then, Captain Shackford stood up, and everybody sort of caught their breath, because you could tell he was entering into the spirit of this business, too, instead of saying to hell with it and kicking everybody out of the store, as he had a legal right to do.

For a minute or two the old man just stood there kind of blinking, so Silas Urdang asked him again what his plea was.

Captain Shackford swallowed and said, Nolo contendere, which broke everybody up into a thousand pieces. You could probably hear the laughter clear over in Kentucky.

It also ended the evening's proceedings, such as they were.

WELL, HE'D PROVED he was a smart old fox, and Isaac Trimble was smart, too, which meant he knew he'd been whipped. He took it like a man and got the next steamboat upriver for Marietta.

People told that story about the mock trial over and over, and it got better and better, the way stories tend to do, so that everybody enjoyed it, even if they'd heard it a score of times before.

Everybody except one, who was Captain Shackford himself. He never took a bow when the subject came up, and never acknowledged that he'd been clever in outwitting Isaac Trimble. In fact, he got more peculiar than ever in some ways, which, when you think about it, was a considerable accomplishment for a man who lived the way he did.

And then something curious happened. It was late one December evening in 1828, the year before the old man died. He was over ninety, now, and he shook like a juggler every time he tried to pick up a pen or a piece of paper. His assistant, name of Nathan Bolitch, ran the store and did an honest job of it too.

What happened was, I was staying late in the store that night and when old Captain Shackford was about ready to climb up his rope ladder and call it a day, he asked me if I'd like to linger a while and join him in a glass of whiskey.

I agreed, and Captain Shackford dismissed Nathan, who went out into the snowy night. There was about three inches, I remember. It was old snow, however, and it had gotten cold. You could hear the river booming and trying to freeze along the shore.

Captain Shackford asked me to pour the whiskey, which I did, and then the two of us eased up next to the fireplace, where customers liked to sit and talk. There was a good cherry log burning. After a long sip, the old man looked at me hard for a minute, and I figured he was going to ask me to help him climb up his rope ladder. I figured he was afraid to give it a try this evening, because of the shakes and misery of old age that had come over him.

But it wasn't that at all. What it was, he asked if I remembered Isaac Trimble's mock trial.

It's not likely anybody in Portsmouth will ever forget such a thing, I told him.

He nodded and said, I often think of it myself.

It's only natural you would, I said. You bested him at his own game. You could have been a great lawyer. Everybody says so.

The world don't need more lawyers, Captain Shackford said, shaking his head. And as for besting Isaac Trimble, in a way that's true, but in another way, it ain't.

What is that supposed to mean? I asked him.

Then it was that Captain Shackford swore me to secrecy and told the whole story. He told it from beginning to end. He didn't leave out a word. It was all there.

That's how I got to be the first man in Portsmouth to know the mystery behind the old man's behavior all those years.

And do you know something? The women were right, all along. I admitted as much to my wife, when it all come out.

A BOUT A YEAR after Captain Shackford died, I ran into Isaac Trimble in a tavern in Gallipolis, and I told him the story exactly the way the old man had told it to me. Isaac listened like a man ready to shake the words out if you stopped.

When I was through, he said, I have never heard such a tale in all my life. Then he grabbed me by my wrist and said, Do you know what?

What? I said.

Isaac Trimble shook my wrist and said, It has the stuff of tragedy in it. Why, Euripides might have written the story you just told!

No, it was what really happened to Captain Shackford all right, I told him. It's no story, I swear.

Isaac Trimble just closed his eyes and breathed in and out a couple of times.

I was surprised by his behavior. Captain Shackford had sworn me to secrecy that cold winter night before the fire, as I've written, and I had kept my word. But when the old man died, a nephew traveled all the way from Portsmouth, New Hampshire, to claim the estate, and he told the story of Captain Shackford's past life, which had made everybody so curious all these years.

And here is that story, the way it happened. Years before, back in the 1700s, Josiah Shackford's mother died, and his father remarried. His new wife had a beautiful grown daughter, who come to live with them, and Josiah fell in love with her. He asked her to marry him, but she said she was still in love with a boy who'd drowned at sea. She said she'd never be able to forget that boy. And even if she did, she couldn't marry a seafaring man because of her horror at the idea of drowning.

But young Josiah kept after her, even though he was old enough to captain a small frigate by this time. After a while, the girl gave in and married him. Her name was Deborah, and when her new husband, Josiah, was at sea, she couldn't sleep because of the drowned boy in her memory; and now her husband was at sea, at the mercy of tide, wind and storm.

They lived like this a few years, until Josiah's father died. Right then, Josiah decided to go west. He told his young wife he had never heard of a ship sunk by a storm in the Ohio River, and he figured that now he would be able to ease her mind, once and for all.

But she didn't take to the news the way he'd figured. She hung back and was quiet. And on the night before they were ready to start on their journey, she told Josiah she couldn't go. She said she couldn't bear the thought of leaving her mother, who was now a widow for a second time and would be all alone.

Josiah Shackford tried to convince her to come with him, as was the proper duty of a wife, but she wouldn't budge. She hardly even listened, in fact. Even though she was a lovely woman to behold, there was something wrong with her deep down inside, and she wasn't moved by his words.

Eventually, his exasperation grew into wrath, and he cursed the poor girl and departed as planned, leaving her there in his father's old house with her mother.

From that time on, he had nothing whatsoever to do with women, as if in her stubbornness he had seen them all. Portsmouth, Ohio, reaped the harvest of that fury and despair, in the way I have explained. Deborah was the cause of his stubborn misogyny.

But their story was not quite over. The old man's nephew, name of Whipple, said that finally when Deborah's mother died, she wrote Captain Shackford a letter. She wrote that she realized she had made a mistake in not coming with him, and she pleaded with him to forgive her and let her come join him where he now lived. She got down on her knees in that letter and begged.

But did this letter ever arrive? Captain Shackford never mentioned it. This was part of the story the nephew told, and he was in a position to know. I am inclined to believe it, because when

Captain Shackford was talking to me there seemed to be more than simple frustration and self-exasperation at work. There seemed to be something missing. There was something he could not bring up that winter evening. In short, I think he had received the letter and did not answer.

I told Isaac Trimble about my idea, and he just sat there breathing in and out like a man who has been climbing a steep path.

The enormity of it, he finally said, doubling up his fists.

It's quite a story, I told him.

Worthy of Euripides, he whispered. Sophocles, perhaps! Yes, worthy of Sophocles of Old. A tragedy in modern dress!

This was fancy, but I let him go on. We had drunk a few glasses of punch, if the truth be told, and Isaac Trimble was not one who went out of his way to avoid oratorical flourishes in his conversation.

But he did carry on about Captain Shackford. He kept at it all that evening and brought several strangers into the conversation, so they could hear it all.

As for me, I just sat there and listened. Once I wondered aloud if Deborah might not still be alive, and Isaac Trimble groaned loudly and clasped his hand over his forehead.

Let us hope not! he whispered, and one of the men, who had a great scar on his chin, grinned and winked at the rest of us.

What did such behavior signify? I was at a loss, and wondered if this man knew something I did not. I was considerably at sea, and it was more than the punch that had put me there.

Isaac Trimble acted peculiar in ways I could not understand. I couldn't help but wonder about him. I wondered what had gotten into his head that he would act so odd, so I put the matter to him.

Do you ask why I am moved? he cried, standing up. His eyes glistened, and I do believe that if he'd had a gentleman's handkerchief with him at the moment, he would have used it.

The fellow who'd grinned and winked at us, did so again, as much as to say: Reverend Trimble is full of notions all of a sudden, let's face it! I learned later that his man was James Ostenfelder, a well-known merchant on the river, widely respected.

But Isaac Trimble saw his look and resented it. Oh, those who have eyes but will not see! he muttered, turning away from us.

Ostenfelder was something of a wag, and he asked, Those who have eyes and will not see *what?*

Euripides would have seen it all, for it required an eagle's vision, sir.

I guess that leaves us out, don't it? Ostenfelder said to me, and we both laughed.

But Isaac Trimble closed his eyes and just breathed in and out, again. A bellows of pondering. I had always liked the man, so to alleviate his hurt feelings, I said, It's strange, all right, but I figure it's the sort of thing that happens every day.

You are wrong, sir, Isaac Trimble told me in a sepulchral voice, opening his eyes wide. As wrong as all men have been from the start. It's the tender sex that understood, and all we could do was just lounge around and laugh at them.

So it was a woman after all, I said, shrugging.

Cherchez la femme, Ostenfelder added, nodding. True enough; it was certain that said Deborah was a woman, and you couldn't hardly cause more mischief than *she* did!

That, too; that, too! Trimble muttered, wiping his chin with his hand.

Women. Ostenfelder sighed, holding his glass up to the light as if toasting their sex: The source and solace of all our ills!

But oh, Isaac Trimble said, groaning, can't you understand that poor woman's tragic fate? The pain and misery she caused, knowing it? And can't you fathom the profound madness of Captain Shackford? Can't you?

I shrugged again, and Ostenfelder raised his eyebrows as he signaled for another round.

The story passes through the both of you, Isaac Trimble stated, with no more effect than a bird troubles the air.

I reckon that's about the size of it, I told him, and Ostenfelder laughed.

Isaac Trimble nodded. The tale belongs to those who understand and savor it in all its truth and power!

It's all right with me, Ostenfelder said, glancing in my direction as he threw his leg over the arm of his chair. How about you?

It's all right with me, too, I said.

Then Ostenfelder told Isaac Trimble that he was welcome to the entire story of Captain Shackford's madness, since it appeared he savored it enough for three people. As for himself, he said, he had other matters to occupy his mind.

I seconded him in this motion, and two other fellows who had come up to join in the raillery agreed, too. It was his story, all right. That was our consensus, and we told him so.

Oh, it is indeed, Isaac Trimble said fervently. It is truly that!

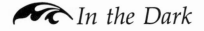 *In the Dark*

DEBBIE AND ALICE are seated together at the front of the room, and whenever Mr. Abbott looks up, their heads go down together real slow, exactly synchronized with Mr. Abbott's head, and I sit there trying to figure out what kind of mechanism would make them move together like that . . . smooth, well-oiled piston, fastened eccentrically to the two wheels of their heads, I figure, so that when his big, black-haired head rolls back and his sad and wrinkled eyes look out over us, their two heads slide downwards away from him—this bilious and troubled old god—and the two of them have nodded, while the rest of us doze onward into the afternoon and pretend to study.

Debbie is big and blank-faced, with ears like hard pink flowers and big hands that she holds tight against her thighs when she walks. Her hair is thick and yellow, like swirled mashed potatoes with too much butter, and her face is pretty. She has always been a good speller, and when she was in junior high school, she won the spelling bee two years in a row. However, her grades aren't very good, because Debbie can't put two ideas together, and she can't count higher than fifty without taking considerable thought.

Alice is small and dark. The two of them, Debbie and Alice, go around together like they try to emphasize each other's impossibility. Once I saw a big bottle of orange and a small Coke sitting together on the aluminum strip of Hermie's Lunchroom, and I thought of Debbie and Alice standing together.

Alice has a pointed nose and long black eyelashes. Her black hair curls in front of her ears, and—in a finer, hazy version—the same fine black hair is scattered in a thousand parentheses and commas along the thin arcs of her forearms. Alice looks angry all the time; Debbie looks bewildered. Alice swings her arms rapidly and walks fast; Debbie keeps her hands flat against her thighs and takes long slow looping strides, like an unhappy grazing animal.

Debbie is a virgin, everybody figures; but Alice is the closest thing to a whore in our class. She screwed four boys one night in September, down by the river. I know, because I was one of them. And then last night, I screwed her down in the furnace room. All the time, she just stared up into the darkness at the cobwebs around the big furnace pipes wrapped in soft gray paper. God, she didn't even blink, but breathed hard through her nose, as if she was in some kind of hurry to get it over with and then murder everything about her.

Once again, Mr. Abbott raises his head, and Debbie's and Alice's heads swing down. He stares at them for an instant, as if for once he's noticed that they aren't fixed in an attitude of deep and reverent study. Of course, this is only a study hall, and most teachers don't care whether you study or not. But Mr. Abbott expects you to look like you're studying. He sometimes acts as if he hates as many things as Alice hates. I sit here thinking that Alice and Mr. Abbott might have a lot in common.

I don't know which one seems strangest to me, but I can't keep my eyes off them—all three of them, arranged in front of me as if for my secret entertainment.

Then the bell rings, and all arise except for the gloomy Abbott, who is staring at the windowpane and tapping his fingers against the oak desk, which someone has stained orange in a distant past.

Debbie's head looms over Alice as the two of them move toward the door in the line of slowly exiting students. I am watching them from four places behind, since I am one of the taller boys in the class, and the three girls and one boy between us don't obstruct my view.

When I am about to veer out into the tumult of the hall, Mr. Abbott calls my name, and I whirl around to see him staring into my eyes, in a spirit of meaningful concentration. He must think that if he stared at me long enough in this way, the subtlest meaning would be conveyed to me. It occurs to me that the Abbott believes in telepathy. It occurs to me that he believes in many things, but believes in nothing that has to do with us.

He speaks my name again. Just my last name, like a question: "Blagg?"

"Yes?" I answer.

"Come here, please."

I angle toward his desk, taking care to look just past his left eye at a hairy ear that reminds me of the drawing of a ganglion in a college biology text I once looked at.

"Yes?" I ask him.

"You know what, don't you?"

"Know what, Mr. Abbott?"

"Blagg, do you have to play dumb with me?"

"I'm not playing dumb."

"You know I know, don't you?"

"Know what, sir?"

Mr. Abbott pauses and taps his fingers. He is waiting until I focus my eyes on his left eye, but I refuse to do this.

"You wasted the whole hour. Do you know that?"

"I guess so," I say. I am in a hurry to get to Social Studies, and want him to finish.

"What have you been doing back there, for God's sake?" he asks me, moving his head a little so as to intercept my vision. But I let my eyes ride with his left ear. Maybe he thinks that's where I can see him, instead of in his big, dark-wrinkled eyes.

"Thinking," I tell him.

"Thinking?"

"Yes sir."

"Thinking about what, if you don't mind my asking?"

"A lot of things, I guess."

"Blagg, is there something wrong with your eyes?"

He surprises me with that, and my vision snaps into place, and I am staring at the Abbott's eyes. They are so old-looking and strange that they almost give me the hiccups when I see them up close. Sometimes they have tears in them, for no reason so far as anyone can tell.

"No sir."

"No, I guess not," he says with a sigh.

"Is that all, sir?"

"Sure, Sure, that's all. Get lost."

"Yes, sir."

But when I get as far as the door, he says, "Blagg?"

I turn and face him once more, staring—from this distance—past the ear so that I am looking at the name "Eric the Red" in Mr. Abbott's own handwriting on the blackboard behind his left ear.

"You know something, Blagg," he says, "you interest me. The fact is, you are a very strange boy."

I tell him yes sir, and dart out into the hall. I want to take a leak before Social Studies, and the second bell is about to ring. The Abbott has probably made me late, damn his wrinkled eyes.

Aᴳᴀɪɴ ɪᴛ ɪs study hall, with the Abbott blowing his nose and then twisting in his chair to gaze at snowflakes swimming lazily against the window. Beyond, the sky is a purple-gray wash.

He looks back at the students before him, and Alice's head goes down. Debbie already has her head buried in a history book before her, studying the very lesson the Abbott assigned only two hours before in another room.

Debbie stands up and begins to walk toward the pencil sharpener, her ears and face burning red, her eyes lowered. She always blushes when she walks, and this only makes things worse, naturally. She walks as if her knees are fastened together, and of course her hands are flat against her thighs as if she is afraid her dress is going to be blown skyward by a sudden gust of wind.

It is a wonder she makes it as far as the pencil sharpener, but she does, and commences grinding away at the long virgin yellow of the pencil, making a noise like a dentist's drill in the silence of the room.

I am not the only one who is compelled to witness her discomfort. All the idle scholars in the study hall have raised their heads to watch—all except for Alice, who is staring at her book as if she is deeply engrossed.

But there is another one watching, too. It is the Abbott himself staring at Debbie as she cranks the whirring pencil sharpener, making the bottom of her skirt jiggle up and down. There is deep concentration on his face, and it occurs to me that, at this instant, the Abbott is not aware of the presence of anyone else in this room.

What is there about Debbie that interests him? We have talked about our teachers before, and have read of occasional scandals at other schools, and we have had to acknowledge that sex is something that extends even as far as they . . . that, to be specific, one of our own teachers, even, might find a student of sexual interest.

But I know from the start it isn't this. Not with the Abbott and this inoffensive camel, Debbie, who can spell so many words correctly without knowing what they mean.

Nevertheless, there is no mistaking the intensity of his stare. Clearly, he sees something in Debbie that no one else can see; and he watches her during the return trip to her seat, without even breathing, it seems.

I have wanted to signal Alice, but for some reason I have waited. Now seems to be the time, so I pull out yesterday's newspaper I have brought from home. Alice is four seats to my left, and two seats in front of me. Debbie sits to her left, one aisle from the cold window that reveals the darkness outside.

I rattle the newspaper and shake it open to the financial page. Then I put it up before my face so the Abbott can't see me, and I glance at Alice. She is looking back at me, and I see her appear to nod once, without lifting her head after the nod, if it was a nod after all. Seeing her angry face, I can't imagine she would consent to anything, let alone this. But of course I know she will.

Alice looks back to the front of the room and drops her eyes immediately. I know the Abbott has been watching her, so I glance past the edge of the newspaper and see him now staring at me, his mouth compressed like a man who's blowing up a balloon.

"Blagg," he says.

"Yes?"

"Will you come up here, please?"

I fold the newspaper carefully and put it on the desk. Then I put both hands on the desk and lift myself slowly—as if I weigh three hundred pounds—out of my seat. My cowboy boots clatter heavily against the iron legs of the seat, and I stumble as I go past Mary Jane Devaney's desk. I know the Abbott flinches with each unnecessary noise I make, but I don't look at him.

By the time I get to the front of the room, the Abbott has gotten up and moved halfway to the door. He wiggles his finger at me, and I follow him out into the hall. The hall smells like an old elevator shaft, and there's a cold breeze flowing down its length.

Abbott whistles at a student council girl walking at the other end of the hall, and yells out, "Close that door, will you?" That's the door that stays open if you push it all the way back. Some of us never fail to push it all the way back, and others—like the Abbott—never fail to expect us to do this.

"Are you interested in current events, Blagg?" the Abbott turns and asks me, raising his eyebrows.

"Not so much," I tell him.

"For a minute there," the Abbott says, "I thought you were suffering from some kind of seizure. Then I saw you were just having trouble straightening your newspaper out. It gave me quite a scare."

"Yes sir." I was looking past his ear at locker number 1486, which would be a girl's locker. North wall; even number.

"What were you reading in the newspaper? Beetle Bailey?"

"No, not exactly."

"Not *exactly*, Blagg?"

"Yes sir."

"Why don't you read your schoolbooks instead of the newspaper? Don't you think that would be wise and . . . judicious, Blagg?"
"Judicious" is the Abbott's favorite word. "Glamorous" is the word he hates most.

"I guess so."

"From my standpoint, Blagg, it would be a refreshing change to see you prepared in world history. In spite of all your effort, you *are* intelligent, Blagg."

The Abbott is always going out of his way to call me by my last name. It's almost like he's trying to put me down, since it's such a goddamn screwy name; but I know it isn't quite like that. The Abbott acts as if he sort of likes the taste of the name . . . and maybe as if he can't quite believe it's a real name, or that I am real, either, for that matter. It seems to me he is always going out of his way to talk to me—most of it criticizing, but interested talk in a way. And I'll have to admit I don't completely dislike the Abbott; as a matter of fact, I don't think too much about him one way or another . . . or wouldn't if he didn't always keep calling me up to his desk or out into the hallway to raise hell or ask me questions.

Now he sighs and pats me on the shoulder, like I would probably do better if I could, and he ushers me back into the study hall, where Alice has her head down, and Debbie is now the one looking up—along with a half dozen others—wondering what's happening with the Abbott and me again.

I go back and sit down and read the newspaper, but leave it flat on my desk. Then, five minutes later, I look up, and the Abbott is again staring out at the snow falling, and I look over at Alice, who feels my look on her, and she lowers her face and looks back at me under her hair and nods.

She knows what the newspaper meant. It was what we had used the other day to keep her from getting dirty on the furnace room floor.

Just thinking about it, the saliva starts squeezing into my mouth and my stomach starts twisting, the way the insides of a clock must feel when somebody's winding it.

Alice takes two fingers and pulls a curl off her ear. The Abbott continues to brood upon the fact of the snow falling.

THE SNOW THAT commenced falling two days ago is now a foot deep, and we all know this is the heart of winter. Store lights go on a little after four o'clock, and in the mornings, we are well into the second class period before it is fully light outside and the cars that pass on the street outside have switched their butter-scotch-colored headlights off.

Last night, the temperature went to eighteen below, and even now it is two or three degrees below zero. There is no wind at all, and when you step in the snow it sometimes cracks as loud as a slat breaking.

All day I am dazed with the enormity of this weather, and I am puzzled by something quite different. During study hall, I tried twice to signal Alice, but she ignored me completely; and after class, she hurried out and I couldn't get to her because the god-damn Abbott intercepted me again and said he wanted to talk to me after school.

I can't figure out what he wants. I am good for a C in history, and I didn't do anything wrong in study hall . . . even though I tried.

When the last bell rings, I go to my locker and throw my books inside. Then I turn around to look for Alice, but she isn't at her locker, so I figure I'd better go up to see the Abbott, and maybe get back in time to talk to Alice.

By the time I get to his homeroom, though, the building is half empty, and I realize that Alice has probably left already.

The Abbott isn't in, but Miss Harshberger says he will return in a few minutes, so I sit down and wait. This is the Abbott's den, where we have world history, and the front of the room is filled with big map stands and a solitary globe that the Abbott likes to spin around when he is making a point. He looks godlike when he does this, and I am sure it gives him a sense of power; but he is wasting his time, because most of the kids in front of him don't get what is happening. They don't realize that the Abbott is spin-ning their world around.

Now, there are footsteps in the hall, and I feel a rush of air as he comes striding in. He has been climbing the steps, and he is breathing hard, so when he greets me, he exhales my name, rather than speaking it.

Halfway toward his desk, he pivots and goes back to close the door. Now, I have an inkling of an inkling, and I am a little bit scared, so I look straight out the window, ten feet in front of the Abbott, while he sits down in his squeaky chair and starts slam-ming and banging at the drawers in his desk. He can never find anything, or remember where he put anything; whereas he can remember everything that ever happened in history. Or at least, it seems he can.

"Blagg," he says, suddenly skidding backward in his chair and crashing against the blackboard.

"Yes sir."

"Will you please for once in your life come over here and sit down in front of me and look me in the eye while I talk to you?"

I pretend that those directions are too complicated to follow, but I shuffle over to a seat nearer the center. I still don't look at him, however.

"You know, I don't like to stay after school any more than you do, Blagg. You know that?"

"Yes sir," I say. I stop chewing my gum, because I don't want to irritate him too much. The halls are quiet already. Alice is gone, and the Abbott and I are practically alone in the building.

"Blagg," Mr. Abbott says, "I know about you two in the furnace room."

I look at his eyes, and, seeing my look, the Abbott nods sadly, with his mouth all drawn up as if this is a dismally grim business for him, too. I am so scared, I really think I might lose control of myself and wet my pants. I am so scared, it feels like electric shocks going up the backs of my arms and legs and all through my stomach.

"I saw you go down with her Tuesday, but you can be sure I didn't spy on you. Nevertheless, I know what's been going on. You can depend on that. Understand?"

I nodded and looked at my hands.

"Good. No denials, Blagg, and I like that. You really have a lot of good qualities to be so . . . well, so mediocre as a student. I've never once doubted your intelligence, for instance. Did you know that? No sir, not once. You have more brains than Edna May Shultz and Vera Bauman put together. Know that?"

"Yes sir," I mumble, although I think I mean to say the opposite.

"Blagg, I don't want to be cruel. I know about the furnace room, but I don't want you to go jumping to conclusions about me having you and Alice Scanlon kicked out of school. Okay?"

"Okay," I tell him.

"But, boy, this is serious. I hope you realize that. Especially since you come from such a good family, and Mr. Altizer feels very strongly about things like this. He'd have you booted out of school quicker than . . ."

He keeps talking, but I am sitting there like somebody has just hit me with a hammer, and I don't really hear what he is saying.

The clock hand jumps another minute above the door, and I realize it has been only nine minutes since the last bell rang, ending classes.

"And why a girl like Alice Scanlon?" the Abbott is asking me. "Why a glamorous little piece of junk like that? For God's sake, don't you have any *pride?* Don't you know she's the biggest little slut in school?"

I would agree to anything now, I am so frightened. The Abbott walks back and forth in front of me, as I sit there alone in a classroom that can seat eighty pupils. I alone am receiving his condemnation, his disgust, his compassion. He is like a great lens of guilt that focuses the sun of wrath upon me, and it is a miracle I don't blacken and curl up in flames, the way toilet paper does when a lens focuses sunlight upon it.

I am trying to swallow, and I think I am nodding at something the Abbott is saying. But he is asking me where I live, and he repeats the question when I don't answer. And when I finally do manage to answer, the Abbott stops pacing and looks thoughtful.

"If you lived two more blocks to the east," he says, "you would be in the Glenview District, instead of this one. That's where my house is, as a matter of fact. Not over a mile from where you live."

He continues to look thoughtful and nods. "Yes," he says, "you'd be going to Glenview High instead of here. That's a better school. Nothing fancy or glamorous about it, but academically a better school . . . take my word for it. My daughter goes there, I'm happy to say."

Can it be that he has forgotten about the furnace room so quickly? He has always been a strange and unpredictable man, but this tangent impresses me as being sinister, in some way.

Suddenly, his hand is on my shoulder and he squeezes it once. "I just don't know what to do, Blagg. What would *you* do if you were in my shoes?"

All I can do is shake my head and finally manage to swallow.

"Something like this," the Abbott intones, turning away from me once more and pacing toward the cold window, "could affect you for the rest of your life. This could make a great difference. God knows there's enough of that sort of thing going on around here, but *in the furnace room!* Do you know how *depraved* that would seem to most people?"

I shake my head no, and have just about decided that I cannot hold the tears back any longer, when the Abbott surprises me once more by saying, "We'll have to talk about it, and the simple fact is we can't discuss it here."

He returns and puts his hand on my shoulder once more. "Why don't you drop by at my house this evening and we can talk this thing over? Maybe you can tell your folks you're going to the library or something. I'm sure you can think of some excuse. But nobody must know about this. Okay?"

"I suppose so," I tell him. "I'll do anything you say."

He squeezes my shoulder one last time and says, "I'm certain we can work things out somehow. I don't want to ruin a boy's whole life. And I have considerable faith in your maturity, underneath all those screwball antics of yours. Understand, Blagg?"

By now, I can hardly see, because my eyes are filled with tears. But I raise my face and nod yes in the direction of the Abbott's face. Naturally, his image appears blurred to me, so that I can't be sure; but it seems that he isn't looking at me at all, but over my head at something in the back of the room.

At any rate, he says all right, gives me his address, and turns back to his desk; and I know that he is through talking to me for now.

I WALK THERE, because my mother is using the car tonight for Christmas shopping, and the branch library is only four blocks from our house. This is where I have told my parents I am going, and as a matter of fact I do start in that direction, because the Abbott's street is beyond the library.

Halfway there, the houses get smaller and a little drab, it seems to me. I haven't paid much attention to them before, but by the time I get to Mr. Abbott's house, I am aware that this is a pretty shabby neighborhood.

The address he gave me belongs to a little two-story frame house with a lighted side porch and a door at the end of that. I stamp the snow off my feet as I go onto the porch. By the doorbell is a little slip of paper, covered with Scotch tape, saying "Out of order."

I knock on the door, and Mr. Abbott immediately lets me in and takes my coat. "Perhaps you didn't know," he says, "but the fact is, I am a widower."

Then, when he shows me into the front room and bids me sit down, he says, "We're informal here. There's just the two of us—Judy and me. Sit down, and I'll call her."

He goes to the stairwell and pauses for an instant; then he seems to change his mind, and he climbs the stairs without calling, leaving me alone in the tiny living room.

I am glad he's gone. There is a card table standing in the entranceway to the small dining room, and it is covered with a tablecloth. In the center of the table, there is a candle burning between two plates and two glasses. To one side, there is another plate heaped with cookies.

Someone is whispering upstairs . . . or at least I think I can hear whispering. Then the stairs squeak once more to the heavy tread of Mr. Abbott as he descends, followed by a terribly thin and pale girl who is staring at her feet as she walks.

"This is my daughter," Mr. Abbott says, not bothering to introduce me at all, so later when I can think it over I realize that she must have already known my name.

Still, the girl does not raise her eyes to me, but mumbles something about being pleased to meet me . . . which is so obvious a lie that even I, at this moment, can see that it is.

"How about having some Cokes with your cookies?" Mr. Abbott says, clapping his hands together nervously. "All kids like Cokes. Right? Go ahead, Judy. They're nice and cold, right there in the refrigerator."

Before she departs for the kitchen, Judy raises her face and looks at me for the first time, and I see that she has an artificial eye. Then, too, for the first time I see how incredibly thin her neck is, and the sight of it almost makes me groan, as if a cruel trick is being played on all of us. Her neck is no thicker than the meaty part of my forearm.

So this is the daughter that he has mentioned several times in class, and the one who he says goes to Glenview High.

Mr. Abbott and I both watch her disappear in the kitchen, and I am thinking almost hysterically that the girl is dying . . . that she has some kind of disease that is infectious, and for the flick of a second in the confusion of this thought, I actually think of her beneath me in the furnace room, and the horror of the thought shocks me back to a realization that Mr. Abbott is talking.

I glance at the Abbott, and he is still staring toward the kitchen, with a look of deep concentration on his face . . . the same look I had noticed there when he had watched Debbie sharpening her pencil.

He slaps his knees, and says, "Yes, perhaps it was injudicious of me to invite you over this evening. But Judy won't bother us. She's quiet like her mother . . . not loud like the old Abbott!"

Saying this, he laughs in a terrible bark. He is seated forward in his chair, so he seems almost to be squatted there, ready to spring out the minute his daughter comes back. He grips one fist with the other hand and slowly cracks his knuckles. In the kitchen, all is silence; and briefly I picture the pale girl lying dead in the darkness, her one artificial eye staring sightlessly upward into the darkness.

"Glenview High doesn't have the glamour we're used to at Shaw," Mr. Abbott says, looking over my head, "but it's more solid academically."

Mr. Abbott's daughter returns, carrying two Cokes on a tray. The candle dips lightly from the ghostly wisp of air her passing has caused. She places the two bottles down on the table, and I notice that the eyelid of her artificial eye does not close entirely when she looks down.

Mr. Abbott stands up and says to his daughter, "I was just saying that Glenview doesn't have the glamour of Shaw, but it's more solid academically."

His daughter lowers her face in a half-nod, reminding me of the way Alice nods. How many times has she heard her father say this to her, alone in the silence of the house? What is the point of his saying it in the first place? I am wondering if she will lift her face and confront me once again with the terrible machinery of her stare.

"Sit down, sit down," the Abbott says now. "And eat up. Kids like Coke and cookies. Eat up!"

He goes out into the kitchen, and I hear the tap start running. Judy has seated herself before I can even think of helping her with her chair, but there is hardly room for me to circle the card table anyway. The water is running fiercely, now, as if the Abbott wants to flood the kichen.

"Isn't your father going to eat with us?" I ask.

She shakes her head and says, "No, he never eats anything."

This surprises me, because I have always thought of him as a big man, but now I realize that he is indeed gaunt . . . that only his head and his bones are big, but that his skin hangs upon him like a sagging wrap of flesh.

She drinks half her Coke and eats one cookie. I drink all of mine, and eat three or four cookies, swallowing them almost whole. The tap is still running in the kitchen. Finally, it shuts off, and Mr. Abbott returns to the front room, looking even more haggard.

"Sometimes," he says, "I get so hot the only thing that seems to help is running cold water over my face. Some of us aren't made for central heating. Some of us would probably be more comfortable living in a cave."

I glance at his eyes, and they are wet; and there is water even on his collar.

"Blagg," he says, "please eat up. I know you eat more than that. Don't forget, I've seen you operate in the cafeteria."

He once more barks out a kind of laugh, and I put another cookie in my mouth.

At this instant, Judy gets up and says, "Excuse me, but I really don't feel well."

Her voice breaks at the end, and she runs upstairs, while Mr. Abbott stands up and looks foolishly upward, as if he can see through the ceiling. Then he follows her, and in another minute or so, I heard her voice say, "But I *told* you I didn't feel well," and then the Abbott is going, "Shhhh, shhhh."

In a few minutes, he returns, smiling like a man about to hiss from pain.

"Blagg," he says, "my daughter is not well at all. The fact of the matter is, she is not a well girl."

The Abbott is standing, and he shakes his head back and forth as he speaks these words, making the loose skin of his neck quiver.

"That's too bad," I say.

"Yes," he says, sitting down on the sofa, slowly and carefully.

I notice the candle is still burning, and I wish he would extinguish it, but he doesn't seem to notice. He merely sighs now and then, and drums his fingers on the arm of the sofa.

"As for the problem we have discussed," he says after a few minutes, "I won't say anything about it if you promise it won't happen again. I mean in the furnace room, of course."

Suddenly he gets up and goes into the kitchen, and I hear the tap turned on once more. When he returns, his tie is pulled to the side and the hair on one side of his head has been mussed up. He looks like a man who has been wrestling, or has just awakened from a nap filled with violent dreams.

"She's had boys call on her before, of course," the Abbott says, closing his eyes. He doesn't open them, and I wonder if he is going to start praying. Outside, someone starts scraping the walk with a snow shovel. Otherwise, there is only silence.

Apparently there is nothing more to be said, and finally I get up enough nerve to stand up and say I have to go. The Abbott nods his head, but he isn't looking at me. "Glenview is really a first-rate school," he says, and I agree with him.

Then when he gets my coat and I am shrugging it on, he mentions that it was probably not a judicious thing to do, inviting me here. When I get out the door, the hair on one side of his head is still wildly tangled. He shakes my hand, and I step out onto the gummy old boards of the porch and off the porch into the cold feathery snow that has been falling once again.

TODAY THE ABBOTT is quiet, and his lecture on the early explorers of the Western world seems distant and half-hearted. He has not once looked at me, and I am wondering if he has withdrawn because I have unwillingly caught him out in something shameful.

When classes change, I move slowly down the hall and pass a gallery of old photographs that have to do with our school's history. One of these photographs shows a winning football team of fifteen years ago. There at the end of the third row is the Abbott, an assistant coach at that time, as round and unwrinkled as a porpoise. There is a grin on his face, and his hands are pushed deep in the pockets of an overcoat that is open to the wind. It looks windy, because the Abbott's hair is mussed and tangled.

After lunch, we go up to the gym and shoot some baskets. Then there is biology and, after that, the study hall with Mr. Abbott. Here there is a lot of whispering, but the Abbott does not seem to notice. I am for the first time aware that often in the past he has come to us as if in an afterthought, leaving the source of his awful brooding somewhere behind. Now I cannot help but remember the sad two-story house and the lighted side porch. I am quiet during the whole hour, and I do not even try to get Alice's attention.

When night comes, there are carolers in our neighborhood, and I borrow the car to go to the library. However I drive past the library and enter a darker neighborhood, where the lights are not as thickly hung around the doors and porches, and where there are no plastic Santa Clauses and reindeer in the lawns, and no expensive wreaths on the doors.

Only here and there a sad little string of red and green lights circling a window, or perhaps an electric candle glowing out of the darkness like a bar of yellow soap. As I pass the Abbott's house, I see a small Christmas tree in the dimly lighted window. It is perfectly symmetrical, and artificial, of course. The rest of the windows are dark.

I turn my head back, as if it is possible that the Abbott and his daughter should be waiting at the windows, looking for me to drive past.

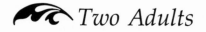

MINTNER SAT DOWN on the blanket and yawned. When he reached over to get the candy bar Goldie had left, he discovered the letter. He lifted it up before his sunglasses and spelled out several words; then he dropped the letter beside the blanket and tried to fake a second yawn, because Goldie was coming back, frowning in the sharp sunlight and sliding her two thin brown feet raspingly, like garden trowels, into the sand with each step.

"Where's my letter?" Goldie asked, sitting down on the blanket. Her hair looked like a peck of confetti; her eyes were deep-set, secretive and as pale as the bleached crab shells under the pier.

"Here it is," Mintner said, tossing the letter toward her hip. He didn't look at her as she picked it up.

"You read it, didn't you, didn't you?" she hissed rapidly.

"Part of it," Mintner said.

"Well, I suppose you think it's crazy."

Somewhere up on the boardwalk, a firecracker exploded. Mintner looked hard, but he didn't see any smoke. Only the anonymous holiday crowds from Philly and Baltimore and D.C.

"Well, don't you?"

"Don't I what?" Mintner asked.

"Think it's crazy," Goldie said.

"Look," Mintner said, closing one eye behind his glasses, the way he often did when he was speaking carefully to a business contact, "we are two independents, you and me. I make no claims on you; you make no claims on me. Two adults with a shared and common need. That's us. Subject dropped."

He opened the closed eye and swung his head around at Goldie, who was chewing her lip nervously and looking around the blanket.

"You lose something?" Mintner asked.

"No, you just make me nervous when you talk like that."

Mintner reached out and patted her ankle. "Two adults," he reminded her. "No claims. Write any kind of letter you want, no matter how kooky."

Goldie lay back with a sigh and felt the hot sunlight flow up over her body and into her face like a tide of scalding water. Mintner was tuning in his pocket radio. She wondered if his one eye was still closed, caught in a stationary wink at the world, as if he, Mintner, figured he was in on the secret.

M‌Y MOTHER WAS an individualist," Goldie would tell people. "She loved flowers—particularly marigolds. That's my real name: Marigold."

"You were precious to your mother," Mintner told her when she first recited this to him. "Precious. *Mère's* gold, you might say."

"Very funny," Goldie said. "Ha, ho hum, ha."

"Well, not bad."

"It's the kind of joke that could give me nightmares," she told him.

"That's not bad, too."

"It's obscene to be as nonconformist as my mother was," Goldie continued. "If I had been named 'Joan' or 'Marcia', I would have been different."

"I had an uncle who wanted to have me named 'Jonah'," Mintner said, "but my mother wouldn't listen to him."

"Don't be funny."

"Then there was a Catholic uncle who said, 'Why don't you name the kid "Judas"? It's got a ring to it.'"

"You like to joke about other people's fixations," Goldie said. "I can certainly see that."

"It passes the time. I have a sister he wanted named Clytemnestra. Now *there's* a name you don't find very often."

"I'm not sure," Goldie said slowly, "but you are just possibly the most hateful, most obnoxious person I have ever met."

"Whatever I do, I try to do well," Mintner said.

Goldie nervously surprised herself and laughed out loud, so hard that a little spray from her mouth struck his chin. She saw it all. It was like a swift, secret little zap of electricity between them, she was to think later; at any rate, here she was in Ocean City, living with him in a second-story motel apartment constructed of hairy slabs of naked, but heavily varnished, wood, overlooking the inlet in back, the tide rip—where in the mornings the brightly colored boats nosed seaward—and beyond, like a hazy streak of watercolor that made her sneeze sometimes when she looked at it, the Atlantic Ocean.

But of course, all this couldn't go on. Mintner had a wife and four kids in an expensive suburb of Trenton, New Jersey, and Goldie was developing a nervous stomach. She had a fine gift for suffering, her mother had told her once when Goldie was complaining about her name to her.

"God shield me from eccentrics!" Goldie had said. "And from making a fool of myself!" She had honestly thought she was about to dedicate her life to the pursuit—the holy pursuit—of normality, solidity and the tangible.

"It gives me comfort," she would tell people, most of whom, it happened, were strange and eccentric, but interested in her, nevertheless, for they didn't often find people who were socially and intellectually centripetal. It was rare for them to find a conformist.

"Go on and read all those screwballs," Goldie said during a literary discussion, her earrings jangling. "I'm sick of all that. Don't you think all of us are ultimately gregarious and have social needs?"

Mintner heard that one, and he said yes, loudly, before the force of the rhetorical question could gather. Mintner was always aborting her rhetoric, as if he was impatient to get on to another topic . . . which topic, incidentally, he had never actually gotten on to.

But Goldie was fascinated by him and had never once in the six months of their relationship lost hope that Mintner would someday stand flatfooted and look into her eyes, with both of *his* eyes open and unwinking, and say, "Goldie, this is what I believe, and when you hear it you will realize that I am as wise and solid and down-to-earth as you are!" Then he might go on to tell her that he was sick of his skinny wife, who kept every letter and circular and bill she'd ever received through the mail and wore her dyed-black hair in a pageboy bob right out of the 1940s, and went on a diet every two months, during which time she ate only parsley, carrots, black coffee, lean pork chops and ice milk.

Goldie's horny feet were tanned to almost the identical color of the varnished wood of the motel; she wore huge prescription sunglasses to correct the astigmatism in her right eye, shield her eyes from the hard brilliance of the sand, sea and sun, make her eyes look vast and mysterious, and hide the fact that one day almost a week before, she had nervously, but unconsciously, in a fit of brooding, plucked almost all of her right eyebrow out. There was another factor, however: she was half-smashed on vodka. But even this had been caused by brooding over that damned Mintner.

This was when she decided to write the letter to Dear Abby. Part of the reason was that all her friends (and Mintner's friends, even more than hers) would have died laughing, or would die laughing, when they found out. But Goldie would calmly and rationally explain to them that one had to get in touch with the mass of people or go mad, and that she, for one, would feel comfort when Abby's million readers shared her problem, anonymously . . . her problem with the voracious, sardonic Mintner, whom she could not leave without the ceremony of advice and media exposure. Even though she had come to him without the ceremony of marriage. Among other things, Marigold would be on the center of the stage, when her letter appeared in Dear Abby's column, and deep in Goldie's opaque heart she knew that there was no more central place than that.

S o when they returned to the motel to change for dinner, Goldie wandered about the room and Mintner lay on the bed, reading a magazine full of pictures of great pink breasty nudes. Looking at them made Goldie feel gray and miserable, even though she was neither, and Mintner had often told her she had "a great built," speaking this way to emphasize his proletarian origins.

"Come here," he kept saying, but Goldie was intent on other things, and Mintner didn't seem interested enough to put down the magazine and really *look* at her. He just kept looking at something on the page before him and chewing a wad of Dentyne gum. He had put half a pack in his mouth two hours ago, on the beach, and he hadn't offered her one stick. She took oblique comfort in the fact that she would have refused it if he had, however.

"Come here," he said again, and turned a page. He was still wearing his open-toed sandals, and there were dark grains of wet sand scattered on the blue bedspread, like frosting on a sloppy cake.

"You haven't mentioned the letter," Goldie said. "Maybe you think it's wacky. A foolish thing to do."

"Listen," Mintner said, closing one eye but not turning away from the magazine. "No strings. Two adults. Like I said."

"The letter isn't strings," Goldie told him passionately. "It's more than those damned silly strings you're always bringing up."

"Read it to me," Mintner said.

For some reason, Goldie felt like crying at the tone in his voice. If she had been his wife, she would have told him to go straight to hell . . . do not pass go, do not collect two hundred dollars. (The allusion to the middle-class game would have really irritated him; *God, what a wife she could have been!*)

But of course Goldie had no legal or moral rights, which fact in itself was one of the reasons for the letter. So she pulled the letter out of a paperback novel she had been leafing through and prepared to read it aloud. Mintner didn't look up from the girlie magazine, but she saw his eyes stop moving, so she knew that he wasn't reading, at least. He was probably looking at the color photograph of a girl's breast.

Goldie stood straight, as if she were in elocution class, and read:

> Dear Abby:
>
> I have decided to write to you because I am now faced with a critical decision—whether or not I should leave this man, whom I sometimes [she emphasized the word, although it wasn't underlined] think [another emphasis] I love, but at other times almost feel indifferent to [further emphasis].
>
> We are of different ethnic backgrounds, his mother being Irish and his father Jewish, whereas I am of Hungarian and low-land Scottish extraction, even though my mother named me after an American flower. My family has lived in this country for several generations, however, and so has his family.
>
> Even though we have these ethnic differences, we get along exceptionally well most of the time. I think it is because of our wit. We seem to have a fantastic talent for punning and making other kinds of jokes. Life with him is really quite exciting, since we both receive stimulation from this sort of thing.
>
> Nevertheless, I am thinking of leaving him, for we are not married. He is, in fact, a married man, so you see I have to accept the fact that so far [emphasis] I must come second. I have a regard for the feelings of others, and it is because of this that I have not once brought up the subject of divorce, even though his wife is an incredible neurotic and he gives absolutely no impression of loving her [great emphasis].

Also, I must admit that I am at heart a very conventional gal, and have always had respect for hearth and home. I love down-to-earth things and am very normal in every way. Some people think I look like Donna Reed, only I am a little heavier.

At present, we are spending several days at the beach. His wife thinks he is attending a convention.

What do you think I should do?

Signed: Troubled

"Whoever told you you looked like Donna Reed?" Mintner asked, when she finished reading. He was looking up from his magazine now, both eyes open, and he seemed genuinely interested.

"Lots of people have," she said. "Only I'm quite a bit heavier than Donna Reed. I'd be the first to admit that."

"I'll say you are. Especially in the milk works."

"Never mind about that," Goldie said. "What do you think of the letter?"

"Fine, fine," Mintner said, snapping a page of the magazine as he turned it. "Who are you sending it to? My wife?"

"I'm sending it to Dear Abby," she said. "Weren't you listening?"

Mintner did not answer. Mintner seemed undisturbed. She watched him as he finally took the gum out of his mouth and methodically mashed it against the back cover of the magazine, without once taking his attention from the page.

Goldie felt saliva squeezing up into her mouth, and she walked swiftly through the screen door and out on the back veranda. It was evening, and the green running lights of the fishing boats lined the channel as they returned to the security of the bay. Down below, in a courtyard beyond the fence, someone was burning trash, and the stinking dark smoke filtered through the breeze into Goldie's face, so she lighted a cigarette to kill the odor.

Back in the room, Mintner loudly turned a page. All else was silence.

MINTNER HAD BLUE eyes, which he said came from his Irish mother. When Goldie had once pointed out that his father had blue eyes, too, "even though he was Jewish," Mintner had gotten impatient, and had said, "Yes, but I get my blue eyes from my mother."

Goldie had laughed at that, whooping a little too loud, and Mintner had not appreciated her reaction. "It's not just the color," he'd told her. "It's the shape and everything. Believe me, if I had my father's eyes, I'd be the first to admit it. But it just isn't true. Facts are facts—a fact you have trouble understanding."

Mintner, who was so proud of his independence and liberation from the claims of both parents, had been hurt, and Goldie had sensed it deeply . . . had felt a spasm of compassion, and had dropped the whole, strangely painful subject. She had let him have his mother's eyes.

Now, Mintner was as invulnerable as a sheik, lying on his back on the bed, gazing torpidly at colored photographs of naked women. Unaware of the desperately normal woman just outside the screen door, contemplating the mailing of a critical letter.

She went back into the room and dressed rapidly, putting on a halter that left her lean midriff bare and emphasized the splendid proportions of her breasts. She put on skintight pants and jabbed an onyx comb in her hair. Then she touched some mascara to her dry eyes, jammed her sunglasses on, and, with her heart breaking, strode out the front door.

Mintner didn't even say good-by. Maybe the nude photographs were enough. Along with a neurotic wife in Trenton, and four innocent children.

Goldie's eyes suddenly flooded with tears, and she almost walked into a baby carriage that was parked outside a pizza parlor next to the motel. When she saw the baby carriage, she naturally felt worse. If she had had a knife in her hand at that instant, she told herself—somewhat hysterically—and Mintner's bare throat beside the knife, she would have sliced a big bloody grin right underneath the cocky one she now pictured him as always wearing.

In the bus station, Goldie bought a Heath bar and sat on a bench, chewing the gummy chocolate while her eyes filled once more with tears. Next to her sat two gigantic black women. One of them wore a red silk cloth wrapped around her head like a bandage, and between her thick knees, looming like watermelons wrapped in hosiery, sat a covered birdcage. The other woman was younger, and her hair was dyed a bright orange.

Goldie was sorry she had worn this outfit, because her bare midriff was cold. She knew her stomach must be all goose-pimply.

At the other end of the station, a young boy sat alone with his arm hanging over a suitcase standing upright beside him on the bench.

An old woman holding a cardboard box with a string tied around it sat several feet away from him.

Otherwise, the bus station was empty. The floor was dirty, and a faint odor of stale urine came from the men's room in back. When the phone rang behind the counter, Goldie could hear the sound reverberate like a school bell in a gym, and she dropped the wrapper of her Heath bar. The man behind the counter leaned out and said, "Phone call for a Miss Marigold Donaldson."

Goldie arose and walked toward the phone. She was not capable of ignoring a ringing phone. Sometimes when she ate too much, she had nightmares in which a phone was ringing and her arms were as heavy as logs, so she could not reach out and lift the receiver. Always, she felt guilty, knowing that somebody wanted to talk to her, and she hadn't responded.

Now she told herself that it might be someone else—her mother, perhaps, or maybe even Rick Shields, whom she had dated back in college, when she'd been second runner-up for Homecoming Queen. Rick had owned an MG and had an expensive stereo.

But when she said hello, she realized that all along she had known it could only be Mintner. Who else could have known she was waiting in a bus station in this little resort town?

"Why can't we act like two adults?" Mintner said.

"I don't know," she answered, sounding so contrite she could have shot the telephone.

"I'll tell you something," Mintner went on. "I am a real son of a bitch. You know that? I admit it. A real goddamn son of a bitch. Go on: call me one!"

"I don't want to."

"Why not? It's the truth. I *am* a son of a bitch!"

"Please don't talk like that," Goldie said. "We're on the telephone."

"You're right," Mintner said. "Q.E.D."

"What's that?"

"Never mind," Mintner said. "It means, that's just exactly what I'm talking about. Look, don't move."

"I'm not moving."

"I mean, stay where you are. In the bus station. I'll come and pick you up, and we'll go out and have beef stroganoff. A real Russian dinner. Vodka before. Moscow mules."

Goldie inhaled and thought deeply. "I don't know," she said.

"Champagne and happy music!" he called out in his mad impresario's voice.

"Oh, the bubbles will tickle my nose," Goldie said, using the silly dumb blonde voice she used when he talked like that.

"Atta girl," Mintner said quietly, his voice mostly breath, like a whisper. "Stay where you are."

When Mintner hung up, Goldie started crying, but by the time he came to the bus station, she was heavily under control, and she greeted him with what she hoped was a stony and dignified silence.

He might have thought it was the way he was dressed, but it wasn't. He was wearing Bermuda shorts, and a South Seas shirt that was at least two sizes too big, so it fit him like a muumuu. His sunburned face was highlighted by inert gobs of white salve on the cheek, nose and forehead.

As he passed in front of the two huge black women, Mintner squinted his eyes at Goldie and held both his hands out, moving them up and down, the way a basketball player guards against a shot. The heads of the two black women turned together, as if they were guided by two compasses toward Mintner's brilliant gravity.

"Now, no more silliness," Mintner announced, grabbing Goldie's hand. "Two adults."

She stood up and, without speaking, walked out of the bus station, smelling Dentyne gum.

Later that evening, Mintner and Goldie drank vodka before dinner. A violinist and a balalaika player played a duet, and Goldie was so high she stood up and sort of danced to the music for a little while. Mintner clapped his hands, but he didn't stand up.

After dinner, Mintner asked her if she had mailed the letter, and when she said yes, Mintner clapped her on the back and said, "Fine. I believe in free expression like everybody else. Let me know when you get an answer."

"I will," Goldie said. "I signed it 'Troubled.'"

Mintner didn't know why she had said that, but he recognized the satisfaction in her voice, and that was communication enough.

Only on one condition had she stayed with him. She told him this six or seven times, each time differently and somewhat incoherently, while Mintner clipped his toenails, or thumbed through the second girlie magazine he had bought on this trip, or sat on the beach with one eye closed over a smoking cigarette as he gazed at the horizon.

"You're not listening," Goldie told him when they were on the beach.

"I'm listening with one ear," Mintner said.

"Is that all I'm worth, one ear?"

"You want me to repeat what you said? Because you've been harping on it all day, you know, and I can repeat it. Verbatim, or with variations on a theme."

"No, just respond; don't repeat."

Mintner vibrated his hands up and down as if he were hefting an invisible weight. "Because I can, you know. I can repeat what you had been saying, but I'll be damned if I can understand any of it."

"Maybe it would take two ears to understand."

"Two years or maybe three. Whatever it would take, I don't have the time."

"Just give me a chance to explain myself. You always seem to crowd me into a position where I appear silly."

"Look," Mintner said. "I think it's a fine idea, if it's still about the ring."

"It's just a symbol, you know."

"I know. You been telling me about the goddamn symbol all morning."

"The least you could do is tell me you understand why I want to buy a ring, even if it *is* a K-Mart ring. There's no reason I should have to put up with the way those bitches stare at me. Just because they have rings on their third fingers and I don't have."

"Goldie," Mintner said, poking her in the ribs, "I will buy you a ring for *all* your fingers if you just give the word. I didn't know you were so much into Queen Victoria, for Christ's sake. Half the married people in this country aren't even married. All right, an exaggeration—say 15 percent. So what? Who gives a shit?"

"I do," Goldie said.

Mintner chewed on that a while and then said, "God knows, this trip hasn't been any goddamn picnic. You been steaming about one thing after another ever since we got here. First it was Dear Abby, and now it's this thing about a ring."

Goldie was sitting up, looking at two women sharing a blanket about forty feet away. One of them was burned to the color of chocolate, and her hair was naturally snow-white. Goldie was thinking she would look stunning in an evening dress. She could see the woman's ring flashing arrogantly in the sunlight, even from that distance. Even through her sunglasses.

AFTER LUNCH, which Mintner had brought in a white sack down to the beach from a stand on the boardwalk, Goldie went back to the motel room and put on a dress. Then she went uptown and bought a few things, while Mintner napped. At a little after four o'clock, she returned to the room—smelling of gin, perfume and sunburned skin—and started taking things out of a sack and putting them in a dresser drawer.

She thought Mintner was still asleep, but suddenly she turned around and saw him lying on his side, watching her.

"Well," he said. "Did you get the ring?"

"No," Goldie said. "I decided against it."

Mintner nodded, as if he had half-expected such an answer. He closed one eye like a man sighting along an invisible rifle barrel.

Goldie started breathing hard. "I suppose you think that's silly, don't you?"

"No, I wouldn't say that," Mintner said, turning over on his back and clasping his hands behind his head.

"I mean, after all the fuss I made," Goldie said, slamming the drawer.

"No, I didn't say a word," Mintner said. "I swear I didn't." He was staring thoughtfully up at the ceiling.

"I didn't say you *said* anything. I said you probably *thought* so."

"Look, live and let live. Okay? A man can only do so much. All right?"

Goldie slouched over to the butterfly wing chair and sat down. Then immediately she jumped up and said, "No, that isn't right. People have to care about one another, and if they care about one another, you can't live and let live."

"Will you stop bobbing around? For God's sake, you bounce up and down, here and there, like some goddamn jack-in-the-box, if you ask me."

Goldie held her hands out, as if beckoning toward him. "Don't you know I can see how silly I am? Do you think I'm so stupid I don't see how brainless I act sometimes and how inconsistent I am? As if I could *help* it!"

"Look, don't start in on that again. I don't know what you're talking about when you get like that."

"We are walking, breathing, living lies, you and me. Your wife, too. I mean, I'm trying to tell you we weren't meant to live the way we do . . . to dissipate our lives and to be this silly and . . . and . . . superficial! Don't you think I can see that?"

"Well, don't look at me. I didn't play any tricks on you. We come together, you and me. I didn't rape you or anything."

"God, that isn't what I'm talking about and you know it!"

"I do? Glad to hear it."

"You refuse to understand, because you know I'm right. Instinctively, you know this, and you know if you faced it the way I'm doing, you'd get hysterical, too."

She ran her hands through her hair and went over to the dresser again.

"Let's get down to brass tacks." Mintner said. "Why didn't you get the ring you were talking so much about this morning?"

"Oh, it isn't the ring," Goldie said. "It never was."

"Not even a symbol?"

"It wasn't the ring."

"You know something? You are really neurotic. I mean, you leave me a thousand miles behind, when it comes to figuring out what your motivations are."

"Leave my motivations out of it. I'm as normal as the next person."

"You are a card-carrying, gold-plated screwball, if I ever saw one," Mintner said. "For all your gab about being normal, you are really a walking fruit cake. It'd be funny if I didn't have a lot of feeling for you."

"You certainly talk like you have feeling for me! I'll certainly say that!"

"Well, you're terrific, for my money. Look, no hysterics. Enough said? Terrific?"

Mintner got up and started to put on his pants.

"No," Goldie said. She took a cigarette out of her pack and tapped it so hard on the bone of her wrist it wrinkled. "I should have taken the bus home last night. I should have left. Only where would I go? Do you know something? Do you?"

She stood by his side, breathing heavily through her nose as she waited for Mintner to answer.

"What?" he said.

"We weren't meant to be what you and I are. *That's* what. And don't start talking about marriage, because that has nothing to do with it. If we were married, you and I, I would still be standing right where I am now, and saying the same things."

"No you wouldn't." Mintner stared at her as she tremblingly lit the cigarette on the side, then he said, "What's the matter with you? Is it your time of the month or something?"

"Oh, Christ," Goldie moaned. "Men!"

"Don't tell me I'm bad at diagnosis. I know how women get when their plumbing goes whacky."

"That doesn't have anything to do with it. And it's not plumbing and it's not whacky."

"I know better. Three weeks out of four you wouldn't understand what you're trying to say now any more than *I* can understand it."

"Then, those three weeks I'm wrong. Because now I'm right, and don't stand there so goddamn wise and cocky and try to tell me I'm wrong or just hysterical in a female way, because. . . ."

She stopped talking as suddenly as if a plug had been pulled somewhere, switching off her thoughts. She went to her purse and pulled out a pint bottle of Gibson's gin and poured some into a water glass. Mintner watched her glumly.

"Sure," he said. "The time of the month has nothing to do with it, and the booze has nothing to do with it. *Nothing* has nothing to do with it!"

"You don't understand anything," Goldie said. She took another drink from the glass and pulled a strand of hair out of her eye. Mintner sat down on the bed, looking tired—his shoulders rounded over his belly.

"At one time," Goldie said, lifting her chin and gazing through wet eyes toward the inlet, "people made sense to one another. And life added up. There were issues, not to mention such things as right and wrong!"

"I don't want to hear any more about it," Mintner said.

๛ *The Ascension of the* Belasco

In 1944, at the age of nineteen, I graduated from the Merchant Marine Academy and was immediately appointed second officer of a little, super-annuated five-hundred-ton coastal freighter named the *Belasco*. Her home port was New Orleans, and her destination when I first boarded her was Caracas, Venezuela.

Because of a back injury I'd gotten wrestling in high school, I had been deferred from regular military service, and had attended college for a year, where I'd hoped to major in philosophy. Fearful of being thought a coward or malingerer, I judged that in view of the losses among merchant seamen recently, I would likely be in as great danger as anyone could hope, and therefore as caught up in the passion of that time. It was important for me to know this.

My record at the academy had been respectable, although it might have been better if I hadn't been so often preoccupied with two matters. One was the fact that I looked far younger than my years: my youthfulness was unnatural. I could have passed for sixteen; and I grew a straggly, shy mustache and worried about how I would ever be able to assume any position of authority without seeming ridiculous. The other was a philosophical problem: I wondered how it is that the Present moment—a slice of time, without dimension—can be said to contain all the Past.

The question had come to me in the following manner: one of my instructors at college—a girl with a limp and a brilliant, nervous mind—had said that in a famous passage Augustine had referred to the Past as always being "present," else how could we ever know it? My instructor dismissed Augustine's perplexity as a semantic evasion; but I embraced it with the passion of startled ignorance, and riddled it over and over in my head, like a popular song.

WHEN I REPORTED to my ship in New Orleans, my disappointment was acute. The *Belasco* was gaudy in its decay, ostentatious in its ugliness. I knew very well how desperate matters were in these days, and had prepared myself for something in the way of compromise in my first assignment. It was well-known, and only natural, that the important and preferable berths were occupied by men with experience, so a new graduate from the academy might well be assigned to a vessel that wouldn't even be chartered in peacetime.

And this was far from being peacetime; and yet, when I first looked upon the old *Belasco*, as scummed and rusty as an old iron bucket festering in some muddy sink, I felt like throwing it all over . . . hailing a taxi and going somewhere to get drunk, changing my name, and not sobering up until I looked old enough to command a crew of heroes.

On the train to New Orleans I had read Edward Galinsky's *The Lyrical Nihilists*, and, when I first gazed upon the *Belasco*, echoes from Galinsky's book resonated in my head. Here, at the age of nineteen, I was confronted with an ontological joke. My despair at this moment was melodramatic, dissociative, and aloof.

What I did, of course, was survive the adolescent impulse toward rhetoric, hitch up my courage, and climb aboard. The impression I then received was odd and powerful. There was an uncanny pull toward some inscrutable recognition. What was it?

Once, at the age of fourteen, I had sneaked into a movie theater that had been closed down and was marked for destruction. I can well remember the unsettling thrill of trespassing (for I had always been a dutiful and obedient boy). I also remember the almost-tangible darkness, the brooding desuetude, the smell of cold, stale air and dusty upholstery rising like the effluvium of *temps perdu* from the rows of desperately anonymous seats. Excepting the odors (*but almost evocative of these*), the *Belasco* had very much the same effect on me when I first climbed aboard.

There was nobody about, so I strolled along the deck, half-hoping that the ship had been taken off the lists at the last minute and I would be sent to another. I paused and took thought. Somewhere to one side of me lay the Gulf of Mexico, where Nazi submarines had recently been operating with uncanny boldness. The gray paint on the bulkhead on the other side of me was peeling in layers, like the skin of an old carp. I felt I could have kicked a hole in it. Shaking my head, I walked on.

Finally, I came upon a sleepy and irascible-looking deck hand, with a Band-Aid on his upper lip and wearing a dirty, faded maroon T-shirt, who volunteered to help me. He took me on a tour of the ship, ostensibly looking for the Captain in every unlikely place, and treating me with a casual contempt that struck me as being a little unfair.

Eventually, having exhausted all other options, this sullen deck hand took me to the Captain's cabin and knocked. A voice from inside said come in, and my guide turned and raised his eyebrows in surprise. Apparently this was the last place he expected to find the Captain. He opened the hatch for me, stepped aside, and motioned me in. Then he closed the hatch and left.

If anything, the Captain himself was even more of a disappointment than the ship. He looked as old as my grandfather, who was retired and living out his days on a sugar beet farm near Lansing, Michigan. The Captain gazed out at me for so long after I'd introduced myself that I almost repeated my self-introduction, thinking that maybe he hadn't heard. But evidently he'd taken in the information, after all. Sitting on his bunk and looking up at me, he finally nodded and lifted up his hand to shake mine, looking the other way, as if he might be too embarrassed to meet the fierce idealism in his new second officer's eyes.

The first night, I went to my cabin and, after settling in, consulted some of the long and complicated notes I had made on a paper I someday hoped to write. The subject was my *idée fixe*, the problem of memory and Time, neither conceivable without the other. Having so little memory then (as I am now tempted to construe the matter), I was fascinated by the problems implicit in accumulating those experiences that would some day fill and define it, overloading each present instant with the relentlessly growing Past. Once, I'd even conceived of the Present as a sort of balloon, expanding constantly with time blown into it . . . for, philosophically speaking, *nothing* can totally disappear. Where is the metaphysical rug we can sweep past events under?

But on that first evening, I might as well have spent my time gazing at a Chaldean script; nothing made sense to me. Even my handwriting seemed alien, and the words I had written were unfathomable. I couldn't concentrate, no matter how hard I tried. The weight of the Belasco oppressed me as if all its five hundred tons were crushing my hope for the future.

PEOPLE ADAPT TO new situations with remarkable promptness. Two or three days in a vacation cabin will make it seem like home, whereas the real home you have left behind has already begun to loom like a dream of the distant past. "The instant they leave," Emerson said, "my guests show as ghosts."

Thus it was that the *Belasco* and its crew were familiar to me by the time of our departure from New Orleans four days later. Nevertheless, my initiation into one of the realities of that time came so soon after that departure, that I had a vague and uneasy feeling that reality was somehow being mismanaged. It was all simply too sudden; we half-expect that great events should be insulated from one another by great, wide sheets of boredom; but the fact is, often they are not.

I was asleep when the U-boat was sighted. One of the crew awakened me with the news, and, like a novice parachutist vaulting through the hatch, I stepped out into the early morning light, giddy with the calm, glowing unreality of what I saw.

The sky was a pale, glassy blue, but the waters of the gulf were still dark, as if the sea had soaked up part of the night. The U-boat was alongside, scarcely a hundred yards away, wallowing sedately in the deep ground swell. This was only our second day out, and I was thinking it wasn't fair; the Gulf of Mexico was *ours;* and not only that, I hadn't had time to adjust to anything.

Numb in the grip of astonishment, I glanced about and saw all the *Belasco*'s deck crew standing silently to my left and right at the rails. On the bridge the Captain was staring heavy-jawed at the U-boat. I quickly mounted the bridge and stood beside him.

"Is that you, boy?" the Captain said in a thick voice, without turning his head.

"Yes, sir," I said.

"This is it," he whispered. "Everything's odd jacks, now!"

I think the old man had felt a need to say something to me at that moment. He spoke to me over a vast distance—the oldest man on board reaching out to the youngest.

The officers of the submarine, dressed only in shorts, were standing about on their own deck. Tanned, they appeared confident and good natured. A stocky, gray-bearded man wearing a tall white cap seemed to be the Captain.

And, indeed, he was the one to yell through a megaphone: "Nice weather," he called out. "But just a bit hot!"

"What is this?" I asked. I turned to look at the profile of the Captain, whose jaw muscles were now convulsing regularly under the loose wrinkles.

"Should we abandon ship, Sir?" I asked.

"Listen! Keep still," the old man said. The submarine captain was speaking again. It was easy to hear his voice over the smoothly

rushing swells that pulsed both of our ships forward in long nudg-
ing arcs.

"I'm just stopping to let you know that I could sink you if I
wanted," the German captain said, "but looking at the size of
you I don't feel it's worth the ammunition it would take. And,
furthermore, now that I can take a good look at the condition of
your vessel, I realize you probably won't get to where you're going
anyway."

At this, all of the U-boat crewmen laughed as if they had just
heard the greatest joke in the world.

I heard it unclearly as if in a dream; and I could hardly swallow.
Once more I asked the Captain if we should abandon ship.

"No," the old man finally said. "That will be all. Stand by on
the bridge. It looks like we're safe."

WHEN PODILLY HEARD of our narrow escape, he made a point
of finding me. I had just come off watch, and I was rubbing
a stinking, yellow ointment on my face and arms. The heat was
like a high, ringing sound in the air; the sea was viscid, dull; the
sky was milky and shadowless.

I was vaguely depressed. I had decided that I was without
discipline. My paper on the problem of "Distributive Memory" (as
I'd decided to name it, for reasons that aren't quite clear at this
time) seemed infinitely remote.

Podilly knocked on the hatch, and, when I opened it, he
pushed inside.

"Now, just a minute!" I said, pointing down at the deck, as if
daring him to step beyond some invisible line.

But the engineer was laughing and didn't seem to hear me.
The cabin was so small that it immediately smelled of Podilly—a
curious mixture of coal dust, sweat, and brandy. As he laughed,
he swayed back and forth in a bearish rhythm.

"Just what in the hell do you want?" I finally whispered.

Podilly then started to repeat the whole story of the U-boat,
exaggerating stupidly, and inventing all kinds of dialogue between
the captains.

"Won't you please sink us?" he had the old man asking with
his hands clasped and tears in his eyes.

"No, sorry," the U-boat Captain answered. "As an officer and
a gentleman, I'd like to oblige, but you see there's the economic
factor and I don't see how I could justify using one of my shells
for your little boat."

"Odd jacks!" he had the Captain shouting; "Odd jacks!"

I was in a rage.

"Get out of my cabin!" I yelled.

Forgetting about my injured back, I grabbed the older and heavier man by his arm and shoved him toward the hatch. For a moment we stumbled there, swaying awkwardly together, and then I managed to shove him out onto the deck, where he started to laugh so hard he ended up coughing.

My back had held up very well, but I realized how foolish it was for me to treat it like that, because Podilly weighed well over two hundred pounds.

For a long time I thought I could still hear him laughing drunkenly, somewhere outside my cabin; and I was sure every member of the crew could hear him.

A light rain fell during the afternoon, but it did not cool the air. Rather, it clouded everything in steam, and the visibility was poor.

I dreamed of a U-boat surfacing, the abandonment of ship, then the U-boat shelling the *Belasco* until she sighed massively, eased over and sank. Such an event would somehow be a vindication, a sort of victory, in contrast to the insult of contemptuous rejection. Later, while I was standing watch, the thoughts at the back of my mind were more and more concerned with Podilly and his mocking, cynical, poisonous attitude.

So when my watch was over, I went to the Captain's cabin and knocked. The old man told me to come in, and for the fourth time on this voyage, I saw Captain Burke writing letters.

There was something inscrutable in the old man's face as he sat there looking up at me. Never had I seen so many wrinkles in a face.

His eyes were almost concealed by two loose folds of skin that hung like rumpled rags at the edges. He looked sagacious, incapable of surprise, monumentally tired.

"What is it, son?" the Captain asked.

"Sir," I said, "I'm concerned about the crew's attitude. And the attitude of the officers, too. I'm talking about the engineer, particularly. Mr. Podilly doesn't seem to have any respect for the ship, since . . ."

"Since the U-boat passed us by, you mean?"

"Yes, sir, I guess that's the way you could put it."

"We should all be grateful, it seems to me."

I thought for a moment. "Yes, sir," I said, "for being afloat; but not for anything else."

The Captain shook his head, making his wattles flap. "Do you know, I've had my master's license for forty years, and to think it would end like this."

Then, before I could build some sort of argument upon this observation, the Captain asked if that was all I'd wanted to talk about, and, unable to find the right words, I said, "Yes sir," and left the cabin.

THE *BELASCO* TIED up at the La Guaira docks of Caracas shortly after noon, amidst a riot of gulls. Captain Burke presented his papers to a small, sleepy-looking official smoking a king-size cigarette. Podilly was nowhere around. I helped supervise the unloading; and by evening chow, the *Belasco* was empty, riding high in the water and listing slightly to starboard.

I wondered about Podilly. Where was he? I'd been dreading the scene the fat engineer would make upon entering port. It would have been impossible for any of us to walk ashore with even a shadow of dignity, after Podilly had told the story of the U-boat in both English and Spanish, to everybody within range of a pistol shot.

But Podilly hadn't appeared.

I dressed in the new uniform I had saved especially for my first trip ashore. I walked off the ship, standing as straight as a mast, into the narrow streets of the city, and didn't stop until I came to a decent-looking restaurant, with red shutters on the windows.

Going in, I ordered an enormous dinner. Feeling somehow hard and competent, almost like a character in one of Conrad's novels, I lighted my pipe and settled back and sipped at some whiskey. Podilly's ghost began to fade. Soon, in fact, *everything* began to seem a bit hazy.

It seems I sat there for at least an hour, drinking whiskey as I ate. I thought hard about things. We had not done badly, when you considered the matter. And I had done my part. No matter what you said, the simple fact was that we had gotten the *Belasco* through.

This thought began to assume the proportions of a great and simple Truth that no one had really considered. I wished I could have explained it to Podilly; if Podilly could have heard me speak it just the way it was formulated in my mind, he might have understood. Heroism is possible in the least likely circumstances. It could happen on board a "floating engine block," as the fat engineer liked to call the *Belasco,* as well as on board an aircraft carrier or a newly minted destroyer.

It suddenly came to me then that all this had to do with Distributive Memory, but I wasn't sure how the parts fit together. Ceiling fans whirled above my head, and somewhere a static-clotted radio was playing a bolero. I took all this in and marveled at the immanence of some inscrutable design, waiting only for my grasp to uncover it.

I asked the waiter to bring me some scrap paper, which, after considerable shared labor over the problem of communication, he did. Then I made several large diagrams and embellished them with words and numerals, until the page began to look like the drawing of a tree, its branches cluttered with notations as thick as leaves.

What all this was meant to signify is still unclear, although at that moment my certainty was great. One connection remains with me: heroism is a covenant with one's past self, and one's future: it is also negotiable, in the sense that it is immediately (within and beyond the reach of the verbal) communicable to others. And this Past and Future are always, somehow, *here in the present moment*, as the Bishop of Hippo had argued. And memory is the telling distribution of Time, as *I* argued.

Contrary to the theories I had only dimly grasped at that moment, I found myself working in the theoretically wrong direction, as if ideas existed beyond human thoughts, let alone language; and we—gropingly, crudely, painfully—strive to accommodate our lives to these tyrannous molds.

I was aware that Plato had expressed a philosophy that was not altogether different from this. But that evening, I could sense certain crucial differences in my idea, and I was so exultant that I could almost feel light coming out of my head. When I paid the waiter, including a lavish tip, I shook his hand and said something like, "It's true that, compared to the stars, we're all floundering in the mud; but right here, right now, it all comes together, don't you see! We're on the only stage there is!"

The waiter, who was old enough to be my father, seemed to have no trouble understanding this: he saw that I was drunk and filled with rhetoric, so in reasonable English he thanked me earnestly and said I talked like a poet and a philosopher. He patted my shoulder and smiled and said he hoped I had a safe voyage back to Kansas City, which was a place I had never visited.

Awesomely fogged from the whiskey, I walked stiffly and numbly back to my hotel room. The voice of the hotel clerk, articulating a careful English, seemed to come to me over a great distance, or perhaps from a closed room.

I was going to ask about a woman, but I decided I couldn't do so with anything like dignity, because my tongue was so thick and the world was shifting so violently.

I know I would have sounded as ridiculous as I must have looked.

PODILLY WAS ASHORE. There was no question about it in my mind, for everyone seemed to know about the *Belasco* and the U-boat the next morning. Of course, under any circumstance, it would be common knowledge; but who but Podilly would have given the story such a grotesque feel? I could hear his voice in every reference.

The hotel clerk in the morning asked me about the incident, grinning as if he had caught me out in a boyish ruse. *"Belasco"* was now synonomous with comic ineptitude. Podilly must have chanted the story about the streets like a drunken old newspaper vendor. While I did some sightseeing that morning, I refused to look at people. I walked swiftly, keeping my pipe going constantly, even though my mouth felt like a furnace, and did nothing for my hangover.

What did they expect? Would they have preferred that we'd all drowned?

In the afternoon, I returned as ordered to the ship to see about emergency loading for a return to New Orleans. The local officials seemed frantic to get rid of the cargo that bulged the wharves.

On board ship, I reported to Captain Burke in his quarters. For once, he was not writing letters, but leaning over to put on his shoes after taking a lukewarm shower. His face was red and swollen, and he panted with the effort of leaning over, which cramped his stomach.

The old man was troubled. "Everything's odd jacks," he said. "It's not just the U-boats. Podilly's sick with fever. He's in the hospital. We're going to have to make do with a fellow laid over from a tanker, an engineer who knows these coal burners. Problem is, he's a drinker. He laid over with the d.t.'s but they can't discipline him now that we need him."

The old man was still panting from the effort of tying his shoes, gasping out his message phrase by phrase.

When he sat up and looked directly at me, he asked, "Do you happen to know what our return cargo is?"

"No, sir," I said.

"Iron. We carry hardware down, and we carry iron back. I had to fight them like the devil. They wanted to overload us. They act like they're afraid the U-boats are going to come right up and torpedo the wharves. We took on more than we ought to, as it is. If we hit bad weather, which is pretty common this time of year, it will be odd jacks, that's what it will be."

I had the feeling that Captain Burke hadn't talked this much for years, and I felt uncomfortable. I didn't know what I was supposed to do or say. The old man seemed to think he was talking to himself half the time, but at other times he would shoot a glance at me—a shrewd glance that really seemed to take me in as a person. This was not at all like his customary mucous stare.

"If we get this iron back," the Captain said shortly before I left, "it will be another miracle. One thing I guess we don't have to worry about, though, is getting sunk by a U-boat."

W E PUT TO sea that night. When we hit the ground swell, I was standing watch and thinking about Podilly. It wasn't serious, they had heard—a recurrence of malaria. What a laugh if Podilly was malingering! But he probably wasn't, because he would have enjoyed coming back just so he could have tormented me.

At that moment, I realized that all this had something to do with age. The Captain was old—far too old for his responsibilities; and even Podilly was too old. With them, too much of the Past clogged the movement of the present moment. An experienced crew of young men, with just a little capacity for idealism, would have made all the difference in the world. It wasn't the *Belasco* which was ridiculous—it was Podilly's cynicism and the Captain's unutility. It was the poison of old age . . . human age, the mocking smile, the memories of one's own youth, which is always safe to idealize in order to make the present seem paltry and comical in contrast. Distributive Memory had something to do with this, I was certain. For each stage of life, there is a right and workable symbol; and these must be distributed properly. The Present, for example, can be known only by means of the proper recipe of Past and Future.

Standing with one foot in each, one could do it right. For instance, I alone—one dedicated man—might conceivably inspire the crew in such a way as to offset Podilly's poison, or drive away the engineer's ghost that still haunted the crew. Wasn't *this* what heroism *was?* And wasn't it possible that I might bring it about?

Under the night stars that swung back and forth to the ship's roll, I silently swore that I would show them how; I vowed that most of the iron in this ship was not in the cargo, but in my own determination to bring us through this trip like men, rather than the motley chorus in some comic opera. I vowed I would create a memory worth possessing, focused and pointed; and yet, this memory would be larger than I was. Or had ever been.

At two bells, the stars and the quarter moon were dulled behind a diaphanous haze. At three bells, no stars could be seen, and the dawn was emerging muddily in the east. The Captain started talking too loud, and I realized that this was symptomatic of more than a hearing problem; he was afraid of the weather. In truth, there might have been a bad one brewing, from the feel and look of the air; and the radio messages from the Coast Guard Fox schedules were vaguely ominous.

It was in this state of preoccupation with the weather, and the signs of a coming storm, that the mast lookout reported a U-boat about a quarter-mile off the starboard beam.

I had just come to the bridge, holding a scalding cup of coffee, when the lookout reported. I saw the Captain's hand tremble for his binoculars. But I could already see the sub's wake in the viscid water; it should have been spotted long before this. If we hadn't all been foolishly ogling the sky and thinking of the weather reports, we would have spotted it from the bridge. And what had the lookout been doing up until this minute?

The officers of the U-boat seemed to sense that they had been detected, and that the *Belasco* concealed no gunnery. She surfaced at about three hundred yards, and all of us—the *Belasco* officers and crew—stood fascinated, watching the submarine crew run to the forward gun, quickly uncover it, poise themselves briefly, and fire a shot about fifty yards over and ahead of the *Belasco*'s bow.

We all remained silent as we stood on the *Belasco*'s bridge while the U-boat circled the ship, then churned within fifty yards of us. A pale gull landed on the gunwhale next to my hand and cocked its eye at me before flying away.

There was no mirth apparent in *this* German crew. I could see the rims of the glasses one bearded man wore, and I could make out a tattoo on the bare arms of another. It was hard to believe that these men were enemies; and yet they seemed to stare at the *Belasco* out of a cold and unblinking malevolence.

"They've lost their sister submarine," the old man said abruptly. "I'll bet that's it. They're looking for vengeance."

Later, I would remember the Captain's words and how ridiculous and melodramatic they sounded. But at that time all I could think was, "Yes, that's it. That's what happened. Probably the victim was the same U-boat that had stopped us on the trip over."

Then I was gripped by a sense of fearful unreality and began to feel the imminence of something larger even than the horizon. It was like the rising of the curtain in a dark theater.

But before I could savor this fantasy, I was interrupted by another. In my mind I could almost hear the Captain's favorite and inscrutable expression: "Now, it's odd jacks for certain!"

Actually, however, the old man was silent. I looked out at the U-boat, gripping my hands on the railing. For what seemed a full minute, the German crew stared back at us. Which man among them was the captain? It was impossible to tell.

There was, however, a slender young man standing next to the conning tower, holding a megaphone. He wore the high peaked cap of a Nazi naval officer. But his face seemed much too young for that of an officer, let alone a U-boat captain. He seemed more like a college basketball player.

Nevertheless, this was the man who eventually raised the megaphone, and called out to us in precise English, that we would be given exactly five minutes to abandon ship.

A ND, OF COURSE, the *Belasco* was abandoned. I was in command of one lifeboat, the Captain commanded the second, and the new engineering officer commanded the third. We lay to several hundred yards away, side by side, nodding somnolently in the swell, while the sharp, unreal report of the U-boat's gun sent a tracer shell into the *Belasco*'s hull about a foot above the water line.

There was another report. I turned to look at Captain Burke in the next boat, but the old man's face showed nothing. It was impossible to tell whether his eyes were teary or merely bleared.

On his deck, the German captain was standing at ease, with his hands locked behind his back. The light had changed, and we were closer to the U-boat than to the *Belasco*. The U-boat Captain was now revealed as older by years than he'd first seemed, as if he had aged in that short interval. But his stance remained military to the last detail, even though he stood relaxed, as he brooded over the spectacle before him in a spirit of vague but heroic insouciance.

Where was Podilly now? Spreading his cynicism in the hospital room to a circle of admiring nurses? Joking about the *Belasco* to a group of men in a Caracas bar? Was he just this moment referring to it as a "floating engine block"?

The real *Belasco* shuddered and clanked loudly as it listed away from the swell, its cargo of iron and flooding seawater putting it unnaturally low in the water. From the lifeboats we could hear her banging internally as her cables broke and the ancient bulkheads burst their sealings.

Suddenly, the old ship seemed to give way to a sudden, impetuous desire to turn over; and it did so, showering white water in erratic hissing fountains when the cold water hit the boilers; then steam shot in crazy geysers into the air, until the sea suddenly began to swallow the ship with an erratic series of enormous gulps.

For a few minutes, the submarine and the three lifeboats swung up and down in irregular patterns. None of us seemed able to believe what had happened, let alone think of rowing. The Captain was staring at the sky to the east, appearing as nonchalant as if he were watching silent fireworks at a Fourth of July picnic.

The young captain of the U-boat looked at us for a moment, then raised one gloved hand and waved a sober good-by.

"Why gloves," I wondered, "in a hot climate?"

B UT I NEVER forgot the gesture. I remembered it long after the storm clouds subsided and our three lifeboats were picked up by a brand-new liberty ship, bound for New Orleans. There had been an odd and irrelevant nobility in that movement, a casual sense of high mission. Never mind the ugliness behind this deadly submarine's existence. Some things are as pure and fine as a cold, bright star appearing suddenly through a mephitic cloud of smoke rolling through the night air.

The captain's face had been young and hard. Oddly familiar. His gesture, a command to stop action and, for an instant reflect. In this instant is a Fate and a Mission. We are all part of it, for it is where the Real surfaces out of all the anonymity of Time. Nothing conceivable could have been more different from Podilly, for instance.

I have often thought of the strange and unexpected fulfillment, the *perfection*, of that instant; and for days afterward I vowed that I myself would someday be an officer like that. Coordinate, but haunted by vastly different politics. That young officer might (I surmised later) not have been more than five years older than I at the time.

For years afterward, whenever I thought of this German captain, I saw his face as something bright and hard, like pounded copper that glinted with sunlight from its faceted planes. It was, I eventually learned, the hardness and integrity of my own youth that shone that way. As if in obscure confirmation of my old theories, this moment arose like a released bird from the particularities of my life.

Do not think I didn't recognize the radiance of a mystical strength and idealism in that supreme moment the young U-boat captain had stood, hands folded in a nonchalant attitude of command as he watched his crew blast the obscene old *Belasco* with shellfire until it sank beneath the waves.

Now, ALL THESE decades later, I am convinced of several things. The *Belasco's* Captain is dead. No doubt he died shortly after the war. Sometimes I think of him at night when I am half-asleep; I see his place as some nameless, unkept graveyard, the tombstones choked with briers and thistles. A purple moon casts a cold, bilious, cyanotic light over the scene. In the distance, the mooing of a great freighter can be heard as it noses its way out into some bay that will in turn lead to the ocean. Even his children are dead. On the tombstone is inscribed one thing only: "Odd Jacks."

Podilly is dead. Beyond question. I imagine his having died in a hospital bed near Altoona, Pennsylvania, lying sunken and wasted, festooned with tubes and monitoring plugs, his glazed eyes half-opened. Deep inside his brain, the *Belasco* is still afloat—a castle of rust. Podilly has grandchildren, I assume; and they have by this time (I speak of the moment in which I write this) not thought of him for almost a decade. Not one of them. But everything was there inside him at that moment.

Who else is there? Oh, many. Many. But their histories will be similarly oblique. And it is not them, anyway, that I am writing about. It is of that Moment, which throws a light over forty years—a beacon of irrelevance, which comes out of a hateful politics in a dubious era.

Even then, at that time (I tell myself), I told myself that I was not deceived. I know that I knew who he was; I was not mistaken, not in the least. The sea is a mirror, they say; but so is time and so is every advent. That young captain's head teemed with enigmas, like a ball of worms in the heart of a dying dog. He had just stepped forth upon the deck of his surfaced U-boat, into an arena whose audience he could never have dreamed of.

Now, I take this time out to savor his past in ways that he would have found incomprehensible. All that he was and had been came to serve that Instant.

I picture him years later dying of emphysema in a Berlin hospital, a thin gray blanket wrapped around his shoulders; all that he has guessed is fading inside his brain, and he is young to be dying, as all old men are.

But even then, in that instant, he became something else: as remote as he is now, dimmed by the years and innumerable irrelevancies. It was all there at *that* instant, too; and the riddle that Augustine posed is still with us.

 *Divorces*

WHEN HE PHONED, it was almost midnight, and I was getting sleepy, and it had been so long since I'd heard from him, I didn't say anything right away. Not even after he'd repeated his name.

"You know—*Duke*," he said. "Duke Slater. Your *brother-in-law*, for Christ's sake!"

"Sure, Duke," I said. "I mean, what the hell."

"It's been that long, hasn't it."

"Well, it has been pretty long. Are you in town?"

"Yes, I'm in town. Look, I know it's late."

"No problem."

"No, it's late, all right. But, listen: could I come over and talk with you? I mean, look, I've *got* to!"

"Sure, Duke," I said, with that sudden emptying feeling you get at such times. It didn't occur to me to ask what it was about. It had to be about my kid sister, Ginny, and I hadn't talked with her for a long time, either. In fact, she was the reason Duke hadn't kept in touch, because Ginny had written me off somewhere, too, six or seven years before, in the complicated accounts she kept in her head.

Duke said he would be right over, so I made coffee, turned on the lights in the front room, and waited. Since he hadn't said anything about Ginny, I assumed she wasn't with him. Maybe gone off somewhere, or possibly, I thought (knowing it couldn't be true), even dead. She had talked melodramatically—oddly smiling—about suicide several years ago, before I'd said something or done something that had turned her away from me. She hadn't even phoned after that, or sent a Christmas card.

Since that time, my wife had left me to start her own career as the owner of a cosmetics shop eighty miles away. She helped finance it with some money she'd inherited from a grandmother.

The stale, late-night silence of the front room depressed me, so I turned on the television set and watched a black-and-white World War II movie until the doorbell rang.

I flipped off the set and went to the door, where Duke stood there in the porch light, shy, awkward, and blocky, wearing a tweed jacket and a lemon-colored shirt open at the neck. He had grown a sickly little mustache and his hair had receded a little, but otherwise it was the same old Duke.

When I opened the door, I said, "Duke Slater, as I live and breathe"; but the heartiness didn't do anything. Duke was as solemn as I'd ever seen him, which was very solemn.

"I know it's late," he said, stepping in.

"No problem, no problem."

Duke nodded and stood in the middle of the living room, looking around at the chairs for some sign that I might have a special chair of my own so that he wouldn't deprive me of it. That was Duke's way; his life was a sustained apology, and he wanted to pass his time on earth without obtruding upon anyone or anything.

Finally, when I motioned toward one of the big puffy ones, he sat down and immediately dropped his face in his hands. "It's Ginny," he said through his fingers. His voice sounded as if it were coming out of a deep hole. "She's left me."

"I was afraid it was something like that," I said.

"I don't know whether I can handle it or not," Duke muttered through his hands.

"What the hell, you can take it," I said. "Others have."

Duke dropped his hands and started at me. "Like you, right? We heard you and Sally had—you know—separated."

"That's right. *Separated.* That's right."

"First you and Sally," Duke said, "and now Ginny and me."

I was going to ask, "Where will it all end?" but Duke wasn't equipped to handle irony even in the best of circumstances; and this was far from being one of the best.

"And do you know something?" Duke said out of a woefully stricken look, "I don't really have any idea why she did it."

"I can tell you why in one word," I said.

"What?"

"She's crazy, Duke, and the fact is, she always has been."

"That's not an explanation," Duke said. There was a heavy, stricken character to his breathing. It was as if somewhere behind that dull, pleasant face his body was laboring at violent exercise.

And his voice was all fairness, in the way he couldn't help. It was terrible.

"She told me I smother her," he finally told me in a choked voice. "What did she mean by that?"

"I don't have any idea, Duke."

I got up and went into the kitchen for coffee, and Duke followed me. "She just kept saying that," he said, "but she never really explained it."

"I don't think she knew herself," I said.

Duke frowned and leaned back against the kitchen counter with his arms crossed. "You shouldn't say that about your own sister," he muttered, shaking his head. "Especially the way she's always idolized you."

I poured coffee in the mugs on the counter. "*Idolized* me!" I repeated. "*She* was the one who cut the goddamn sibling thread, not *me!*"

Duke nodded sadly and accepted the mug I handed him. He blew in it and thought. Finally, he said, "Yes, she idolized you, all right. I don't think that part ever ended. You were eight years older, so it's only natural she'd look up to you."

"What do you mean I *was* eight years older. You talk like she's dead and gone."

Duke sipped from his mug and swallowed. It was too bad he had to look so forlorn; insidiously, it sooner or later brought out the nastiness in people. "It's like she's been gone for two years instead of two weeks," he said. "And I can't make any sense out of it at all. She said I smothered her, but that's just not true. I let her do anything she wanted. And I don't want to brag, but I've made a good living for her. We've got the kids in good colleges. But she says I *smother* her. And then she just takes off. Like that."

He snapped his fingers and then looked down at his coffee. Maybe he saw his features reflected in it for a moment, because he dipped his face in the blackness and drank, as if to destroy the image.

"Well, I feel for you," I said slowly, "but the fact is, I never even understood what had ticked her off with me. I couldn't figure out why she suddenly cut me off as if I'd *wronged* her in some way. And after I phoned several times and she'd just answer questions as briefly as possible and nothing else, why I thought, to hell with it."

"I know," Duke muttered sorrowfully. "I couldn't figure that out either, at the time."

"At the time?"

Without looking up, he nodded and sipped some more coffee from his mug.

"But now you've figured it out. Is that it?"

Duke narrowed his eyes and stared into the blackness of the window. It troubled him to work himself into a situation that might suggest duplicity. "You know, she practically looked up to you as a father, your being older than her and everything. And being a successful lawyer. She really respected you for that, too."

"I don't seem to hear you answering my question," I said.

Duke nodded and put his mug back on the counter, as if he'd already finished his coffee. "I guess what it was, from the way she talked about it to me . . . I guess maybe she felt that you smothered her, too. That's why she cut loose. I've given it a lot of thought, and that's the only explanation. She had to get out from under you and be her own person. That's the way she started talking back then, you know. So I figure it's the same thing, essentially."

"Good God!"

"I know," Duke said.

He stayed there for another two hours, going over and over the same thing, but not telling me anything new. Finally, when he left, he said, "I hate to be a pain in the ass, but who else could I turn to, except you?"

"That's right," I said. "And I'm glad you did."

He nodded, but then in one phase of the nod, simply let his face hang. "I only hope things work out," he said.

And I told him I was sure they would, which was a lie if I've ever told one.

G INNY DROPPED OUT of sight, as far as I could see, but Duke phoned me now and then during the next few years, sometimes talking for over an hour and monopolizing the phone. It was as if his need to talk the problem over grew until he had to express it. As he kept saying, over and over, there wasn't anybody else he could turn to. "With your parents gone," he said, "there isn't anybody else I can discuss it with." This was true, but it sounded a little ridiculous coming from a man who was now approaching fifty and had made a fair success of his electrical contracting business.

One night he called at 11:20, when I'd just climbed out of the shower. All day I'd weeded the flower borders—a chore at one time never consummated until my ex-wife had nagged me into it. I told Duke I was still wet, but he didn't seem to catch on, so I stood there and listened to him for just under one hour and ten minutes. Several times he mentioned how well his business seemed to be going. "If Ginny were still with me," he said, "we'd have everything we need."

That was ambiguous enough to give me pause, but one of the answers I sorted through my mind and rejected was: "For God's sake, go out and get another woman. The world's full of disheartened and lonely widows and divorcees." Then I thought: Yes, *like Ginny*, and managed to keep my mouth shut. But Duke wouldn't have heard, anyway, because he was still following his own line of thinking. "I don't really know what she's up to," he said. "I phone her every now and then, but she just listens and hardly says a word. She won't even tell me what she's doing for a living or anything. But do you know what?"

"What?"

"I think she isn't doing *anything*, I think she's just, you know, going around and breathing. I don't think she's shacking up with a man, or anything. Not that a woman with her looks wouldn't have opportunities."

"How about your own love life," I interrupted. "Seems to me you could do all right."

After a pause, Duke said, "You know, I don't think along those lines. All I want is for things to be like they were. I was never what you'd call *macho*, I guess, but that's never really bothered me. I know pretty much what I want."

"Sure," I said.

"And I guess she does too. If she isn't doing anything but just living, well, I guess she prefers that to living with me."

"I don't think it's that simple, Duke."

"Maybe not. You're probably right. I don't think she ever did anything simple."

"Or sensible."

"Who are we to say? All I know is, the way she's kept her looks, she could get just about any man she wants."

"She's kept her looks, all right."

"And figure. Face and figure. Don't think I don't know her faults. I know all about her vanity. But do you know something?"

"What?"

"It doesn't make any difference to me. Not a bit."

"Duke," I said, "you're something else."

He was quiet a moment, then he told me that he was sending her money every month. He said he *wanted* to send the money. He emphasized the fact. He insisted that she had never once asked him for a cent; but when he said this, I thought: of *course* she's never asked: she doesn't *have* to; and she *knows* she doesn't have to.

This was not a charitable thought, but I was disgusted with both of them, especially in view of my own recent marital problems. I didn't have much room left in me for tolerance, let alone sympathy.

Something else I learned during that conservation was that if Ginny had made a father surrogate out of me, even as she'd rejected me, so had Duke. It was implausible, in a way; but I couldn't think otherwise. Because, whatever was true for her, had to have *some* truth for him.

But what advice did I have to give him? What could a real father (Ginny's, say—*ours*) have done to give him courage and wisdom. Or clear away the mud in her thinking?

But there was one other thing Duke mentioned during that long phone call: all the references she'd made to suicide before leaving him. This only added to his worry, of course. And then he said something that sounded so odd coming from Duke that it took my breath away and I had no response whatever to give him.

He said, "In a way, she killed herself by leaving me, didn't she? She cut everything off, which was like killing her old life. You could almost see her making up her mind. She didn't say ten words to me the week before she left. I was busy then, I'll admit; but don't think I didn't notice. Then it happened: just like that. She cut everything off, the way you pull a switch."

Everything but the money, I thought.

Along with poor old Duke, bewildered and numb from the whole business.

WHEN IT WAS finally evident that Sally was not going to return, I sold our house and moved to an apartment that was approximately an equal distance on the other side of the city, making something like an equilateral triangle. I felt too old to play the part of bachelor with much conviction, but this doesn't mean that I did without female companionship entirely.

Still, my life was lonely enough for me to have long and solitary hours in which to think about things. Our grown children phoned once a month, which was just about often enough. And occasionally Sally would phone, and we'd discuss things in a fairly civilized manner. I don't think we ever missed each other very much, which might suggest that we had missed a whole lot all those years we had lived together.

But then one late summer night, the inevitable happened.

Duke phoned and said he'd just learned that my kid sister had killed herself. That's exactly the way he put it: he said, "your kid sister."

"Took about four pounds of sleeping tablets," he said, sounding like he was fighting back a yawn. "Looks like she really wasn't kidding around all those times."

Long after the event, I have often thought of how he'd broken the news to me; and looking back, I think that even then—absorbing the shock and horror of Ginny's death—I was aware that this was something else that didn't sound like Duke.

"You better drop everything and come right away," he said.

"Of course."

"How fast can you get here?"

I told him I'd leave as soon as I could throw my shaving gear together.

"There's something else," Duke said.

"Like what?"

"I don't want to tell you over the phone."

Then I could hear Duke taking deep breaths, and I knew he was going to start crying.

"Look," I said, "for Christ's sake, get control of yourself!"

"What are you talking about?" he gasped. "It's like I can't even *find* myself!"

"Are the kids there?"

After two or three deep breaths, he managed to say, "They'll be on their way, as soon as I break the news to them. But for God's sake, hurry up, will you?"

"I'll be there as soon as possible," I told him.

I DECIDED TO drive rather than wait for a plane, because even with close connections, I wouldn't arrive any sooner by flying. Also there was the necessity to concentrate on driving, which helped focus my mind and diminish the awful sense of helplessness you have at such times.

As I drove, I kept trying out this new truth: Ginny is dead. I thought of her as she grew up, eight years behind me, and tried to remember specific things about her. I tried to think of how good I'd been to her, or how bad . . . and decided that I hadn't been either very understanding or particularly insensitive. About average, which gave a dull sort of comfort to me, for some reason. By its very nature, morality lures us to the average, to the norm; we do not want to excel or fail, either one.

Of course I tried to avoid the seepage of guilt that begins the instant you know one of your family has died, but I knew there would be some of that, inevitably, and this was natural, too.

But all the way, I kept hearing Duke's voice, and couldn't help wondering what the "something else" was.

Then, shortly before I arrived at the house where Duke and Ginny had lived all those years, I began to think about one of the first things I had thought when I first met my future brother-in-law coming to date my kid sister. If parents had worked hard at coming up with an inappropriate name for a child, they couldn't have done any worse than naming this unobtrusive, decent, dull, and hard-working boy "Duke"—for that was his name, his *Christian* name, in fact.

Now, he was waiting at the door for me, and when I stepped inside, Duke asked if I wanted a brandy, and I said no, not right away.

He looked mussed and shaken, but he was often that way, as if he had a gift for small miseries. Nevertheless, he seemed to be pretty much in control.

"Have the kids gotten here?" I asked.

"Not yet," Duke said. "Nobody. As a matter of fact, I wanted you to get here first."

"Why?"

Duke shook his head and swallowed. Then he looked away and passed his hand through his thick patch of receding hair. "She left a note," he said.

The awful unreality of everything came back to me suddenly, at that instant, and I couldn't speak for a minute. *My kid sister's suicide note!* I was thinking. *My God!*

"She left a note," Duke repeated. "Do you want to read it?"

"Not right now," I said. "Look, maybe I'll have some brandy, after all."

"Sure," Duke said, going out to his liquor cabinet in the alcove. While his back was turned, he said, "You can read it when you want, but what I want to do right now is talk it over with you."

"Talk what over?"

For an instant, Duke just stood there with his back to me. He wasn't pouring brandy or doing anything. I thought maybe he was going to start crying again, but he didn't. Finally, without turning back to me, he said, "One time you and I were talking over the phone, do you remember? And you said Ginny was crazy."

"I remember," I said.

"Well, maybe you were right. Because do you know what she said in the note?"

"What?"

"She said she wanted to be buried in her red bra and bikini. She even had them out there on the bed, beside her."

"You've got to be kidding."

"You know I wouldn't kid about a thing like that," Duke said, his voice beginning to yodel. "That's what she said, all right."

"Good God almighty!"

"That's just the way *I* felt about it."

"Buried in a *bikini*? *Why*, for sweet Jesus Christ's sake?"

"God only knows! But that's what she said."

"Jesus!" I whispered.

"I don't know what to do, with the kids and everything."

"What do *they* have to do with it?"

Duke poured brandy in two snifters and turned around to hand one to me. "You know, I'd hate like hell not to give her her last wish, even if it is crazy."

"It's worse than that," I said. "It's obscene."

Duke nodded sadly and sipped his brandy. "I figured you'd feel that way about it. I guess that's pretty much how I feel, too."

"Just get rid of the fucking note," I said.

"I haven't told anybody but you about it, as a matter of fact. You know, she phoned me right after she took the pills, and I rushed right over. When I got there, she was dead. I called the emergency squad, then I put it in my pocket. The note."

"Get rid of it," I whispered.

Duke shook his head. "You know something, though? She was always proud of her figure. When you look at most women her age, and then . . . look . . . looked at her, the difference was incredible."

I cleared my throat. "Get rid of the note."

Duke blinked slowly as he stared at me. "Do you think she really was crazy?"

"I know she was," I said.

"Really? Like in a *clinical* sense?"

"Yes."

Duke nodded. "You don't have any authority to attach a label like that to her."

"She was crazy."

"I don't think I'll tell the kids. I mean, Jesus, they don't have to know, do they?"

"Of course they don't. Get rid of the goddamn note!"

He nodded again. "I figured she'd listen to you, if she were alive. Even after she cut things off with you. She always looked up to you like a father. Especially after your dad died."

"It's the only thing to do," I said.

"I guess you're right. Only I wonder why she would want to do anything as odd as that. Something that kooky. And, I don't know, sacrilegious. Even though we didn't, you know, go to church very often. Somehow even the idea sickens me. I try to think of her corpse lying there practically naked, in that red bra and bikini of hers. You know what I mean?"

I'd finished my brandy, and I shuddered. "Yes," I said, "me too. And I don't have the least idea what she had in mind."

"I do, sort of," Duke said. But I closed my eyes and just stood there breathing, and Duke didn't say anything more about it.

Twenty minutes later, their oldest daughter, Crissy, arrived.

By then, Duke had burned the note. I hadn't even read it. I didn't want to. I don't think I could have even looked at it.

THAT WINTER I met a woman named Kristi Krider, who after her divorce had returned to college to study special education. We met at the church that Sally and I had attended years before, and things seemed to go very well for the two of us. We soon got to be so comfortable with each other that it was more than comfort; there was a sort of beauty in it.

We were married in the spring, and of course Duke was invited to the wedding. He came, wearing a bow tie, blue blazer, and dark brown slacks. He had grown thick graying sideburns since I'd last seen him, and the result was unfortunate.

At the reception I introduced him to Kristi, and the two of them hugged each other with stiff backs. Kristi was smiling, but Duke's expression was earnest and distant.

When we talked briefly later on, I asked if he couldn't come and stay with us a few days after we were settled in.

"No," he said seriously, "I'm still pretty much a loner, I guess."

This seemed odd to me, because I'd never thought of him as a *loner*, exactly. In fact, there had always been something wistful and pathetic about him, like a fat boy who follows other boys around and watches, yearning to be invited to play. More *abandoned*, I guess, rather than a loner. But I guessed he was talking about Ginny, so I gripped his arm and squeezed it in a gesture of affection.

Several days later when I was talking about Duke to Kristi, I said, "You know, if I'd had a brother, I guess I would have wanted him to be like Duke."

"Why is that?" she asked.

I tried to explain it, but it didn't make much sense. When I finished, Kristi said, "Well, he did seem awfully nice in a low-key sort of way."

I glanced at her. She was filing her nails and had spoken in an abstracted manner, but in a tone I hadn't noticed before.

"There's more to him than meets the eye," I said.

"I don't doubt it," Kristi said. "He impressed me as being a very sweet and decent man. I mean it."

All of this transpired on our honeymoon in Las Vegas, where we lost over $1,800 at various tables, and had one hell of a good time, even though we left agreeing that this wasn't our sort of place and that one trip per decade would be plenty.

FOUR YEARS LATER, Duke committed suicide with a .38 Police Special. He shot himself under the ear, kneeling by his bed in the apartment he had been renting.

The shock of the event left odd debris in my mind. In some sad way he hadn't seemed to have the flair or imagination to do a thing like that; but I knew how pathetically stereotyped such a notion is. And yet, the awesome incompatibility that existed between Ginny and him was, after all, a gulf; and one would have thought the separation, the profound difference, between them would have established in him some sort of immunity from suicide.

Of course, that, too, was an unstable idea. So I tried to rest on some such conclusion that Duke had been weaker—which is to say, more vulnerable, more "sensitive" than I had realized. And yet, in another way, I had been right all along, for it was true: everyone *had* underestimated him. Kristi had, certainly; she had done so immediately, with some sort of feminine instinct I was not likely to understand. And my poor kid sister Ginny certainly had, without living long enough to realize the fact. And yet, what ghosts had haunted her I will never know about.

For his funeral, Duke left no instructions. I don't think he'd thought that far ahead. And the basic message he'd left in his suicide note was that he was sorry. Sorry. *Sorry!*

He hadn't elaborated upon this: he hadn't said exactly what it was he was sorry about. Maybe Ginny would have understood that part; but I certainly did not. Rather, I could think of several things, whereas I'm sure she would have fastened upon only one. And—who can say?—maybe she would have been right, after all.

⟢ *Inviolate on Shawnee Street*

I wouldn't be surprised," Mrs. Hanawalt said to June on the fourth day of the old man's illness, "that it was worry over the Rettingers that brought all of this on."

Mrs. Hanawalt had said this as if the idea had just then flashed in her mind. But in fact, she had mentioned it three times before to her daughter, who by now had difficulty in finding an adequate response to her mother's words.

The woman frowned at her daughter, seeming to wonder how she could be so heartlessly phlegmatic when her elderly father was dying. After staring at her for a moment, Clara Hanawalt went upstairs to see if Pierce was doing as well as could be expected. She stayed upstairs about forty-five minutes, then came down looking deeply troubled.

"June," she said, standing expectantly until her daughter looked up. "June, he admitted that what the Rettingers are doing has made him sick. In so many words he has now admitted it."

"I don't know what we can do to stop them," June said. There were strings in her neck when she raised her face, and Clara noticed them; whereas she herself was as plump and smooth as a filled balloon, and didn't have a wrinkle in her face.

"It's David Rettinger," Clara said, sitting so heavily in the chair that her heels bounced off the floor. "I told you, didn't I, that I phoned him two or three weeks ago, and he came right out and admitted that he was going to turn their old place into an apartment house?"

June was silent. She was filing her nails busily, and she suddenly realized that her hands were so close to her face that she was staring at them almost cross-eyed.

"Well, didn't I tell you?" her mother asked, half with hope that she might be able to tell the story again, and half with irritation.

"Yes, I think you told me."

"He *admitted it.* 'Yes,' he said. 'That's what I plan to do, Mrs. Hanawalt.' As big as you please. If he goes through with it, June, it will *kill* your father. Honestly, I can't really understand what you people in that generation of yours think you're doing!"

June rubbed a tender spot on her finger with the emory board.

"Pierce's grandfather made this estate," her mother intoned, looking around with some of the bland unconsciousness of a person petting a dog. "And his father helped build it up, and then finally Pierce lent his hand. The Hanawalts made Shawnee Street what it is, and they have always been prominent in town; the fact is we've made Shawnee Street into the heart of our community. It is really a form of desecration to . . . somehow *gratuitously* destroy the beauty and calm we've created here."

Her eyes were glazed with a vision that her words, presumably, only adumbrated. For another minute she sat silently, then she asked in a whisper: "Why, do you know what apartments would bring? The kind of people, I mean?"

"It is a shame!" June said, still staring at her fingers.

Her mother nodded and then told her what kind of people would come to live beside their estate if David Rettinger did such a thing.

UPSTAIRS IN HER ROOM, late that night, June lay down with her clothes on and stared at the ceiling. After a few minutes, she started humming a song she had known as a girl. It seemed years since she'd even thought of the song.

There was a knock at the door.

"June?"

"Yes?"

"Let me in. It's your mother."

Who else might it be?

"Did I hear you crying, June?" Her mother asked, her eyes dark with interest as she stared at her daughter lying on the bed.

"Of course not. When did you ever hear me cry?"

"I heard you make a sound."

"I make sounds all the time. You know I like to hum when I'm alone."

But her mother didn't hear this answer. She stood there looking vaguely about, and June was momentarily aware that her mother had never been comfortable in this room. Both she and her father had always made much of the fact that this room was June's *very own, to do with as she pleased.* But what, after all, could a girl have done, when the room was a mere oasis in this deserted estate? Who, for instance, could have come here without their knowing and approval?

"June, we haven't talked together since you've had your divorce," her mother said.

"I know."

"Was he . . . was he *mean* to you, June?"

"I don't feel like talking about it. It seems so far away and completely done with, that I don't think I could say anything sensible about it."

Her mother removed her glasses and wiped her eyes with a handkerchief. She walked heavily over to the cushioned rocker and sat down, sighing. "I didn't think you'd tell me anything," she said. "It seems you've always been remote from me. And now that Papa's dying, it hurts to have you act that way."

June turned her head away from her mother and gazed at the familiar metal hinge that the old fashioned window swung upon. The hinge was a fantastic thing, shaped like an ugly hand, an eagle's head, a stingray, a comet . . . and in the interior of the hinge, one bolt stood out like an unblinking eye. As a child she had been fascinated, and at times terrified, by the dented old piece of metal that her imagination kept insisting upon bringing to life.

She heard the rocker start to work back and forth with a no-nonsense squeak and then a thud from her mother's oxfords smacking the floor.

"I called again," Clara Hanawalt said.

"Called who?"

"David Rettinger."

"Oh."

"He can't be influenced," she said. "If we could afford it, we might be able to buy the old place; but what about the taxes? And the upkeep? Why, David's got enough money! You know very well he doesn't have to turn it into an apartment house to keep it up! He just wants to make it pay. That's the trouble with your generation: they want everything they do to pay. Money, money, money. Where's ideals?"

Suddenly, she jumped out of the rocker and left the room. June got out of bed, looked at her face in the mirror, and started combing her hair. Then she looked at her comb and saw three hairs, as coarse as banjo strings. She jerked them out one by one and stared at them, wondering what it was that her mother was plotting.

ALL THAT NIGHT, June could hear old Pierce mumbling and crying out in his sleep. Her mother was silent, but it was her mother, after all, who had done something that night. She had come up with a plan, while they were sitting in front of the television set that evening. June could sense it the minute she glanced at her mother and saw she was not looking at the set, but staring slightly over it into the distant shadows of the room.

But Clara didn't actually say anything, and June realized that she would have to wait. She stood there with her hankie plastered tightly against her mouth, while her mother glanced at her warily and leaned over to turn the television to another channel.

"I think I'll go up and see Daddy," June said, after a while.

"That's all right," her mother said. "Ask him if he wants me for anything. If he's awake, that is."

June climbed the steps and went to her father's room. Inside, it was dark and warm, smelling of the oldness of his flesh as well as the secondary smells of mussed pillowcases and sheets. His false teeth grinned up at the ceiling from a water glass on the nightstand, and the profile of his bald old eagle head was thrust back, eyes closed, as if he were poised at the brink of a colossal sneeze.

June sat down and whispered "Daddy" at the old man for a few minutes; then she got up and went back downstairs.

"I think you can persuade him," her mother said triumphantly. "After all, at one time he liked you."

"What are you talking about?" June asked.

"Liked you. *Liked you!* You know—boyfriend. Birds and bees." Clara seemed outraged at her daughter's slow-wittedness.

June looked above her mother's head.

"What are you grinning for? You know it's the truth."

"Why, it was *never* true! Dave never liked me. I was never his girlfriend. We didn't even have one date."

"Can't you think beyond dates?" Her mother asked. "Why I remember seeing that boy walk home from school by your side a hundred times. If that isn't liking, I don't know what is!"

June whooped with laughter. "Why, we *lived* side by side. Did you expect us to pretend we didn't know each other?"

"There were other ways," Clara Hanawalt said, nodding with her eyes narrowed. "Edith Rettinger told me ten times if she told me once that David had a crush on you. He would've asked you for your precious dates if . . . if . . ."

"If what?" June asked in a loud voice.

"Why, if you had been *interested*. The Rettingers didn't have anything like the background you had. The advantages, you might say, and family. And all the things that matter. I don't think Edith Rettinger could have forgotten this difference. She was very, very impressed by it. She was an awfully nice person, Edith Rettinger was!"

June whooped. "You *hated* her! Don't you think I remember? You *hated* the woman. How can you forget so much?"

Such an unavoidable and unpleasant truth as this touched a mysterious switch in her mother's mind and emptied it. For a curious instant June now watched her mother as she blinked vaguely and seemed to listen to the wind. She knew that Clara now remembered nothing. The subject of Edith Rettinger was ended.

So her mother went back to her plan, saying, "You must go and see him."

"Who?" June asked.

"David Rettinger. Who else have I been talking about? He had a crush on you, June, and he will still listen to what you say."

"I don't want to do it," June said.

For a moment, her mother was silent. Then she said, "You are the most selfish person I have ever met. When is the last time, pray tell, that you ever did *anything* for someone else?"

For an instant, June was aware that the television set was on, and there was a man there talking rapidly about a new floor cleaner and wax combined. He seemed so earnest that June wondered momentarily which of their two worlds was the real one— hers, in this high-ceiling old house, or his, in the walnut box, with everything appearing either in shadow or glowing forth in a solder-like brilliance.

"You know, of course, that his wife left him."

"Of course I know it!"

"Well, don't jump at me like that. I don't know if you know things or not, you're so unconscious most of the time. And then you've been away, you know."

"Well, I don't see how that alters things," June said, running her hand lightly through her hair.

"Don't be silly."

"I don't care to listen any more. It's a ridiculous idea."

"I haven't given you my idea yet. You just listen. You can invite him over for dinner. And then you can talk to him. You don't get over these feelings you've had when you're young; they always stay with you. I've found that out in life."

"Ridiculous," June said.

"Just keep still and listen. Do you know your father is *dying* upstairs? Aren't you at all concerned about giving him a little peace before he dies, and the knowledge that *something* he has worked for all his life will rest safe and unchanged beyond his death?"

"Why do you have to bring me into all of this? If it would do some good, why, I might do it; but this is just ridiculous."

"Just listen to me, for once in your life, while I explain to you how your father feels."

June sat down and stared off into the darkness, facing the empty dining room, while her mother sat behind her and recited the saga she had so often recited, about Pierce and his home on Shawnee Street, and the ideals of this twisted, water-drinking aristocracy, worshipful of two things: money and ignorance of the world beyond Shawnee Street and the town.

Once, during her mother's recital, June heard old Pierce groan upstairs and cry out. She pictured him as a great king, lost in the wilderness of age. She turned and stared curiously at her mother. But Clara merely paused long enough to identify the sound— glanced up, as if seeing through the floor into Pierce's room, then continued with the tale of the old man's investments in real estate in the 1920s.

Why, Clara herself didn't care about Pierce! It was a compulsion she was acting out. And for the first time, June detected a look of actual stupidity on her mother's face. It explained so much; the riddle of her character was clearing up, bit by bit, year by year; if June were to come back and live with her long enough, she might someday know her mother's every dimension, as clearly as the antique decorations in the two-acre Hanawalt lawn, or the symboled and ornate furniture that stood Ozymandias-like in the darkness of the hall, the parlor, the library and the sitting room.

"You can *buy* the Rettinger house," June suddenly cried out. "You know goddamn *well* you can!"

"It isn't practical," her mother said, in a voice that coiled inside her mouth, guarded and shrewd. And June knew, then, that there was something else . . . something as yet intangible to her, as she faced into the whirring, complex machinery of her mother's planning.

T HEY TALKED UNTIL 11:25 P.M., at which time June gave in and said, yes, for the sake of peace and quiet she would consent to David Rettinger's being invited to dinner, and she would even do her best to influence him not to make an apartment out of his house. But she was also curious. She wanted to observe how far her mother would go. It was clear that, iceberglike, the plan was ponderously fixed like a small continent beneath the surface of her mother's words.

"The doctor said he must never be interrupted while he is sleeping," her mother said. "Like I've told you before."

"You've never told me that."

"You don't listen to me, that's the trouble. I know very well I told you."

"Well, what's the difference. I just thought I would go in to see him this morning."

"You just concentrate on making yourself as attractive as possible. I want David to be impressed tonight. You look tired and a little hard today."

"Thanks a lot."

"I only say it to help."

"Is Daddy excited about the dinner?" June asked.

"He doesn't know about the dinner. And that's one reason I don't want you to go in there today. He'll be able to tell from your face, and the excitement will be bad for him."

"He doesn't know? You said you told him yesterday."

"I did not."

"You did *so.*"

"I did not! And when I say I don't want his sleep disturbed, I mean exactly what I say. I want him to sleep today to gain strength for tomorrow. We'll tell him then, and I hope we'll also be able to tell him that David Rettinger has changed his mind. And stop staring at me like an absolute ninny."

"I'll leave him alone. Get off your high horse."

"All right," her mother said, vibrating her hands up and down, like an angry pianist. "All right."

L ATE IN THE AFTERNOON, June sat massaging her face with cold cream, staring into her mirror.

She thought of old Pierce in his room. She opened her door to the hallway, and heard the television set chattering in the deep distance of the first floor. Her mother was either there, sunk in apathy before the set, or—more likely—excitedly plotting things as her glazed vision fastened upon whatever program was playing. Or perhaps she was out in the kitchen.

There was something additionally odd about her mother today. Her face was harder, more set, shinier. Her distractions more astronomical; the signs of inner resolve more intense.

For an instant, June had considered putting on her raincoat

and hat and going out a half-hour before David was supposed to arrive, leaving her mother there alone with him. She was still considering it, in fact; the only thing that was wrong was that she would never know exactly how the foolishness turned out. Her mother would never tell the truth about anything . . . was congenitally incapable of even knowing what the truth is. The whole world was altered to fantasy and lies the minute it was reflected in the crazy mirrors of her mind.

Maybe June would stay for the meal, only she didn't really know. Wouldn't know, in fact, until she saw herself doing one thing or the other, and then would know, and watch herself as she acted.

But now, she was disturbed about something else, too. Knowing the fantastic ability of her mother to spin plots and entangle— not only those nearest—but whole neighborhoods and communities in the involute consequences of her acts . . . knowing this, June was thinking of her father who lay dying in the other room.

Distance between them was inevitable, because of Pierce Hanawalt's age. But in one way, he had been more perfect in her eyes than a father who might have shared her games and bickered with her. Although he had been a known presence throughout her childhood, he had always come to her as an aged relative visiting from his remote second-story office or returning from a business trip. He was tolerant, calm, and huge, in contrast to her mother, who was always wearing the armor of a thousand schemes and swiftly brandishing small weapons of malevolent concern. As a girl, June had loved her daddy and had indulged herself in his vast acceptances as if he had been a kind of human playground for her—made for her pleasure, but also accommodating whole populations of other times, things, and people beyond her understanding.

So now she was deeply, if mutely, sorrowful that her father was dying; and yet found herself considering his death as something secondary to what her mother was trying to bring about. She had felt ashamed for this feeling ever since she had come back to share in the death watch and waiting.

She wiped the cold cream off her face and went out into the hall and down to old Pierce's room. Putting her hand on the knob and starting to turn it quietly, she discovered that the door had been locked.

For an instant, she stood in the hall trembling with an awful suspicion. Then she walked to her mother's room and searched until she found the key that led to Pierce's bedroom through his private bathroom.

June walked down the hall to the bathroom door beyond, and walked in. The smell of the bathroom was flat, a little like the basement of an empty house. No smell of soap or shaving cream. She tried the door opposite, which led into her father's room, and found it locked, as she had expected. Quietly, she put the key in the keyhole and turned it until she heard the latch click. She moved the door open slowly, and stepped three times into the cold darkness. Then she stared for a moment at the marblelike corpse of her father . . . having expected such a sight, almost in every detail. And yet she heard herself panting as if she had just run an enormous distance. She stepped backward through the door into the bathroom and locked the door after her. Then she returned to her room.

THE DINNER FLOWERED before her like an island of thick weeds, and David Rettinger, who had gotten bald and fat, was sitting at the table talking, and her mother was smiling sweetly and prodding her occasionally with looks to come to life and be charming with David.

But the discovery she had made affected her like a hammer blow, and June hardly opened her mouth all evening. Once she stumbled on the rug going from the dining room into the front room. Her mother pinched her arm hard and whispered through gritted teeth: "You act like you're drunk or something! Will you please act *right?*"

She walked slowly into the front room, where David was sitting on the sofa, smoking a cigar and letting his fat belly tumble like a filled hot water bottle over his belt. Once he belched out loud and didn't excuse himself.

"Nothing will move him, Mother," June heard herself whisper. She was carrying a glass tray with three glasses too full of sherry tilted dangerously on the glistening surface. At least she had meant to whisper, for David was only about thirty feet away, still lumped on the sofa in the grandiose aftermath of his gluttony.

But her voice had been loud, and David had asked, "What's that?" and her mother had gasped and had half-turned toward her in confusion.

Then June heard her mother talking rapidly to David about her feelings with regard to his plans . . . how *beneath* David it was to convert his old home into a boarding house.

"But there are these college kids who need places to live," David said, scattering cigar ashes on his pant leg as he gestured.

Then Clara commenced talking about old Pierce . . . his dying wishes concerning the neighborhood, his years of greatness in the building of Shawnee Street into what it was . . . all the arguments she had intoned during the past few days. For June, the evening had already lasted too long. The big clock ticked the seconds away, and her mother's words snowed into her mind like something dislodged from the calcium edges of a dream.

But suddenly David was saying it was past eleven o'clock (staring with a frown at a gold watch on his fat, hairless wrist), and Clara was standing tilted backward, her mouth pursed in a permanent flinch of anger, her eyes glassy and unfocused with wrath.

June arose and shook hands with someone, and spoke words of leave-taking. She could smell David Rettinger's cigar, mixed with stale sweat from his clothes. She could hardly understand that this man had once been a child and she had once played with him and accepted him as a friend.

June turned back into the house when the door finally closed and heard her mother whisper one word: "Failed!"

The word smacked the surface of her mind like a tossed brick, rippling cold waves of terror up and down her body until even her vision of the room began to ripple and waver; and then it seemed as if someone turned the lights down halfway from a secret master switch.

She was dimly aware of her head striking the waferlike carpet; and then, for only an instant, she dreamed a furious little dream. A dream in which David Rettinger as a child was standing knee-deep in her mother's geraniums, holding his hands up to his mouth, and shouting in a voice as faraway as water dripping deep under earth: "All-ee, all-ee in free!"

June felt herself trying to run, only she was not trying to run toward home base so that she could touch it safely, but trying instead to run away from David and the thick nightmare of the flowers, for ever and ever.

Then she was lying on the sofa . . . on her back, and something cold and squashy was splashing on her forehead. She looked up into her mother's dilated eyes. Her mother was dipping the wet cloth upon her eyebrows, letting the still-soapy water run down into her ears, and whispering, "Weak! Selfish! Why, you ninny, you actually *fainted!* If I didn't know you better, I'd have thought you were drunk."

༄ Medicinal Enchantments

WHEN RON BIXLER came out of the McDonald's at a little past six o'clock one cold winter evening, he was surprised to find Ralph Waldo Emerson sitting in the passenger seat of his green Porsche. Although his unexpected visitor's clothes were not obviously of the nineteenth century, they were obviously not of this time and place, either.

Ron was on his way home from an afternoon hack party, where he'd met Sandra Fuller, one of the cutest girls (with fantastic eyes, not to mention hips and calf muscles) he'd ever seen in his whole mostly misspent existence (as he liked to phrase it), and she was so entirely in tune with him that he'd felt an overlay of something almost mystical, which the hack (not to be confused with smack, crack or sack, as he also liked to put it) alone could not have accounted for, although God knows it could account for a great deal, including soda-pop sky rides, lavender picnics, and camels on deserts where there is neither sun nor sand. Still, hack was the sort of hallucinogen that they claimed didn't radically interfere with motor skills, and he was sure he hadn't taken too much for driving. Everyone agreed that hack was pretty good that way.

Nevertheless, much business had been transacted, and much pleasure, and they could not have been easily distinguished as to which was which. It was that kind of party. A number of couples had drifted off, and when Ron was thinking of doing some drifting off himself, with Sandra Fuller . . . wham, she was no longer there, and he couldn't find anyone who'd seen her leave, or with whom. This was a numbing realization, for the two of them had been showing vital signs of becoming obsessively, fatedly simpatico (as he thought of it).

Ron had told her more about himself in an hour than he usually told others in weeks or months. He talked about how he'd spent two years in grad school, majoring in English until the bulb went on and he'd gotten this opportunity from an old friend, who was already making it big, to go out into the real word, which is to say, advertising, where, if he did say so himself, he was doing okay. "Very much okay," he'd emphasized to Sandra, winking and almost *feeling* the sunlight reflected from the gold chain showing above his imported, shimmering, gray, silk, drop-necked Carlucci shirt.

Then, only half an hour later, when he'd looked up, there was this whoosh, and cute little Sandra Fuller was no more. At least, she was no more *there*. So Ron shrugged (did he really shrug? Yes, he did.) and found his way out to his Porsche, with several people calling out, "Be cool, Ron! Be cool!" Which was their way of saying good-by, sort of. And take it easy, man.

He knew what they were saying and was not about to fly in his Porsche. Slow and easy. Moderation is best. Keep it in between the white lines and stop when the traffic lights turn red. Focus on the here and now, hard and clear.

But, then, twenty minutes later, he stopped in at a McDonald's (wait till he told *them* that!) to take a leak and get a cup of coffee, because his bladder could stand draining and his head could stand waking up and sort of washing out.

And when he emerged, carrying the insulated paper cup of coffee in his hand, there was this business with Ralph Waldo Emerson, sitting up, practically as lifelike as anyone he'd seen at the party, maybe more.

Ron's first response was one of indignation as well as astonishment. This was partly due to the fact that he hadn't clearly identified the figure right away; at first, he'd thought it was just some smartass who'd somehow jimmied the lock and gotten into his Porsche and made himself at home. A practical joker. Or maybe a thief. Porsches are high-visibility targets, theft-wise, as everyone knows.

The driver's door was locked, and Ron had to unlock it to get in, and by the time he'd settled himself, he was certain that the man in the passenger seat was none other than the Sage of Concord himself. Back in grad school, he'd seen too many pictures of that wrinkled, wise, lopsided face ever to mistake it for another— even after dark, in a McDonald's lot with late-twentieth-century traffic speeding past beyond the yew bushes and crab-apple trees that were growing out of the decorative white gravel. As a graduate assistant he'd taught freshman courses, with considerable emphasis on nineteenth-century American lit. Which rhymes, he sometimes liked to point out cynically, with you-know-what.

The shock of this particular moment, however, was such that Ron couldn't find anything whatsoever to say. Which rhymes with nothing. All of the available responses ("Just what do you think you're doing in my car, asshole?" or "Good God, are you who I think you are?") seemed inappropriate or inadequate, so Ron Bixler didn't say anything. He simply nodded (the expression on his face that of a man who's just lost a $50 bet), put his key into the ignition, and started the car.

It would be rude, goddamn it, even to stare. And yet, his first glance showed that Ralph Waldo Emerson was wearing his seat belt fastened, obviously ready to go and as calm as an old transcendentalist daddy *should* be on a visit to what we like to think of as the real world.

The first words spoken were of course by Ron, leveraged on a familiar joke. He said, "It isn't that I couldn't, you know, *hack* it, but I just felt myself drifting off a little, you know, which can be bad news, so I decided I needed a cup of coffee." He paused, thinking. "And to take two things: a break and a piss."

This seemed a bit curious, even to Ron, for it almost had the sound of an excuse for not bringing something out to his passenger. Or perhaps for not inviting him to come inside with him, where they could have shared quarter-pounders with cheese or Chicken McNuggets, along with large coffees and maybe a hot fudge sundae without nuts. Still, the Wisest American hadn't *been* there then, so how could Ron have invited him in?

"God, won't this traffic ever let up?" Ron asked rhetorically before whipping his Porsche out into the second lane.

Ralph Waldo Emerson said nothing to this, and Ron had a sudden feeling of panic. He had seventy more miles to go. It might prove to be a long trip.

He worked his car over into the right lane again, looking for the Plainfield turnoff. The precision handling necessary for this maneuver helped calm his mind, and, after negotiating the turn, Ron felt pretty much in control of things. As anyone *should* be, driving his own car.

"Well," he said finally, "what's new?"

"The exercise of the will or the lesson of power is taught in every event," Emerson said.

Ron turned this over in his mind. Its obliquity to the question asked was inescapably evident. Not only that, he had not really ever particularly cared for Emerson. Or, for that matter, *read* him.

"I don't suppose you would be surprised to know that I'm surprised," Ron said after a moment's silence, when he swerved and passed a green semi pulled by an Autocar cab-over, groaning up the incline near Kettle Marsh.

"Nature," Emerson said, "is thoroughly mediate. It is meant to serve."

"Jesus Christ," Ron muttered, half to himself, "it's going to be a longer drive than I'd thought!"

For the next few minutes they were silent. Occasionally, when an oncoming vehicle's headlights flashed through his car's interior, illuminating it, Ron glanced over at his passenger's face, possessed of the same benign gaze that revealed a sensibility upon which nothing was lost. Sort of like Henry James a generation or two later.

"Well," Ron said after perhaps five minutes had elapsed, "I can't help it: I *am* surprised, and the truth of the matter is, I think it's only natural."

"That is always best," his passenger stated, "which gives me to myself."

Thinking back upon this, Ron was as perplexed as he should have been. But he covered up his confusion by clearing his throat. What did he know about Emerson? What could he retrieve from his graduate school days? Not very much. Emerson wasn't fashionable any more. He wasn't *being taught* these days. (Comment: "I taught Melville last quarter." Question: "What kind of student was he?" Nothing quite like the bad old gags.)

But somehow, somewhere, there was an opportunity in this occasion, and Ron Bixler would be a damned fool if he didn't make the most of it. In a way it was a pity that Dixon Westlake couldn't have picked Emerson up; Westlake had been the department's man in American Renaissance and would probably have known how to heat up a pretty good conversation with R.W., and would have profited handsomely from the experience. He would have gleaned a fistful of articles, at least, in spite of Emerson's decline in the opinion of modern scholarship.

Well, maybe he should resort to the sort of comments you were driven to with any writer. Emerson *was* a writer after all—or had been (whatever), and would presumably be approachable through the standard ploys. In fact, being in advertising, Ron was sort of a writer himself. Not like one of the *real* ones—a journalist or writer for films or even books.

"I'm in advertising," he said, "but that doesn't mean I'm an illiterate. I still read, now and then. But I'm sorry to admit . . ."
Ron interrupted himself, leaning forward to see if the van before

him was really turning or the driver had simply forgotten to flick back the turn signal after it had merged onto the highway.

"I'm sorry to admit," he said, "that there's a lot of your work I haven't read. You know, just haven't gotten around to it."

"Ah," his passenger uttered, "a new disease has fallen on the life of man."

"What?" Ron Bixler asked, flashing his brights to signal some oncoming nerd to dim his.

But his venerable companion did not repeat what he'd said, and for a moment they proceeded in silence. Overhead, a battery of turnoff signs glowed handsomely vernal in their mint green and white luminescence.

Another quick glance to the side revealed nothing new; Emerson remained in his comfortable posture, his seat belt securely fastened, smiling rather frostily and whimsically out upon the passing show. Weren't all these speeding cars and bright lights frighteningly new to him? Not so far as Ron Bixler could tell.

He swallowed and tried again, pinning his comment upon the other, even though it had not gone very well. "As a matter of fact," he said, sounding more tentative than he felt, "what things of yours I *have* read didn't really, you know, *do* much for me."

"Do much?" the voice beside him inquired.

Ron shrugged, jogging his own seat belt sufficiently for him to be aware of its casual, strong, paternal hand ready to hold him fast should some abrupt vehicular violence try to thrust him forward into the steering wheel and windshield.

"You know," he went on. "*Move* me, particularly. I mean, I'm sure it's great work—everybody says so—or *used* to say so—but it just doesn't seem to be my sort of thing."

"Can we not learn the lesson of self-help?"

Ron frowned and bit his lip. "Let me admit something else," he said. "I'm not getting a whole lot from your answers, either. Couldn't you be a little more direct? Explicit? I mean I know that language is inherently metaphorical, which, if I'm not mistaken, was something you used to harp on; but for Christ's sake, Ralph, or Waldo . . . say, what *do* they call you, anyway?"

That question, one would think, could not tolerate other than a direct answer, but all it did evoke was a murmured, "Throughout nature the past combines in every creature with the present."

Feeling like his dullest undergraduate trying to cope with the mandarin allusiveness of Wallace Stevens, Ron sulked, while the lights of passing semis flashed through the tiny, once-cosy interior of his Porsche. Maybe he'd gotten out of touch and should change the subject to advertising or current events. But, no, that wouldn't work, either.

So, after several minutes of silence, he turned on the radio, but couldn't get clear reception on any band except one lonely FM station playing a medley of Strauss waltzes, of all things. Maybe there were solar disturbances, and irrelevant, old-fashioned oddities had been let loose upon the world. He snapped the radio off.

"Actually," he said, "I'm not entirely alone in my prejudice. If it *is* a prejudice, that is."

To this bulletin his companion said nothing. Indeed, nothing was required, although some sort of vital response would certainly have been welcome.

Nodding, Ron continued. "Posterity hasn't been very kind to you, Ralph. If I'm not mistaken, you were lionized to the point of idolatry in your mellow years. But then, that was the same generation that canonized Longfellow and Whittier. Good Lord, how far from the mainstream can you *stray*, I ask you!"

The truth was, however, he was not really asking his auditor anything. He was merely playing out a set of implications . . . which is pretty much what life is, if you think about it. Not to mention conversation, though done collaboratively.

"Funny thing about reputations, Ralph." He had decided that his friends would call him by his first name. After all, he suddenly remembered, it was his son—the cute and genial little prodigy who had died at the age of five—who had been called Waldo.

Ron shook his head. If he hadn't been doing sixty after dark, and if the traffic hadn't been so heavy, he would have packed and lighted his pipe. "Yes sir, a funny business! I'll bet you'd be surprised at how just about everybody has forgotten 'the Wisest American,' as somebody once called you. Say, who was that, anyway? Do you have any idea?"

When Emerson didn't answer, Ron glanced over at him again and was both oddly surprised and somewhat irritated to see that the Sage of Concord bore an expression that seemed even more genial and sagacious than the earlier one. The thought that right at this moment he might have been with Sandra Fuller sent a wave of demoralizing frustration and self-pity over him. Maybe what the old dude needed was a sting.

"Yep, they've pretty well swept your heartwarmy axioms under the rug," he said, shaking his head as if at the perfidy of fate.

"Or into the dust heap. Choose whichever metaphor you wish. You *do* dig metaphor, as I seem to remember. Am I right?"

So clearly was this a question that Ron vowed to wait until there was an articulate and complete, if not necessarily relevant, answer. And he was not disappointed.

"The flower of courtesy," the figure beside him intoned, "does not very well bide handling, but if we dare open another leaf, and explore what parts go to its conformation, we shall find also an intellectual quality."

Well, that was bizarre enough! And yet, it verged upon pointedness. Ron had the feeling that there might be something to it, after all. God knows what sorts of buttons the old sage was pushing, but this answer seemed to come dangerously close to engaging the question, in the way that one gear engages another, and as all right answers must do, engaged by the ratchets of the question.

That metaphor was bizarre enough to have originated with his ghostly hitch-hiker, with a little refinement, and it made Ron pause to think over the implications.

Perhaps a change of pace was called for. "Do you do this sort of thing very often?" he asked breezily. "You know, hitchhike? Travel?" *Or,* a voice inside his head uttered, *materialize in the front seats of Porsches at some local McDonald's?*

"The incommunicable trees begin to persuade us to live with them, and quit our life of solemn trifles."

Ron laughed. "Solemn trifles, eh? Jesus, nobody's ever accused *me* of being solemn!" But after saying this, he fell silent, thinking of another way the sentence might be taken.

"Listen," he said, sounding as earnest as an ad consultant or Student Senate president, "I'm really sorry I don't know your work better. I mean, what the hell, this should be a rich opportunity. Sort of." Again, he thought of Dixon Westlake and silently deleted the word *rich* from the statement. The son of a bitch had not just given him a B, he'd given him a B−, which struck Ron as a gratuitous fillip on the humiliation scale.

For a while the drone (the *solemn* drone) of the engine occupied his mind. With this preoccupation another began to emerge: What was he going to do with Ralph when he reached home? What about his plans for Sandra Fuller? He could imagine phoning her and trying to talk seriously, with Ralph Waldo sitting like a sack of groceries somewhere in his bachelor's pad.

"Listen," he said conversationally, "I forgot to ask where

you're headed. You know, where are you headed *tonight?* I'm not asking in a teleological sense."

Going under the overhead lights marking another freeway exit, Ron looked to the side once again and discovered what seemed to be an absolutely *hilarious calm* in his passenger's expression. *My God,* he thought, *I'm going bonkers!*

"Whither do we tend?" his companion asked.

"Look, goddamnit, I'm talking about *places!* I'm talking about where I let you off, at the Sunoco station at Forest Lane, which should still be open at this hour, or maybe taking you to the Day's Inn over on Freemarket Boulevard. I'm talking about ham and eggs, and you keep giving me ambrosia and nectar and shit like that!"

Under the next battery of overhead lights, Ron looked at his wristwatch (the Porsche clock didn't work, which seemed only natural for a car clock, even if it was a Porsche that was scarcely twenty months old) and saw that it was going on eight.

"It's going on eight," he said, saying it so loudly that he might have been speaking to somebody on the other side of a motel balcony.

But a glance at the serene object beside him confirmed his suspicion that Emerson was every bit as unflappable as his contemporaries had reported, and, his reviving memory hinted, his essays implied. It was impressive how much he could remember after all these years. "A lot better than B−, Westlake!" he muttered to his old prof, as if he were there to hear.

"I find that the fascination resides in the symbol."

"Do you know something, Ralph?" Ron said, pausing to work his lips back and forth as if warming them up for the delivery of a resoundingly conclusive statement. "Back when people read your stuff, the feeling was that you were too goddamn, you know, optimistic. 'Too fucking ethereal,' as I remember somebody saying one time back when we were in graduate school and had to read your essays. I must have missed that course, because as I said, I haven't really gotten to know your work as well as . . . well, I wouldn't say *should,* but well enough to hold an intelligent conversation with you now, under the present circumstances."

Present circumstances! The phrase triggered something, and, for a moment, Ron's head seemed to have fallen out onto the highway, where it was bouncing along behind the car, as if held more or less in tow by thick, fantastically strong rubber bands. Well, not exactly like that, but somewhat like that, in its impressionistic totality.

"You see," he plunged on, as if having just retrieved his battered, tar-caked head, "the world isn't all that fucking *spiritual,* pal, if you want to know the truth. Maybe back then, with the old village smithy under the spreading chestnut tree, or wherever it was, but not these days, it isn't. It's a whole new ball game, fella, and somebody ought to wise you up to the fact."

He honestly hadn't meant to sound so finger-popping hip, but he supposed it was too late now to change his tack. Not only that, wasn't Emerson always great on the marriage of contraries? It just came to Ron, right then: he was. Or had been.

But all this talk didn't seem to inspire anything in the way of response, and when some oncoming headlight illuminated the interior of the Porsche, he glanced over again, just to be sure that Ralph was still, you know, *there* . . . and, well, *alive,* if that's what he was. Present, anyway.

"Not that you didn't get off some good ones," he muttered after a moment. Then he sort of laughed and shook his head, as if remembering things that, in their capacity to amuse, were condign with Pete the Tramp and Tillie the Toiler, and the one about the poor battered male spouse who wanted to get a divorce, and when the judge asked if his violent wife still held a grudge, said, no, she had a carport.

Once again he tried the radio, this time wondering if such sudden outbursts of sound from an object scarcely larger than one of his volumes of essays didn't somehow pose a threat to his passenger's nerves. *How odd it must all seem to him!*

But the great man's marmoreal serenity was not shattered. His face glided between the flickers of illumination from traffic and the occasional overhead lights, and the instability of light merely emphasized the thin, shrewd, quirky stubbornness of his presence. Why couldn't the old duck have been Sandra Fuller, and why couldn't they be headed for old Ron's Passion Pad, and Sandra could hardly sit still, she was so excited!

But fantasies got you nowhere. So Ron leaned forward and turned on the radio again, but it was not indulgent. Several rock stations vented their mindless discharges upon the patient, silent air, and the Porsche continued in its swift and undeviating course. Well, at least they were out of range of those damned Strauss waltzes!

Another semi passed, its carriage of lights gliding forward like a swift constellation of falling stars. Then another. Odd to say, Ron was all of a sudden not in any particular hurry. He could hardly understand why this should be so. It wasn't like him, and it almost made him a bit uneasy.

Finally, after a long silence, he said, "Well, what do you think of it?"

"Think of it?" the figure beside him echoed. For the first time, those conversational ratchets seemed to have engaged one another. Furthermore, Ron fancied he could detect a certain perplexity in Emerson's tone, a certain uncertainty.

Ron swept his hand about him expansively. He noticed a grid of lights ahead and to the right—what had once been called "skyscrapers," but which were not often called that any longer. It was a term that had come into being after Emerson's death and had now passed its life span into another oblivion, this one crepuscular rather than absolute.

"What?"

Ron nodded. "The world out there," he said. "*Our* world."

"All persons," the Sage of Concord uttered, pointing his index finger heavenward, "all things which we have known are here present, and many more than we see; the world is full."

"*Full!* Why, shit *yes* it's full!" Ron Bixler said. "How could it be otherwise? I don't quite get your point, Ralph."

"These enchantments are medicinal, they sober and heal us."

I'll drink to that, Ron muttered, but he knew that his voice had not really carried. Then he spoke more loudly. "You see," he said, making a face at either the unpleasantness or the difficulty in what he had to say, "I just don't *know* your work. Furthermore, I don't know of anybody who *does*. I'm sure this must be something of a shock to you, but there it is. No sage worth his salt would want to close his eyes on the truth, would he?"

"And why not, when the truth is present as much then as otherwise?"

Ron laughed. "You're pretty hard to pin down, it seems to me. But I'll tell you something, Ralph: that cuts both ways. Being hard to pin down is fine, so far as polemics goes, but it doesn't build you any mansions or garner ad accounts. Not in this world, it doesn't."

"Is not time a pretty toy?" his passenger cried. "Life will show you masks that are worth all your carnivals. Yonder mountain must migrate into your mind."

Ron made a face. "Shit, that's not what I was talking about! I mean, this is too fantastic a, you know, *opportunity*, not to take advantage of. I'm sure if I mention that you're available, the deans at my old alma mater can come up with the money. You've never heard of it, but it's there, all right. And I'm not totally without influence . . . which would give Westlake the shits, if he knew about it, which he probably wouldn't, being out of it, and all."

"Let the realist not mind appearances."

Ron shook his head. "There you go again! Do you know something, Ralph?"

When his companion did not answer, Ron said, "Hey, I just asked you a question."

"I know what the child knows, and the boy who herds cows into the evening mists. Mankind all tend toward sleep as surely as the world turns."

"Wild," Ron said, "Maybe I could get a feel for it and sell the dean on a, you know, reading or something. No promises. They probably still have their old poetry series, which draws about four people per reading; but, shit, the way I feel is, something like this shouldn't be passed by!"

The interior of the car pulsed rapidly with lights, and Ron was suddenly aware of a semi that had come up behind him in the left lane, flashing to pass. He sped up and passed the car to his right so he could ease over and let the semi go by.

"I don't know how much student turnout they could expect, though," he said thoughtfully, tapping his steering wheel with the heel of his hand. "They don't turn out for much unless it's, you know, contemporary and sort of with it. Of course, if you were a rock group, the sky's the limit. But with what you've got to offer, I guess the best way to go might be commercial TV, although they might not be interested . . . except maybe for the ghost angle. Still, I've got contacts with ten or fifteen program directors, but to be truthful, probably half of them haven't even heard of you, Ralph. And so far as the ones who *have* heard of you, they're gonna figure it on ratings, and their audience would rather watch game shows or soaps. Hey, are you tracking me, Ralph?"

"I embrace these words as we must embrace lost children."

Ron glanced quickly, to see if the old man was slipping something past him, for this answer sounded disconcertingly apt, although still not entirely clear as to meaning.

"The key to every age is imbecility."

Ron laughed. "Jesus, you can say that again!"

Suddenly, there was a loud thumping noise, and the Porsche started to bump as if going over speed breakers.

"Shit," Ron muttered. "I *knew* that fucking tire was going to blow! And only thirty-two thousand miles on this baby!"

He pulled over onto the shoulder of the highway, while the traffic roared past. "Sorry, Ralph,'" he said, "It's just a flat tire. My right rear. I'm pretty sure it's defective, and you can't say that about many things on a Porsche. Hey, let me ask you something: do you know what a flat tire is?"

When there was no answer, he muttered, "Of course, you don't! Anyway, this won't take very long."

"The religious," Emerson said, "which is to guide and fulfill the present and coming ages, whatever else it be, must be intellectual."

Ron nodded. "You can say that again." Then he turned off the radio, got out of the car, closed the door, and got ready to change the tire.

When he was jacking it up, he could almost see the old sage start to lean sideways a little as the car tilted. He pictured him still gazing straight ahead. Then he wondered if maybe he shouldn't pull in at the next rest stop. Old men have trouble with their bladders, he'd heard. Or maybe read. Whatever, he didn't want some goddamn accident on his upholstery.

He removed the flat tire and put the spare on. Fastening the lugs, he realized how helpless and truly out of it the curious old dude was.

"What a screwy thing to happen!" he said half aloud before throwing the flat tire back inside, not bothering to lock it into the rack. "Let it rattle," he mumbled, dusting his hands vigorously.

"Goddamn cars," he said, opening the door and climbing back in behind the steering wheel. "Always something going wrong with them! Now, who would've thought that with a *Porsche,* for God's sake. . . ."

At the moment, he could feel something slightly, almost impalpably different, like a change in air pressure. He turned and gazed at utter darkness in the empty seat beside him, fascinated despite himself when a car's headlights passed, flushing that emptiness with light.

"Well," he said, "it looks like the old bird has finally flown. Whither, no man could guess. Or woman."

Saying which, he seemed to remember a line from one of the old cat's poems. He frowned and worked his Porsche out into the second lane as he accelerated, passing a truck very much like that one which had flashed its lights to pass only a few minutes before.

"What is it?" he said, frowning still harder as he tried to remember. "How does it go?"

Then something snapped as sharply as fingers in his mind, and he remembered: "When me they fly, I am the wings."

Kind of neat, maybe; but then, that wasn't Ralph talking at all, Ron remembered. It was the Buddha or Atman or something.

No sir, he told himself, feeling a great and inscrutable relief. That had been something else. Or *someone* else. Whatever. But it had not been Ralph. Not at all.

Then he slapped the steering wheel with his palm and said, "Look out, Sandra Fuller, wherever you are, because Old Ron has got you in his sights."

But then, so softly it might have been a squibble of hallucination, fired by what little hack remained in his system, he heard the old man's voice say, "Men, like children, should mind their toys, for they are always the vessels wherein their minds and hearts journey forth."

"Jesus, ain't *that* the goddamn truth!" Ron said, reaching over to turn on the radio again.

Lovely Things That Should Not Pass Away

WHEN MY WIFE departed abruptly early last spring, she not only abandoned me, she abandoned her position as chairman of the local school board as well. Our twins were grown and in college, so they weren't immediately, tangibly affected by her actions.

But the school board had an emergency meeting and asked if I would serve out my wife's unexpired term. They pointed out that I had served on the board recently and had continued to participate in school affairs. They said they knew me and knew my ideas, and my taking over for her would be the simplest solution for all concerned, since the charter stated that a spouse may serve out the unexpired term of a member when his or her position has been vacated by death or similar emergency. I agreed to this, and at the last meeting of the school year we voted unanimously to sell at public auction all the property and real estate of the old Kingsville High School, where my wife and I had been students together.

The school itself had been defunct since consolidation with a county school, four years before, and the building was in miserable condition. The lawn had not been mowed, and it was now overgrown with thistles and weeds. All the windows of the building had been broken out by vandals. Inside, things had deteriorated even worse. Plaster was falling from the ceilings, blinds were shredded from the windows, seats had come unscrewed from the floor and were now turned awry—broken and covered with pale dust. Books had been scattered everywhere. It was a depressing sight.

As for my wife, she settled in the Desert Sands Motel, forty miles from Santa Fe, New Mexico, and phoned me every night to explain in exhaustive detail why our marriage was not working out. It was not anyone's fault, she explained; but it was inevitable.

Considering the fact that people change differently and at different rates, the chances of two people remaining compatible over a twenty-year period are practically nonexistent, she explained. I told her that this was true, but not the only truth. I also told her she was too inflexible; and she explained that she was not a rubber band—which was another truth. She also told me that my medical practice came first, which meant that she had always had to come second. Maybe this was true, also; but *why* was it true? And of what use was such a congestion of truths, anyway?

By this time, our conversations had necessarily become formulaic, and I could have read or watched television with her voice in my ear and not really missed anything. (I can imagine her reading what I've just written and saying, "That's part of the problem, too!" And maybe it was. Or is.) Where did the school board come into all this? I don't know. All I know is, if our loyalties are partitioned in any way that can be adequately expressed arithmetically, something is lost and we're in trouble.

As for the school board, we voted to salvage what we could from the old building, where we had once moved and talked and fooled around under the terrible spell of adolescence. There had been liens on the real estate—therefore litigation that had delayed the sale—but by July the land title was clear, and we advertised a public auction in a score of newspapers.

I CAME EARLY to the building that morning. I met Henry Billicoe, the auctioneer, and we lighted cigars and went over the list of items to be auctioned, while two of Billicoe's helpers carried out junky desks, old wooden cabinets, sour-smelling stacks of yellowing files, pictures, and sundry other articles and placed them along the single, overgrown walk that led to the front door.

The auction was to begin at ten o'clock, but people started arriving about nine. Billicoe and I soon finished with the list, and we stood on the walk chatting. I saw a few people I hadn't seen since our graduation from this very school twenty-two years before. It was strange to contemplate that the high school we had gone to wouldn't be standing much longer.

An old woman wearing an orange pants suit and dangling silver earrings came up and told me, with a lost, broken gesture of her hand and tears in her eyes, that her happiest days had been spent in this school. For a wild moment, I thought of my wife in the Desert Sands Motel and felt a seizure of guilt. "It's been closed for four years," I said. "It isn't doing anybody any good just rotting here on the ground."

"I know," the old woman said, shaking her earrings in obscure denial, "but as long as it was here, I felt that just maybe it would be fixed up and used again. I know it's silly, but I just had that feeling."

I puffed on my cigar and nodded. I had nothing to say to that. She *was* a little bit silly; but then again she had a point. Like my wife in New Mexico.

Right before ten o'clock, a man whispered to me that he had just seen Verne Mitchell. I stopped in the middle of a sentence and asked where, and he pointed to a group of people next to the road. The day had gotten hot by now, and flies and wild honeybees were circling above the dilapidated desks that Billicoe's helpers had put in the thick green weeds and thistles along the walk.

I worked my way slowly through the crowd out to the road, shaking hands with a few people and nodding to others, and then I saw Verne talking to a woman. I hadn't seen him for years, but news had gotten back about his divorce, his drinking, and his being let go from his selling job. Old Verne wasn't doing so well, and he looked it. Still, it wasn't hard to recognize him; he was heavier and his face was an unhealthy red. A typical middle-aged hypertensive blood-blister face. We shook hands and talked about the auction.

Verne lighted a cigarette and puffed hard on it a moment. Then he pointed the burning end at the school. "You know," he said, "I thought I was King Shit when I went here. Remember? I got a honest-to-God medal for football. They said I was the best who ever played at Kingsville High. Now, there isn't going to be no Kingsville High at all. Nothing left." He thought a moment and then flipped his cigarette, half smoked, out onto the road. We watched it as it lay there burning in the glare of the sun.

"It seems to me there are a few of your old pictures in that stack," I said, motioning toward the building. "You can bid on them if you want. And your trophy's around here somewhere. The Most Valuable Player in the County. You were the only one from Kingsville ever to get that one, if I remember."

Verne nodded slowly and belched. His eyes were red, and I got a sudden whiff of bourbon.

"Didn't you marry Ginny Schattner?" he asked.

I nodded.

"How's she doing?"

"She's doing all right, so far as I know."

"Like that, is it?"

I thought about it and nodded. "That's the way it looks from here."

"Well, what the hell: join the club."

"Thanks."

"I hear you're a doctor and everything."

"Well, I'm a doctor."

"And chairman of the school board, too. I guess you showed you had it in you even back then." Verne motioned toward the old school, as if the past still existed inside.

Just then, Billicoe started auctioning seven long green blinds that had been put aside. He leaned back and the vein in his neck bulged. "Let's have a seven-dollar bill!" he bellowed, waving a rolled-up blind above the heads of the people. He was standing on a chair where everyone could see him. Another of his helpers had arrived—a tall, rooster-faced man wearing a bow tie. As Billicoe chanted and boomed, this man would scan the audience, and, if a bidder wiggled a finger, or nodded, this helper was sure to see him and yell, "Whup!" so loudly that Billicoe could hear him even through the hoarse torrent of his own chanting.

Billicoe sold the blinds and then a dusty box of nuts and bolts. Just as he was about to reach for the great stack of pictures at his side, I felt a tiny, steely clutch at my arm and I looked around to see Miss Emory. Although she was grasping my arm and smiling, she was looking directly at Billicoe and stepping toward him.

I spoke to her, and she patted my arm, but still she didn't look at me. We were standing in the shade of a catalpa tree, but at that minute Miss Emory limped out into the sun, and her white hair pulsed once into a burning cocoon, and even her tiny face seemed suffused by fire. Her back was no longer straight, but her grip was strong on my arm, and her glance was still alert. She had been lame all her life (I remembered staring often at her foot—curled like a hawk's talon—as she stood at the blackboard diagraming sentences) and had taught at Kingsville for almost fifty years.

She continued to work her way through the crowd by squeezing arms and smiling. People stood aside and some spoke to her, but she did not turn her head away from Billicoe. And when that man had raised that first large picture, showing individual oval portraits of the whole graduating class of 1909, and was about to start his chant, he glanced down at Miss Emory and saw her gesture with her open hand. He stopped, exhaling audibly, and leaned over to listen.

But it was clear that Miss Emory wanted to speak to the crowd.

She motioned Billicoe to silence, limped past him, and climbed the first two steps at the entrance of the old school. Everyone was quiet as she looked out upon us. I could hear birds chirping and grasshoppers whirring in the high, hot grass.

"Ladies and gentlemen," she said. "I have in mind a project, which I'd like to share with you. I would like to buy all the mementos and documents pertaining to Kingsville High, along with all the pictures and trophies, and display them in one of my downstairs rooms. I would like to keep this room as our museum. I am sure that many of you have deep and fond memories of Kingsville, but I don't think there is anyone who has invested more of himself in this school—if I may put it that way—than I have."

There was complete silence now; Billicoe was staring at the old lady with his heavy jaw relaxed as she spoke softly, smiling constantly. She stated her proposal as something rational and practical. Perhaps it was her manner—the tidy, neat way she closed her lips after each sentence (you could almost see her making a period in her mind), the subtle cadence in her voice.

Miss Emory continued after a pause in which she looked at several of us to see if we were paying attention. I don't think she would have been too surprised if somebody had raised his hand or one of us had shot a paper wad at Billicoe.

"Perhaps I am excessively sentimental," she said, "but it seems to me sad and unfortunate that Kingsville High should disappear entirely with so many of us still alive to remember what a truly lovely school it was for us in its day. Things that are lovely should not be allowed to pass away, if we can at all prevent their doing so.

"It is for this reason that I am planning the museum. I plan to bid on all of the pictures, trophies and records that are offered here today. I have no interest in the remainder, which is the bulk of today's sale. But I shall even bid on the Gilbert Stuart portrait of George Washington. Even though its duplicate has hung for years in virtually every schoolroom in the country, this particular picture is nevertheless *ours*; therefore it is part of Kingsville High."

I don't know how most people were responding to the old lady's speech. Everybody respected her, but not everybody liked her. She had been a perfectionist, in life as well as in the schoolroom; and she had always been an outspoken person. A man ahead of me snapped his Zippo lighter sharply as he lighted a cigarette. Visibly, Billicoe was beginning to be impatient.

"All I have remaining to say, is this," Miss Emory continued.

"Everybody will be welcome to visit my little museum. Always; and of course, free of charge. Even though I propose to buy these things, personally, I shall feel that they belong to all of us who have invested part of our lives in Kingsville High."

She stepped down, then, and for a wild moment I half expected the crowd to applaud.

Billicoe, sweating and exasperated, looked down at me, and I nodded assent. Instantly, he waved his arms and bellowed: "You heard the lady. Ladies and gentlemen, you heard this fine old lady. Do I hear any bids on this? Get it all together there, Marvin. Do I hear any bids? How about a ten-dollar bill for the whole lot? Lemme hear ten dollars! All right then, how about a five? Lemme hear a five-dollar bill!"

"Wait a minute!"

Everybody turned to the rear, and there was Verne Mitchell coming forward, a cigarette dangling from his lip.

"I don't care about the rest of this crap," he said, still pushing through the crowd. "She can have it all." He motioned offhand to Miss Emory, without looking at her. "But there's two things I *do* want. I want my picture that hung in the hallway beside the principal's office, and I want that trophy they give to me as the most valuable player in the county. I figure they're mine by rights. After all, I won them."

Miss Emory's smile faded. I doubt if she was sure who Verne was. She frowned hard into the sun. Somebody beside her whispered in her ear, and then quite clearly she said: "Verne Mitchell? Yes, I remember him. He was a football player."

There was general laughter at this, and even Verne laughed, turning his head around to the others in acknowledgment. But Miss Emory hadn't laughed.

"We'll put 'em aside," Billicoe said. "Now we'll bid on the rest. Anybody bid a dollar? Single-dollar bill!"

Miss Emory raised her finger, and Billicoe's assistant yelled: "Whup!" Billicoe chanted for another half-minute, but no one was willing to bid against Miss Emory and what was apparently considered an altruistic act, even though one woman wanted to bid on her class picture. She and her mother were standing in front of me.

"Go on and bid," her mother whispered rapidly several times.

"I don't think I ought to," the woman said, staring at Miss Emory.

So all of the records, all of the pictures except one, and all of the trophies except one went to Miss Emory for one dollar. She opened her purse and paid the clerk immediately and turned back to Billicoe, who was already calling out for bids on the picture of Verne Mitchell in football uniform in one hand and the large Most Valuable Player trophy held in the other.

"Let's go!" the assistant yelled. He was chewing tobacco now and the sweat stood out on his face. Billicoe's shirt was completely soaked with perspiration, and his eyes and neck vein bulged as he yelled for bids.

"Let's have a twenty-dollar bill!" he yelled. Verne and Miss Emory glanced at each other then looked back at Billicoe.

"Five dollars," Verne called out.

"Whup!"

"Five dollars!" Billicoe shouted in response. "Now lemmehear-asevenfiftyandawannafiftyanafiftyanafiftyanawannahearafifty-anafifty...."

"Seven-fifty," Miss Emory said.

"Whup!"

"Andawannatenandatenanawannaten. . . ."

"Ten," Verne said. "By God, they're mine!"

By now the crowd was tense and silent. I suspect that most people were aware that there was an odd sort of contest between the old lady teacher and this aging, drunken man who had once been the hero of Kingsville High. And I suspect that most were hoping that Miss Emory would win, because there had been something ugly in the reception Verne had received. No doubt he'd deserved it. It was as if he expected to step back into the image of a seventeen-year-old hero when he stepped back into this school-yard. He was old-looking and wretched-looking; he had failed in important ways, and everybody knew that he had failed. How could he be fool enough to expect us to look at him as a hero now? I had noticed it when Miss Emory had identified him as "a football player," and Verne had turned around and looked at people with a deep chuckle of amusement. "Imagine her not being sure of who I am!" the smile seemed to say.

The bidding continued, and the tension mounted. Sweat had gathered on Verne's face, even though he was standing in the shade of the catalpa tree. Miss Emory, however, seemed as dry as an artificial flower, though she was still standing in the sun, reflecting light like glass or metal. The bidding mounted to a preposterous twenty-five dollars, and then Miss Emory let twenty-seven-fifty pass. My guess was that she didn't have any more money.

Verne got the bid and, a few minutes later, went to the clerk and laid out the money from his wallet. It was obvious by now that he was really drunk. He weaved above the table where the clerk was working, and when he turned away from it, he said to no one in particular, "By God, they're mine anyway!"

Miss Emory was gone. I had gotten one glimpse of her telling Charley Collins to bring everything over in his truck. Then she turned back toward the crowd to stare for an instant, her expression grim and tired, but undefeated.

I couldn't help thinking about the poor old woman. It was obvious that she had been planning her museum for weeks, possibly months. And since she was a perfectionist, I could imagine that everything was now ruined for her. Her collection was not complete. It was a little ironic that her museum was missing only those two items that pertained to Verne Mitchell, whom, I now remembered, she had never liked. And obviously Verne had felt the same way about her. Their bidding against each other had been more than bidding. It was strange that their distrust of each other was still alive after all these years.

B Y Thanksgiving, my wife—whom Verne Mitchell had known as Ginny Schattner—had stopped phoning from the Desert Sands Motel. Maybe she was no longer living there. Maybe she had moved into Santa Fe, where her aunt lived and operated a modeling agency. I worked hard at my practice, and eventually what I was doing became more important than the loss of my wife. Maybe she had been right, after all; or maybe all the popular, best-seller psycho-crap she'd been absorbing through the years had provided her with what everybody needs, now and then: a self-fulfilling prophecy.

I had started "keeping company" (to use the courting phrase favored by the old-time Methodists of my childhood) with a woman named Angela Kreber. She was also divorced, which seemed to mean something to me, when I considered that here was one fact that connected Verne Mitchell, Angela Kreber, and myself—three utterly disparate types, one would think. But such speculations lead only so far, and, if you are as busy as I am, the luxury of making tenuous connections seems as expendable as Monopoly or Chinese checkers.

The winter came, and it was uncommonly cold. The old high-school building remained untouched—having been sold to a firm in Piqua; and when I passed it one day, it loomed above the barren white oaks in front like some Gothic relic. I don't think it would have looked so dreary and vacant if the weather hadn't been so cold.

One Saturday at the small clinic I run with another physician, I received word that Miss Emory had tried to phone me. I hadn't been able to answer the phone, so she told the nurse that she didn't want me for professional reasons, but asked if I could drop by on my way home that afternoon.

I had seen Miss Emory only once or twice since the auction, but I had often thought of her quixotic little museum. For some reason, the idea had stayed with me. Once, when I saw her at the Kroger store, the old lady had chided me for not coming to see it; and I had promised to drop by. But I hadn't; so I felt guilty and was now determined to go there directly from the clinic after her phone call.

It was a very cold day, and the snow lay almost a foot deep in the fields. The snowbank in front of Miss Emory's house was as smooth as a cement ramp. Something caused me to hesitate before driving my car through the immaculate, white, pristine apron of snow. But I parked the car there anyway, and got out into a drift slightly above my arctics. I stomped up to the front door and turned the old-fashioned, clock-wind bell handle.

Miss Emory let me in and took my coat. The interior of the house was warm, bright, and immaculately clean. Her curtains were starched and white, and sunlight seemed to collect inside the living room, making her old clocks glisten and twinkle (needless to say, they all kept excellent time) and her antique chinaware glow.

She had an old bottle-gas burner in the fireplace, rather than logs, but the effect was much the same as that of an open fireplace. No two pieces of furniture matched, and much of it was Lilliputian and rather fragile looking. For this reason, I sat on a footstool whose squattiness suggested strength. We chatted a little while, and then she insisted on making hot cocoa. When she was in the kitchen, she called out for me to go into the museum through the door to my left.

I did as she suggested. The room was somewhat dim and cold, compared to the living room, but I could easily make out the rows of pictures I had seen at the auction and, years before, in the halls of Kingsville High. On a library table at one end of the room stood the trophies, and underneath were stacks of ledgers and school records. I looked around the wall again and was suddenly confronted by the large photograph of Verne Mitchell in his football uniform.

"I see you're looking at it," Miss Emory said as she limped into the room with the tray of hot cocoa. She placed the tray on the table and handed me a cup. "He sent the trophy, too," she said, gesturing faintly toward the cluster of trophies. There was a slight frown on her face.

"That's a surprise," I said. "You must be pleased."

She sipped her cocoa, and turned her eyes aside thoughtfully. "I am," she said in her precise diction, "and I am not."

A train passed at that moment—the track was not far behind Miss Emory's house—and I could feel the floor vibrating gently. The disturbance was like the intrusion of a harsher, cruder world. Miss Emory sucked her cheeks in and waited, while the china and glassware tinkled. When the noise had subsided, she said, "Naturally, I'm pleased to complete my collection for the museum. It isn't that. It was the manner—the spirit—of his note. Wait a minute; I'll get it for you. I have left it out for you to read. That's one of the reasons I asked you to drop by."

She left the room for an instant and returned with the letter. She handed it to me. It was typewritten, and it said:

> Miss Emory:
>
> I don't suppose I should have bid against you, but then it seemed important at the time. I guess I have had these souvenirs long enough. They don't bring back any of my passed happiness when I was "a big shot" at Kingsville. But maybe they will you. I wish you every success with your museum. I hope these things will bring somebody a little bit of pleasure.
>
> Verne Mitchell

I handed the note back to her.

She frowned. "I don't think it had occurred to me why he *really* wanted those things."

I nodded.

She gave me a sharp, tiny glance. "You know . . . you've heard about his trouble, haven't you?"

"Yes, I've heard about it. If you mean his drinking and . . . well, his divorce."

Miss Emory made a face and looked to the side. "I didn't want to remind you of your own difficulties," she said in a small voice.

"Don't worry. The fact isn't any worse than what led up to it."

She nodded. "I suppose a lot of people feel that way about it. Maybe it's necessary; I wouldn't know."

"Well, we do what we can," I said.

"I don't like the futility implicit in that argument," the old lady said, shaking her head no and gazing out the window. "But I really don't want to raise painful issues. You must know that."

"I do," I said.

"Was he drunk that day at the auction? He was, wasn't he?"

"Well . . . a little bit, maybe."

Miss Emory sighed. "The poor boy," she said.

"Well, some things can't be helped."

"Don't say that!" Miss Emory said, frowning even more deeply. For the first time, in all the years I had known her, I detected something almost girlish and helpless about her. In a way, I suppose this had to be part of the truth.

"You know what I keep thinking about?" she asked suddenly.

"What?"

"Well, he lives all alone, doesn't he? Now that he's divorced. I mean, his parents live in Bellefountaine and . . . I suppose he's all alone, isn't he?"

"I don't know," I said. "I suppose so."

"Well, maybe this was all he had. Don't you see, I keep thinking about what a silly, foolish boy he's always been and all this trouble. . . . . The plain truth is, Verne could never *think* straight. Maybe that's why he and I didn't get along. He was always so puffed up about his athletic prowess and his good looks. And he misled so many others by his loud and obvious system of values. He was a threat, you know. To all of us. A threat to all we stood for. And the problem was, he just couldn't think. He was important to everyone, but *he couldn't think*."

Miss Emory was now shaking her fists up and down, and two tiny little spots of red showed on her cheeks. Far in the distance, I fancied I could hear the whistle of the train that had recently passed.

"Can't you see?" she said. "I'm afraid he might do something foolish, such as . . . well, *kill* himself!"

I was surprised when she said this, because it sounded awfully melodramatic; but of course I managed to make the appropriate sounds of comfort. And Miss Emory seemed to accept my assurances. But after all, what did *I* know about Verne Mitchell?

The two of us were unnaturally silent for a while. Miss Emory was staring at the cup that she held gently in her lap. Eventually, she smiled a little out of the side of her mouth. "You know, it's quite ironic," she said.

"What is?"

"First let me ask you if you like this." She waved her hand at the things in the room. "Do you think I've been silly? Was all this worth doing?"

"Of course it was. What was it you said at the auction? I remember the sense of it . . . something about fine things not passing away."

"Lovely things should not pass away," she murmured. "I have always believed that, and will always cling to the belief; but evidently others don't. Except Verne Mitchell. That's the irony, don't you see? He had a need to hang onto something of the excellence that isn't with us any more. That's what the bidding was about. But then he found out the trophy and the picture weren't enough; *they had to be shared.* So he sent them to me. The poor boy!"

"Of course they have to be shared," I said. "And I think it's appropriate that it should finally sink into his head that those things belong here. But what's the irony?"

She continued smiling as she placed her cup on the table. "In the six months since I started this museum, how many ex-students of Kingsville would you guess have come to see it?"

'I wouldn't have any idea."

"You're the first," she said. Something cold and bitter came into her face, and she was staring at me as if I personally held the strings to the hearts of people and prompted their ingratitude. *"Sic transit . . ."* she began, but let it hang.

I cleared my throat. "Well, you've got to understand that life has to go on. What we value in the past is the life that we had then, and if we are lost in that now, we have ceased to live . . . paradoxically, we have renounced that very thing we worship, or value. . . ."

My words snarled like a backlash in my head. I hadn't thought of the cruelty of my saying such a thing to this lame old woman who had no family, nothing beyond this ridiculous little room full of drab trophies. "I didn't mean to sound . . ." I started to say, but she waved her hand at me.

"I know," she said. "I know all of your arguments. But when you analyze too much, what *is* there left?"

I closed my eyes and risked it. "Everything you ever had," I said.

For a moment she stared at me with no more expression on her face than if she'd been sleeping.

I stood up. "And look what you have here. It *is* something. It is all that is left of those fine days at Kingsville, outside of what is in the hearts of a few people. A . . . a few of us."

I sensed that we were both over our heads in something that bothered us even when we weren't thinking about it. Maybe it was best not to try to articulate what it was. No doubt. I'll take the other kinds of diagnosis any day. The mysteries are just as great, but the results of your decisions are usually clearer.

Miss Emory was silent as I pulled my arctics on. She shook my hand politely when I said good-by. "I may write him and ask him to come," she said.

"Yes," I said, "I think that's a fine idea." Then I went out of the house, waded through the snowdrifts, and got back into my car with a feeling of relief that the whole business was over with, and I could forget about the poor, crazy old woman, at least for a while.

But when I got home, there was a letter from my wife, which began: "In case you're wondering where I've got to and what I'm doing, let me satisfy your curiosity. I'm now living with Judy and Ron Wechler (you do remember *them*, don't you?) in Santa Barbara, and things seem to be working out wonderfully for all of us. Ron is president of a foundation dedicated to the effects of aging upon social ideals; and as I told both of them (Judy's very much into their work together), I could serve as a living sample of some of the things that go wrong."

As for the rest of the letter, it doesn't bear quoting. At least, that's my opinion, because I can't make the least bit of sense out of it. But then, I'm not really sure what Miss Emory's about, either, so maybe my testimony doesn't mean much.

The Thunder and the Grass

O NCE THERE WAS a king who reigned peacefully over a flourishing Kingdom, but he was so morbidly afraid of death that nothing could ease his spirit. His preoccupation was so great that he took his food and drink grudgingly and was often oblivious to the words of others. When he labored in council, he did so as one whose thoughts were always elsewhere. And the darkness of his nights was crossed by cold pale bands of waking, during which times the terrified King lay in his bed, counting his heartbeats.

Knowing that every step he took carried him nearer to his end, he hardly ventured forth from his chamber. And during his long vigils, he began to think of Death as another Empire, the shadow of his own; he pictured it as an awesome kingdom—one that he was destined to visit one day when his time upon this earth ran out.

His Queen, who was a grave, lovely woman, with a gift for pacifying birds and dogs, could do nothing for her Master. She, better than most, understood how the King spent his hours. He was so fearful he often seemed to her more of a demon than a man—one of those trolls whose wrath is said to wash tirelessly back and forth in a grotto of molten darkness.

Then one day the King heard of a magician, who lived in a distant part of his Kingdom and was supposed to command great and unnatural powers. It was said that with a flick of his finger he could whiten the ground shadow under a laurel thicket; and by merely speaking certain words he could change the day of the week, so subtly that no one knew it had happened.

"What is this man's name?" the King demanded.

"His name is Enobarbus, Immortal Majesty," his Chief Councilor answered.

"What kind of name is that?" the King muttered; but it was

155

clear he was not really asking a question, so his Chief Councilor remained silent.

The King walked to his window, counting his steps—knowing that they could never be repeated. Never. Not even the supremacy of his throne could recall those steps, or allow the King to relive the interval they had occupied.

Finally, still gazing through the window, the King said, "Bring him to us."

"Enobarbus, the magician?" the Chief Councilor asked.

"Yes. At once."

Bowing, the Chief Councilor, started to turn away, but paused. Noticing this, the King said, "What is it?"

"Immortal Sire," the Chief Councilor said, "there is something else about Enobarbus, according to what they say."

"Something else?" the King asked, raising his eyebrows. "As if changing the world were not enough? What is it? Are you going to tell us he can talk with dogs and birds? If he can, we'll say it's no wonder: then he can talk with our Queen. Tell us what else this Enobarbus can do—as if taking away shadows isn't enough for one man!"

The Chief Councilor bowed gravely, accepting the King's banter unperturbedly.

"Immortal Sire," he said, "Enobarbus is also a prophet."

"A what?"

"A prophet, Immortal Sire."

The King frowned and shook his head. "Oh, is that all," he muttered. "As if there weren't enough of those around."

"Yes, Immortal Sire."

The Chief Councilor was once again ready to turn and leave, when the King stopped him, saying, "And one more thing: Don't call us that any more."

The Chief Councilor did not understand but, afraid of offending in some way, merely raised his eyebrows in an expression of inquiry.

"'Immortal Sire,'" the King said disgustedly. "No more. Not the *immortal* part. You understand?"

"Yes, Sire."

"We know it's been done for centuries, but we've had enough of it ourselves. To hell with custom in this case."

"Yes, Sire."

"And you may leave."

"Yes, Sire."

When his Chief Councilor was gone, the King turned back to the window and, facing the sky, said, "It mocks us."

THREE EMISSARIES WERE dispatched the next morning, and with nine attendants they rode jangling down the road from the castle. The King stood at his window, gazing after them, thinking of all that clutter of steps among the twelve horses—none ever to be repeated.

Behind him, his Queen asked if he did not feel better, knowing that such a great magician had been sent for. The King turned to her and sighed, shaking his head. "Our griefs are all in here," he said, tapping his finger against his head. "We know that!"

"But that's where all griefs lie, my Lord," the Queen said, meditatively touching her cheek with the tips of her fingers.

The King looked at her, then shook his head. "It's because death seeps in," he said. "We learn of it too young, and never understand it. It seeps into our heads and poisons everything that's there. Nothing escapes. You look at a sunrise or watch a falcon swoop high up over the oak trees or listen to the oxen as they pant and plod their way on the worn path—they're all moving inside death. Death surrounds all the things of this world."

"Surely not the sun, my Lord!"

"Yes, that too! Who could conceive of it going on forever?"

"But who would want to last longer than the sun, anyway?" the Queen asked.

"That's it!" he hissed. "Don't you see? Beyond that, there's the night. Darkness. Nothing but that black void. And do you know something?"

"What, my Lord?"

"That's where *God* is waiting. Who can abide a thought like that? We ask you, *who could ever tolerate such a thought?*"

"I don't know, my Lord."

The King stared at her as if her answer had surprised him momentarily; or as if he himself had just that instant taken in the enormity of the question he'd posed.

"Are they out of sight yet?" the Queen asked, stepping up beside him so she could gaze out the window.

Without turning to look, the King said, "No, they are still in sight."

Then he reached over and tenderly stroked the Queen's breast with his fingertip, gazing at it wonderingly.

Smiling, she said to him, "Does my Lord wish anything?"

"Immortality," the King muttered sadly, turning to look out the window.

Two crows were now circling high above the party of emissaries, which had proceeded so far they were almost out of sight.

"They feed on corpses," the King whispered.

Holding her hand beside her eye, the Queen began silently to weep, and turned away from the King.

Later, he did not notice when she left the room.

O N THE NEXT day, when the emissaries returned, the King received them. They approached his throne slowly, appearing glum and frightened.

"Oh, Sire," the first one said, "we have failed in our charge. Have mercy on us, we pray!"

"Why, what is the matter?" said the King.

"Enobarbus is an old man," the first one said.

"And he is bearded and mad from all his mystic arts," the second one said.

"And full of dreams, so that it is hard to make him speak," the third added.

"You're talking in circles," the King thundered. "All of this is nothing to us. Tell us why he isn't standing here this instant, as we commanded."

"He said he could not come," the first emissary whispered.

"Could not?" the King thundered. "Or *would* not!"

"Could, could, could," the emissaries all repeated together, like a columbarium over which the shadow of a great fox has fallen.

The King clasped his hand over his eyes and thought about their words; and the emissaries stood trembling, knowing well that messengers had been killed for bringing unfortunate news. But when the King took his hand away from his eyes, his expression was not wrathful.

"And he gave no further reason?" he finally asked, barely louder than a whisper and with a small note of wonder in his voice.

"None, Sire," the first emissary answered.

The King shook his head violently as if to scatter the words from his ears. But finally, he nodded, and in a matter-of-fact tone said to his Chief Councilor, "Then we ourselves will go to visit Enobarbus. We will travel forth and visit the old magician and speak to him out of Our Own Mouth."

The Chief Councilor nodded and said that horse and attendants would be ready to travel by noon, with which assurance the King strode out of the hall.

The instant he'd left, the second emissary was the first to speak, saying, "I would like to see what that wretched old magical bastard will do when the King appears before him!"

The third emissary nodded and said, "Yes, it will be hard for him to say anything, after he's beheaded."

Not hearing any of this, the King went to his chamber, where he sat on his couch with his head in his hands.

"You won't need to travel, Sire," a child's voice said.

Astonished, the King looked up to see a small boy standing before him, clutching by its tail a dead cat, which dangled limply from his hand. The cat's head looked smeared, somehow, as if it had been crushed under the wheel of a cart.

"Who are you?" the King cried. "And what are you doing in my chamber?"

The little boy closed his eyes and made a face. He strained until his face turned red.

"What on earth are you up to?" the King asked.

"I am Enobarbus," the child said. "I arrive in my own fashion and no other."

Then he held his breath and strained again, like an infant at stool, until he grew taller and, at the same time, turned old before the King's eyes.

Speechless, the King lifted both hands before him, as if to ward off the sight of this miraculous transformation.

But Enobarbus did not appear to notice. He muttered briefly in Latin, and then stroked the cat, which suddenly convulsed into life and scampered away.

"We hope never to see that creature again in our whole life," the King said in a hushed voice.

"If you live forever, you'll see everything again," Enobarbus said. "And again and again. There'll be no end to it. Not the least thing."

The King nodded soberly, but then shook his head. "We don't care," he cried. "No matter what the cost. The fact is, we can't abide the thought of dying. Death . . . death is something we can't. . . ."

"Fathom?" Enobarbus asked.

"Accept," the King said.

The old magician closed his eyes and raked his beard with his fingers.

"Are you as powerful as they say?" the King asked in a small voice after a moment's silence.

"Probably," Enobarbus answered.

"You can turn darkness to light, and change the day of the week, as they tell?"

Enobarbus shrugged. "Those are trifles, oh King. Ask me what it is you want."

"And you have prophetic powers?"

Again the magician nodded. "For definite events I have definite foresight. What is it you wish to know?"

The King then reached forth and clutched the old man's robes. "Tell us what day we are fated to die on!"

"What?"

"There are seven days in the week," the King said. "Everything that happens in this world has to happen on one of those days. If it is destined, as we suppose it must be, that our death will happen, then it must happen on a certain day. Tell us what day it will be: Sunday, Monday. . . ."

Enobarbus held his hand up and closed his eyes again. "I know all seven," he said. "And I understand your question. It's an odd one: I don't mind admitting that, but not beyond all probing."

"You mean you can do it?"

"Quiet," Enobarbus said, wetting his finger and holding it in the air. He opened his eyes and said, "It's not a Sunday. Nor a Monday. Wait a minute. Let me look."

For a moment, the room seemed to shrink in size, and Enobarbus himself appeared no larger than the dead cat he'd brought back to life; but then, in an instant, everything returned to normal; and the old magician announced, "Tuesday."

For a moment, the King was silent. Then he said, "Are you sure, Enobarbus?"

The old man nodded.

"You understood what we were asking? And you say that you know for a fact that we are destined to die on a Tuesday?"

Again Enobarbus nodded. "You won't die on any other day, Sire. This is a certainty."

For a long while, the King sat on his couch and brooded. Then he shook his head wonderingly, as if unable to believe the enormity of his own vision.

"And it is true what they say?" he muttered slowly: "You can change days, the way others change their mind?"

"There's a close connection between the two," Enobarbus said. "But, to answer your question, yes."

"Then, Enobarbus, could you erase a day from the week?"

"What?"

"Could you make a day disappear from the week?"

"Just any day?"

"No, I mean the day itself. The reality, the word. Take one of the seven days of the week and remove it from reality, just as if it had never existed. Change the world so that from this instant on people will not even *think* of referring to 'the seven days of the week,' but to the *six!*"

Slowly, Enobarbus smiled. Then he smiled a little more broadly and almost opened his mouth to speak, but appeared to change his mind. The King watched him closely, not daring to interrupt the flow of thoughts that were going through the old magician's mind.

But eventually, he could wait no longer, so he whispered, "Enobarbus, *could* you?"

Enobarbus nodded.

"However," he said, after a moment's pause, "if I take away all the Tuesdays, it will have to be *all* of them. I mean, before as well as after."

"I don't understand," said the King.

"Such a radical transformation of reality can't be partial; it isn't like slicing off the end of a cheese. This means that everyone now living born on a Tuesday will cease to exist, Sire. They won't be killed, mind you; it will simply be as if they had never been."

The King's face lengthened. "But I was born on a Monday," he said. "I'm sure of it."

Enobarbus appeared to think a moment, and then he nodded. "That's right. You were. It was a Monday 11,238 days ago."

"Can you really do it?" the King cried.

"Yes," Enobarbus said.

"We'll see that you have anything you want!"

"Maybe. On the other hand, that may not be necessary."

"But you'll do it."

"I said I would," Enobarbus stated, articulating the words very carefully.

"And no one will know the difference?"

"No one."

"When can you do it?"

"When you go to sleep next Monday night," Enobarbus said, "you will sleep deeply, for only the accustomed time; but when you awaken, it will be Wednesday."

"For everybody?" the King asked.

"For everybody," Enobarbus answered. "Tuesday will never exist again. Tuesdays *before* that time will continue to have existed, for there is no one alive who does not have ancestors born on Tuesdays, but all references to them will disappear. At this time, even the word will have ceased to exist. And all things that were to have happened on Tuesdays, or have happened on Tuesdays, or were begun on Tuesdays, will not exist."

The King shook his head vigorously, "Not *die. . . .*"

"No," Enobarbus said. "Not die. They will simply not be and, given the new state of affairs, will never have been."

"How strange it seems to us."

"Indeed it must seem strange. Also irrational. So it is best that others don't find out. You must never tell anyone."

"Not even my Queen?"

"No one, my Lord."

"All right. I swear it."

"Very well."

"What a miracle!" the King cried.

"It is that, indeed, Immortal Sire," Enobarbus said.

WHEN WEDNESDAY MORNING arrived, the King awoke with the realization that two nights, instead of one, had passed. In addition, he knew that an entire day had been carved out of reality by the magician, Enobarbus; although, for the life of him, the King could not remember what that day had been called.

Happily, he lay in bed and counted the six days of the week on his fingers, knowing that his Death Day—whatever it had been named—no longer existed. He counted the six days of the week silently, and then aloud: Sunday, Monday, Wednesday, Thursday, Friday, Saturday.

He arose in a state of wonder. So much of the old world remained for him: exactly six-sevenths, of course—which is enough to represent a world.

And then, in a brief instant of darkness, he relized that one out of every seven people he had known would now not exist, and he would not even know who they were. He would not even have the sad luxury of missing them. Still, human habit is such that he felt compelled to ask his Seneschal if the Chief Councilor was all right.

"Indeed, Immortal Sire," the Seneschal answered.

"And the three emissaries," the King added, as he shrugged on his tunic.

"Indeed, Immortal Sire," the Seneschal answered.

And after that, the King went over the whole list of his retainers; but of course, any he could remember were alive and well, or he would not have remembered them. There was, in all honesty, a certain uneasiness in this fact.

"And Enobarbus!" the King cried, almost forgetting. "Is *he* well?"

The Seneschal gestured subtly with his open hand as he nodded, and the King remembered that none of his household had liked or trusted the Old Wizard from the instant he had appeared among them.

Dressing slowly, the King was calm and light-hearted. It seemed he could hear better than before—at least better than that six-sevenths he could remember from the old life he had lived. Even the birds beyond the window sang more spiritedly. And the sun might have been created that very morning, so beautifully did it evoke the things of this world!

Then, briefly, the King was troubled by something in his arithmetic. Arithmetic was not the precise art to measure what might have been sacrificed. He suddenly understood this. Therefore, sensing that it was not exactly true that six-sevenths—and only six-sevenths—of his memory had been forfeited, he called for Enobarbus.

Appearing older than the King had remembered, Enobarbus listened to all that the King had to say about this one small trouble that remained.

"Although," the King concluded warmly, "you must understand that the main thing has been accomplished: we do not fear death at all, now; it doesn't exist for us any longer."

"Understandably, Sire."

"In fact, we are immortal."

"Along with all others who were once destined to die on that certain day," Enobarbus said.

The King frowned and motioned the idea away with his hand. "Of course. That, too. But the important thing is: we are finally released from the terror that had saddled our heart for years."

"Yes, Immortal Sire," Enobarbus said, bowing.

But the King was not satisfied. Frowning, he said, "But what about this other part we mentioned: what about the vague uneasiness? The fact is, we don't like not knowing about that one-seventh of the old life we lived in."

"The old reality," Enobarbus said, nodding.

"Exactly. What about it?"

Sadly, the old magician shook his head. "I don't know," he finally said.

"You don't *know?*" the King roared. "How can that be? Aren't you wise beyond all others?"

Enobarbus closed one eye in a doleful wink. "No Sire, I am not. I am not wise at all. I am merely clever."

"Clever?"

Enobarbus nodded.

"But doesn't that become the same thing, when all is said and done?"

Enobarbus frowned. "If I said no, you would ask how I could know that it wasn't the same thing, unless part of me stood beyond what I now am."

The King threw his hand aside. "We don't like riddles, Enobarbus. Speak plainly."

Enobarbus closed both of his eyes. "If," he said slowly, "there were a vast meadow of grass that extended as far as the eye could see, and it was known that by plucking one particular blade of grass from all this meadow one could bring about a rainstorm, I could go out into that meadow and walk until I stopped in a particular place, where I would lean over and pluck a blade of grass, and at that very instant thunder would rumble throughout the heavens and the air would turn dark."

The King thought a moment and then said, "You cannot be any clearer than that, Enobarbus?"

"No, Immortal Sire, I cannot. I don't know how the blade of grass is connected to the thunder."

"Well," the King said, "we will not concern ourselves over needless subtleties when there is a kingdom to govern."

"Prudent," Enobarbus said, nodding. Then he continued: "Judicious, wise, sagacious, and politic."

"What?" the King asked.

But before Enobarbus could answer, the King's Seneschal appeared at the door, bowing gravely.

"Well, what is it?" the King said to him.

"Immortal Sire, the Chief Councilor is waiting."

"What about?" the King asked.

"About the woman you must choose as your Queen," the Seneschal said. "You were to discuss the matter with him, in view of the gravity of the choice you must make. I mean, Immortal Sire, for the sake of the Kingdom. The law states you must take a Queen before you grow older."

Irritated by such an officious reminder, the King waved the Seneschal away. Then he muttered, "Of course, we remember! Don't you think we know it's time we chose a Queen?"

"He's gone, Immortal Sire," Enobarbus said.

The King turned and looked at the old magician, and then nodded and left the room, so that he could meet with his Chief Councilor on this most important matter.

A LTHOUGH THE KINGDOM continued to flourish in the following years, there was a mysterious unrest among the people. Outwardly, all was well: the King took unto himself a Queen, and she was favored by all. The Kingdom itself was at peace with its neighbors, and the crops each year were full and heavy.

But in spite of all outward good fortune, there was a growing suspicion that something was not as it should be. Even though the King himself was content, and ruled with wisdom and compassion, there was a chill of discomfort in the hearts of people that found expression in odd and unlikely ways.

Old women began to awake from nightmares in which they suffered from a feeling that someone they had once known was missing. Guilt and fear were often evident in the most casual situations; and once a knight was seen to draw his sword and slaughter his own hound, for no apparent reason.

"Whom the gods destroy, they first drive mad," the Chief Councilor intoned when he heard the story.

But beyond agreeing with him, the Under Councilors did nothing, suggested nothing. Later, it was noted that this particular knight seemed oddly at peace after killing his dog, as if he couldn't remember the outrageous thing he'd done—worse, in its way, than killing a human enemy in combat.

Most unsettling was the darkness that had come into the lives of the people. The very existence of all those who had been born on the lost day had been annihilated; and yet the consequences of their existence remained. Thus it was that a woman found herself the mother of children whose father she could not remember; and yet, knowing the laws that govern the birth of children, she could not understand how she had become what she was, or how her children had come into being.

Of course, such mysteries prevailed over roughly one-seventh of the Kingdom, so there was a certain comfort and acceptance simply in their familiarity. And, not having words for this sudden void in their lives—which they could not precisely identify *as* a void—they began to use those words which were available, so that the mystery could be named and thus, in the way of human necessity, understood.

Those whose existence had been annihilated, were called "ghosts" and "ancestors" equally. A woman whose husband had been taken away from her would sometimes contemplate one of her children and say, "I wonder who your ghost could have been!" The word "father" was almost never used in such a reference, for that word designated something quite different in the minds of the people.

As for Enobarbus, he lived for a while among the court, but steadfastly refused whatever riches or advancement the King offered. He claimed he was not in need of anything; and indeed, his behavior was so odd that no one could doubt that he spoke the truth. His needs were not those of others.

Most of his time he spent walking about with his hands clasped behind him—smiling or mumbling or sometimes humming a little tune. When spoken to, he more often than not answered in an unknown language. Occasionally, he would stop and talk to the ground at his feet, or address the knuckles of his hand. Several times the night guards came upon him standing motionless upon the parapets, an arm outstretched and his eyes closed. He was a disquieting sight, looming there in utter silence, his beard and robe stirring in the night breeze. The guards sometimes said that he looked like a man about to fly; and no one in the castle doubted but what the old magician could have done so, if he'd wished.

Although neither the King nor Enobarbus ever spoke of their Secret, no one doubted but what Enobarbus bore some responsibility for the change that had come over their lives. And soon, the atmosphere of fear and distrust grew so great that Enobarbus left the castle. It was not known exactly how or when he left; the court simply awoke one morning to find that Enobarbus was not there.

And no one mentioned the fact at all; not even the King.

E NOBARBUS, WHOSE DEATH day was Sunday, lived to be a very old man. It is said that several generations passed away before he himself was called, but this fact was not given much emphasis, in view of the extraordinary longevity of certain people in that period, for when Enobarbus had wrought his marvelous change, some of those who would normally have died within a handful of Tuesdays were already old. Moreover, now that weeks had only six days in them, time appeared to move more swiftly, and the year contained only 313 days.

Some of the people lived miraculously long: one woman was said to be almost a century and a half old; while many were beginning to live into the second century of their existence. Some predicted that in the cycle of years, biblical times were returning, so that a few might even live to the reputed ages of Noah and Methusaleh.

But others began to say other things, and because the Under Councilors—now growing old under the shadow of the Chief Councilor (whose death day also happened to be Tuesday) and under the King . . . some of these Under Councilors began to suspect that something was not as it had been before. Therefore, they met in secret and devised various theories to account for what had happened. In these theories, the feared and hated Enobarbus began to play a greater and greater role.

Meanwhile, the King himself was growing old, although he seemed as vigorous as ever, and was never known to express a fear of death. His Queen grew old, too, along with the children she had borne him. The castle stood as vast as a cliff and with each passing decade, appeared stronger and more obviously invulnerable than ever.

From his old habitation, Enobarbus heard about these things, for gossip spread quickly throughout the Kingdom. And yet, he seemed indifferent to all that was told him. Living alone, without human attachments, Enobarbus was scarcely noticed by those about him. And he seemed content to remain anonymous, for most of his realities were inside his head, and he had little need for a world to entertain him.

Then one day, two emissaries came from the King and asked Enobarbus if he would not come with them to see his Monarch. They asked politely, almost diffidently, as if they well knew the story of how he had mocked those other emissaries so long ago.

Enobarbus agreed, and was carried in a coach to the King's castle, where the King awaited him in his private chambers. The Seneschal who greeted him was a much younger man than the previous Seneschal, who had died on a dark Friday long ago.

When Enobarbus was admitted to the King's chamber, he was shocked by how old and decayed the King looked. But there was a surprising vigor in his speech, for he greeted the old magician in so loud a voice he might have been shouting from one hilltop to another.

"This time you came properly," the King shouted, with an expression of grotesque intensity on his face. He paused and breathed several times, as if gathering his thoughts. "This time you didn't appear as an urchin," he went on. "None of your tricks this time, eh?"

"None, Immortal Sire," Enobarbus said, realizing that the King was drunk.

Frowning, the King nodded, accepting this fact and pondering over it with a lugubrious expression of gravity. Finally, inhaling again, he said, "Well, we knew you still lived. In fact, Enobarbus, we have been protecting you all these years."

Enobarbus bowed and said, "That is true, Immortal Sire. I was aware of your protection."

"Aware of our protection, eh?"

"Yes, Immortal Sire."

For a moment, only the sound of the King's heavy breathing could be heard. Then he stirred and said, "Why have you never asked for anything else?"

Without hesitating, Enobarbus said, "I could never determine exactly what I wanted, Immortal Sire."

Astonished, the King stared at the magician. "So wise, and yet lacking that essential wisdom?"

"As I told you once, my Lord, I am not wise."

The King nodded, saying he remembered well. "But still you live on. Was that part of it?"

"Part of what, Immortal Sire?"

"Part of why you did it," the King said. "We've often thought that the reason you served us so willingly, and asked for nothing in return, was that you too were destined to die on that day . . . whatever it was called."

"No," Enobarbus said, shaking his beard, "my death day is coming upon me. I can sometimes feel it rising like water, when the river begins to flood, Immortal Sire."

"Yes, yes," the King said. "You needn't be so . . . what do you call it: *vivid*. We understand what you're saying."

Enobarbus bowed. "And now," he said, "you want something else."

The King half-closed his eyes: "You knew all along, didn't you?"

Enobarbus shrugged. "I suspected," he said. "It's lovely for a while, but like everything else, it begins to seem . . . how shall I say it?"

"Vulgar?" the King suggested.

"Somewhat, Immortal Sire. But more than that."

"Predictable? Repetitious? Without point?"

"That comes closer to it, Immortal Sire."

"'Immortal Sire,'" the King repeated heavily, savoring the words. "How that title beguiled us at one time!"

"It was with you as it would have been with others," Enobarbus said.

"So you know what I am about to ask, don't you?"

Enobarbus nodded.

And then, with passionate suddenness, the King reached forth and clasped the old man's robes and cried, "Put it back, Enobarbus! Put it back!"

"As you wish, Sire," Enobarbus said.

And before the King could say anything else, the old magician began muttering and touching his fingers, as if he were trying to count to seven.

"And what will you call it?" the King asked, staggering over to the window and gazing out as he had done so often for so long.

"Tuesday, Sire," Enobarbus said.

The King blinked slowly. "What did you say?"

"Tuesday, Sire."

"Of course!" the King whispered. "Now I remember!"

"Your Majesty will say when?"

The King nodded. "Something has been missing in our life, Enobarbus. Did you know it would be like that, too?"

"No, I couldn't have predicted that."

"I know: you said as much. This thing we're speaking of is. . . . I don't know how to say it: like something we once had; or maybe *were*. It's impossible to describe it, but the emptiness is frightening. Tell me: if you bring back this lost day, will I have a chance to grasp it once again?"

Sadly, Enobarbus shook his head. "No, Sire," he said. "I can bring back the lost day, but whatever came about on that day is lost forever."

"Why?" the King cried. "Why?"

"Because," Enobarbus said, "without this loss, oh Sire, you wouldn't know what it is to be a man."

Parlez-vous *Means "Good-by"*

EDITORIAL:
JEFFERSONVILLE COURIER
Jeffersonville, Ohio
APRIL 19, 1934

SOMETHING'S GOT TO BE DONE!

Southeast of our little city, right beyond the railroad yards, exists a cluster of small, twisted, tar-paper shacks, known to every bum west of Pittsburgh as the "Jeff Jungle." Indeed, you would have to look hard to determine the nature of these tiny edifices, for they seem hardly fit for human habitation. They are beds of squalor, filth, disease, wretchedness, and immorality. They are a blight upon Jeffersonville.

Actually, if this "jungle" existed in another section of town it wouldn't affect the lives of the people of Jeffersonville the way it does. We might then be able to ignore it, although the legions of bums that accost our backdoors for handouts are not the least of the irritations.

But as it is, businessmen coming into Jeffersonville get their first impression of our little city as their train passes the glinting galvanized iron used for the roofs of these shacks, and the first introduction to our local citizenry by the sight of a whiskered and disreputable hobo squatting by the tracks and staring dumbly at the train.

We of the Courier *herewith announce our intent to take up the crusade to drive these social leeches from Jeffersonville.*

THE TWO OF THEM were carrying boxes of canned goods east across the railroad flats toward the hobo jungle. It was early morning, and the bright sun made Preacher squint and draw up his mouth. He had a bad cough; and Frank, the man in front, heard him expectorating with regularity as he followed him across the flats. Preacher was still pretty young. He was gaunt, though, and his clothes flapped on his body. His dark face was prematurely lined in an expression of high rhetorical anguish.

As they neared the path that led down into the jungle, they could hear the birds chirping. A whiff of green came into their nostrils, and the cinders under their feet suddenly disappeared, and they were on the clay bank. The words "Wall Street" had been written in tar on a board stuck in the ground.

"Let's put 'em down and take a rest," Frank said, blowing through his mouth. He was tall and he had once been fat; but now there was fat left only in his face, which was red and blotched.

"Them cans is heavy," he said tonelessly. A dirty robin skipped in front of him, and Frank kicked at it aimlessly, almost losing his balance.

Preacher pulled his old felt snap-brim hat off and squinted up at the glare of sky. "I still don't like it. They wouldn't leave no good food stacked out there in a shed like that. It must be spoiled."

Frank leaned over at him and said, "I tell you, that's just their storage shed back there! Ain't you even *looked* at that restaurant? They ain't got no room to store things inside. They got to put 'em out back in that shed."

"How about that ketchup you got there once?"

"Hell, a little mold! Honest to Christ, what's a little mold? Mold gets on the best of food!"

"Yeah, but people throw it away. Especially restaurant people."

"I told you, one of them bottles of ketchup was all right. Hell, the other one sat around the shack for a week. And it rained every God-blessed day. No wonder it got moldy."

"It just don't look good," Preacher said. Nevertheless, he threw the box onto his shoulder and walked down the clay path into the jungle. He went past the shack where old McGuffey lived. McGuffey thought he was Pershing on Sundays and Edgar Guest the rest of the week, and he wrote sentimental poems about our doughboys stopping the Hun on the battlefields in France, and recited dreamy, wet-eyed tales of his life Over There.

Now, seeing that McGuffey's shack was silent, Preacher stood still and sniffed with his eyes closed. "I can smell sickness," he said.

"You and your goddamn nose!" Frank said, putting his case down and pulling a tin out. "It says *Isobeney Sardines:* fine quality at low cost."

"Somebody's sick with a fever," Preacher said, gloomily.

Frank raised his head and thought a moment. "I tell you, Preacher, your nose is imagining things."

"Maybe so," Preacher muttered, shaking his head.

Frank sat down on the ground. "Come on and help me open one of these here cans." He grabbed one and pried at it with a broken screwdriver. His face got redder than usual, and, after a minute, he stopped, panting.

"Damn, I'm weak from hunger! I think I'm almost starved to death. Kiss me, if I don't! Come on and give me a hand!" he cried, his voice rising. He strained once more with the screwdriver, his dry lower lip stuck out like a piece of frayed cardboard.

"Open the blessed cans by yourself!" Preacher said tardily. "If you live, I'll try some."

"You're some friend, Preacher!"

The can sighed and split open. Inside, the sardines were covered by a frothy gray liquid.

"That looks awful!" Preacher said. "I ain't hungry no more. Just one look cured my hunger."

"Hell, all sardines smell like that," Frank said, frowning. Then he stared at the can a little bit and put it down on the ground.

"Where's a cat?" he asked.

"How would *I* know? I ain't seen no cats down here for a long time. Even a cat would starve down here."

"Christ, I can't eat it without being sure!" Frank looked this way and that. Then he slowly rubbed his long, white shinbone and stared at the can.

"Preacher, it must be all right. Wouldn't they destroy it if it wasn't?"

"How would they destroy it? Throw it down into some garbage dump like this? Or come right out and give the stuff to us, so that we'd be killed off?"

"If I don't get me some chow before long, I'm just gonna curl up and die. Like that." Frank snapped his fingers soundlessly and stared at McGuffey's shack. "Even if we *could* get a cat to eat it," he mused, "the son of a bitch would leave when he got his bellyful, and we wouldn't have no way of telling whether he died or not."

"I say chuck the stuff and let's go try and get us a handout."

"In this town? Are you crazy?"

"Let's get locked up, then. I can almost smell them franks and home fries."

"Quit your dreaming; they ain't got jail room!"

Preacher sat down, then lay back on the warm grass and watched a line of smoke rise into the air from a neighboring settlement. It was like a tree trunk, with no limbs, nothing attached, nothing issuing from the trunk of its existence, but simply rising until it faded into nothing in the still air. Birds could fly through it then, and it would hold no reminder of fire or wood. Just like him; birds could fly through his mind now, and not even disturb the still curtains that hung at the windows.

Grunting, scuffing one shoe in a patch of gravel, Frank struggled to his feet. "Come on," he said. "Let's go see McGuffey."

McGuffey's tar-paper shack was off the path about twenty feet. He slept on an automobile seat, which wasn't so bad, because McGuffey was a small man. He had a large nose, however, which gave him a haughty air. His manners seemed to have an odd touch of the aristocratic. When he walked, he held his head back, emphasizing some notion he had of gentility. His clothes were black and entire, and if they'd been cleaned and pressed, he would have seemed like a poor worker instead of a bum. McGuffey had been a great cardplayer in his day, and there were times when he sat for hours upon end, cutting a deck and blinking out at the transformation that had unaccountably come over his world.

But now, McGuffey was not abstracted, not dreaming. Maybe he had just come out of delirium, or maybe he was just about ready to go into it . . . but at the moment, his face was strained and pale, and his hair stood out from his head like ruffled feathers.

"I'm going to kick off, fellows," he said when they entered.

Preacher shuffled uneasily in the closeness of the shack.

"Only time I was sick before was in France. But that was after all the action." The idea pleased him, and he smiled with a kind of weak pride.

"I just had me a dream," he said, looking at them as if he were already speaking from the Beyond, and therefore knew things they didn't know. "I dreamed about my dear old mother. She was a hunchback, you know. Came from overwork, and being on her knees, praying so much. Yes, boys, it was her prayers that got me back safe. I've lived a hard life, but now I'm going to meet my mother, over yonder, on the other side, where the sunlight is."

McGuffey cleared his throat and blinked up at the ceiling, such as it was. Frank and Preacher could see a harmonica sticking out of his shirt pocket. Next to his deck of cards, he liked that harmonica better than anything else on this earth.

Frank touched the old man's forehead."Why, it ain't so bad, old timer. It's just reachin' the dew point. I wouldn't be surprised but what you outlive all the rest of us!"

"How about some drinking water?" Preacher asked.

McGuffey smiled feebly and shook his head no. "You boys can't fool me. I kin feel the Angel's breath a chilling my breastbone. My mother is calling, boys. It's all right."

"For God's sake," Frank said, "all you need's a little food. You just run out of strength, is what's wrong. You need some strong food in your body."

"No, boys. I don't crave no food. No, thank you just the same. *Parlez-vous*, boys. That's French for 'good-by.' "

"The hell it is," Frank said. But Preacher shut him up and motioned with his head, signifying that they should leave the hut.

Frank thought a moment, then nodded, and the two of them said good-by to McGuffey.

"He's a sure-as-hell goner," Frank whispered when they were outside. "I think it's the influenza."

"He might pull out of it," Preacher said, frowning up at the sky.

"The hell he will! His head's as hot and dry as a hayfield in August. He'll be dead in another day or two."

"Well, then we might just as well not think about it. He won't be no worse off."

"That's the goddamned truth!"

Preacher picked up one of the unopened cans of sardines and studied it. Then, he reached back and flung it far over the treetops. They heard it clatter when it landed somewhere on the tracks beyond. Then they heard a freight train chuffing in the distance.

Frank was holding the opened can in his hand and gazing back at McGuffey's shack.

"Preacher," he said, "he's going to die anyway."

"What are you thinking about?" Preacher asked.

"Why not? Jesus, we got to find out if this is good or not. My mind's beginning to wander, I'm so far gone."

Preacher gazed at him a moment, then looked over at McGuffey's shack.

Frank put his hand on his shoulder. "Would *you* mind eatin' it, if *you* was dying?"

Preacher frowned and slowly shook his head. "No, I reckon not, Frank."

BULLETIN:
JEFFERSONVILLE COURIER
MAY 12, 1934

POISONED SARDINES STOLEN

If Hoboes Culprits, May Be "Bum" Steal

Mrs. Edna Gregory, of Edna's Cafe on Main Street, reports that two cases of spoiled sardines were stolen from a utility shed at the rear of her restaurant early Thursday morning. If anybody reading this paper knows or hears of anyone who has seen these sardines, they should be warned.

Mrs. Gregory, however, theorized that somebody from the hobo jungle might have stolen the sardines."In which case," she commented laughingly, "there will be adequate punishment for the theft."

"Still, it just don't seem right."

Frank's hand shook as he held the can and looked at it. "Don't sardines always smell like that? It's been a long time since I ever ate any."

"Not the way I remember it," Preacher said. "I couldn't eat those things. They're poison, Frank."

Frank got up and went over to McGuffey's shack. Preacher lay back on the grass again and dozed, jerking the muscle in his cheek when a sleepy fly buzzed around his face.

In a few minutes, Frank returned. Preacher sat up and asked him, "Did you give it to him?"

"Jesus, no," Frank muttered, his voice cracking. There were tears in his eyes. "The son of a bitch says he's feeling better. Can you imagine that? He's even hungry. How can he feel better when only half an hour ago he was sure he was riding on the train of no return? I might have give him the sardines anyway, but I got to thinking. *You* know."

"You done right," Preacher said.

Frank started to cry softly in his sleeve. Then he took a deep breath and got control of himself. He cleared his throat. His eyes didn't look right. They seemed far away.

"I'm glad, Frank," Preacher said. "They're poisoned. I'm glad you didn't give him none of them sardines."

Frank stood up and tottered in the sunlight.

Preacher stood up, too, and they both faced the clay path that led back up to the rail flats.

"Well," Preacher said slowly, "they ain't nothing to do but just go into town and see if we can get us a handout. Maybe we can bring McGuffey something back."

Frank nodded. "But first, let's put these here boxes of sardines in our shack so's no one gets into them."

They carried them in and laid them on the ground. Then, Frank started walking up the path, and Preacher fell in behind, going "Aha, aha!" with phlegm rattling in his head. He stopped, took his hat off, and squinted up into the brightness of the sky. Ahead of him, Frank was teetering over the rails, and Preacher could hear him humming "There's a Long, Long Trail a Winding."

The two of them went into town and started knocking on doors, but there was nothing doing. Late in the afternoon, Frank stole some potatoes out of a backyard garden; and in a back alley, Preacher managed to catch and strangle a wasted pullet that skittered in the dust ahead of him.

The sun was slanting low when they walked across the railroad back to the jungle. A freight whistle wailed in the distance, and the heat rose in shimmering waves over the tracks.

"Summer's here for sure," Frank said. "It's come mighty early!"

"This weather's what's cured old McGuffey," Preacher said. Then he paused at the top of the path.

"They's something wrong," he said. "I smell something wrong."

"You and your goddamn nose," Frank said.

"I mean it, Frank." He was stock-still, looking at McGuffey's shack.

"This ain't no time to smell out trouble," Frank said. "We're eating."

When they had eaten, they took a cooked potato and the back of the chicken up to McGuffey.

"I'll be a son of a bitch!" Frank cried, as soon as he entered the door.

They straightened McGuffey's body out on the car seat. With his hat in his hand, Preacher put the deck of cards in one pocket

of the corpse and the harmonica in the other. "It's symbolic,"
Preacher said, with his voice low.

"Well, let's get up and report it. He's got to be buried."

"It's the least we can do," Preacher agreed.

"Yes. That's the truth."

Preacher frowned. "Even if the son of a bitch *did* steal some of
our cans!"

Frank stopped and glared at his partner. "You're awful fond of
that goddamn fish all of a sudden!"

"Look who's talking! You were the one who stole it, and who
wanted to try it out on that poor old fellow in there! Let's not be
tryin' to give *me* any guff!"

"Who you think you're talking to, Preacher?"

"I'm talking to *you*, you greasy son of a bitch!"

The two men hit each other simultaneously, and struggled in
dull, vague effort. Frank hit Preacher on the jaw, and his hat sailed
to the earth. Then Preacher hit Frank and the big man sat down
with a grunt, holding his jaw and looking distressed. He sat there
for a moment and finally spit some blood out of his mouth. Then
he got to his feet and the two of them went up the clay path to
the flats, starting on the long trip to the Court House to report a
death on Wall Street.

JEFFERSONVILLE COURIER
MAY 14, 1934

VERDUN HERO DIES FROM POISONED SARDINES

Exdoughboy Poet Succumbs in "Jungle"

*Walter McGuffey, a small, shy man who had been down on his
luck for many years, died in quiet anguish in his little shack in
"Wall Street," a section of the hobo jungle yesterday.*

*His death terminated a brilliant and tragic career for the
doughboy poet, who, if reports are true, spoke four languages
fluently and had mastered higher mathematics. His modest
ways, his quiet harmonica playing, his silent absorption in his
faded old deck of cards gave no indication to many of his con-
freres that here was a man who might have been a genius and
lived in affluence and comfort had fate been more kind to him.*

*In his paltry store of belongings, one item stood out in
lonely, if tawdry, splendor. It was a poem written in pencil on*

the back of the label of the very sardine can that was instrumental in striking him down. Here is that simple verse:

> *Just before the battle, Mother,*
> *Yes, those words are true!*
> *Just before the battle*
> *My thoughts fly home to you!*
>
> *For if this doughboy falls, Mother,*
> *Remember in your heart,*
> *He fell for you and home, Mother,*
> *Though we are far apart!*

Only one more word need be said about this lonely figure . . . something that was once said about another poet who lived in quiet obscurity:

> *Nine cities claimed the name of Homer dead,*
> *Through which the living Homer begged his bread.*

Frank and Preacher were walking along the railroad track just outside of town, headed north. Frank had heard that they were hiring on the docks in Toledo.

Neither man had spoken for almost half an hour, although Frank had done a little whistling to pass the time away. And then they heard a man call out to them. They looked and saw a little fat man, wearing a sailor-straw hat, pin-stripe pants, and a matching vest. His shirt sleeves were rolled up, and he was motioning to them.

They stepped down off the tracks and proceeded a little cautiously toward the man, who was standing beside a Model A Ford. Behind him was a frame building, painted white, and beside that a gigantic mound of coal.

"Just climb right over that there fence," the man said. "I've got a deal for you. Go ahead. Climb on over, I'm the owner, and I won't say anything."

"What's up?" Frank asked.

The little fat man closed his eye in a wink and stared at the two of them. "It isn't what's *up*," he said, "it's what's *out*. Namely and to wit, that mountain of coal you boys see over there." He waved his hand behind him carelessly, sure that the coal was where his hand pointed. Frank and Preacher would have looked before pointing to it. That was the difference between them.

"Do you boys want to make fifty cents apiece?"

"We wouldn't half mind," Frank said.

"Well, they dumped that coal on me without shoveling it into the bin, where it belongs. You shovel that coal in, and you get fifty cents apiece, United States of America coins. My name's Wallace. Mr. Bud Wallace."

Frank pinched his lips in his fingers. "That sure is a lot of coal for fifty cents."

"You boys in a bargaining position? You've had too much work lately? You don't think you can work it in, your schedule's so busy?"

"He didn't say that," Preacher said resentfully.

"I know he didn't, brother!" Bud Wallace said, pointing his finger at Preacher to let him know he'd heard. "But money is scarce as hen's teeth, these days, which is what I have inside that there building: about twelve hundred laying hens, and I have got to keep them warm."

"Shouldn't be much of a problem in this weather," Preacher said, pretending to wipe sweat off his forehead.

Frank said, "Why don't you just shut up and listen to Mr. Wallace?"

The little fat man nodded and said, "All right, I know when I'm beat. Seventy-five cents apiece, if you shovel every bit of that coal in there, and get it in by noon. I've got to go drum up some business, and I can't afford to stand here and argue with labor."

"It's a deal," Frank said, and Preacher nodded.

When Bud Wallace drove off in the Model A Ford, Frank started in shoveling like he had an itch. He bent over and just went crazy, and the coal started to fly.

"What in the world is the matter with you?" Preacher asked after a few minutes, when he'd stopped to catch his breath.

"You heard what he said about getting it all shoveled in by noon, didn't you?" Frank said.

Preacher nodded. "I did, but the way you're going, you'll finish by yesterday morning. I never seen such a frenzy to work. Are you sick or something?"

"I just feel like working, that's all," Frank said.

Preacher stood there a minute with the shovel in his two hands, watching Frank after he'd said this.

T HAT WAS THE beginning of a great change in Frank. That morning, Frank worked like a madman, and what's more, he acted like he enjoyed it.

When Mr. Bud Wallace returned, he was impressed. Frank asked if there wasn't more work he could do, and Mr. Wallace was impressed even more. Preacher just drifted off and watched things, and before long the two of them forgot all about him. Frank pointed at the roof of the hatchery and said there was a shingle loose, which he could fix faster than Mr. Wallace could say "Jack Robinson." He pointed out that the downspouts were rusted and needed painting, and he knew just the primer that would stop that rust in its tracks. He mentioned that weeds had grown up in the gravel of the driveway and asked if Mr. Wallace wouldn't like to have the driveway weeded, unless he'd rather have it freshly graveled, which Frank could spread for him with the same shovel he'd just used to get the coal in the bin.

Preacher was considerably disgusted, and when Mr. Wallace left them again, saying he'd be happy to hire Frank for some odd jobs, he told Frank about it.

Frank nodded and said he understood. He said he was aware that he wasn't acting right, but he couldn't help it. He said he was all fired up with ambition and for some reason wanted to get work. He couldn't help himself.

Preacher didn't say a word, but just glared at his old friend and listened. You could tell by the expression on his face that he had probably never in his whole life heard so much nonsense poured out of a human mouth in such a short time.

When Frank stopped, Preacher shook hands with him and said that this was it. There wasn't any point in their being buddies any longer, because a rift had opened up between them that nothing could bridge.

Frank agreed that this was so, and said he was sorry, only even when he said it, there was a gleam of excitement in his eyes, because he had finally, at the age of thirty-one years, discovered the Gospel of Hard Work.

Preacher just shook his head and took off, and that night he slept under the trestle over the Olentangy River, where a B. & O. freight was supposed to pass by at 4:20 the next morning, headed toward Marion, Upper Sandusky, and Toledo.

JEFFERSON COURIER
JUNE 11, 1938

MAN, 35, GETS HIGH SCHOOL DIPLOMA

A 35-year-old Jeffersonville man was among those half his age to receive a high school diploma at the Jeffersonville High

School Commencement exercises yesterday. Frank Goshen, who was forced to drop out of school in the eighth grade back in his hometown of Reynolds, Indiana, finally passed the milestone that is denied to so many.

Long out of work, Frank settled in Jeffersonville only four years ago, having become an employee of Harley "Bud" Wallace, local owner of the Wallace Hatchery. "Frank is an inspiration to other men who think the world is down on them," Mr. Wallace said, "because instead of complaining, he just gets down to work and makes things happen. If there were more Frank Goshens in this world, there would be less unemployment."

Frank just shrugs and grins when he hears such praise. He says he's always wanted a high school diploma, and the opportunity in Jeffersonville was just too good to pass by. Some day, he theorizes, he wants to open his own hatchery. He claims he's learned a great deal from his work at the Wallace establishment.

As far as his fellow students are concerned, Frank is just "one of the guys," even though he is old enough to be their father.

"I mind my business, and they mind theirs," the big, friendly, sandy-haired hatchery worker says with a grin.

ONE NIGHT SHORTLY AFTER this story about him appeared in the *Jeffersonville Courier*, Frank was working late at the hatchery.

Bud Wallace had phoned from Columbus, saying he'd been held up on business and asking Frank to call his wife and explain things. Frank could tell by the way he talked that he was drunk, but he didn't mind. He phoned Mrs. Wallace and said that Bud was going to have to stay over, and Mrs. Wallace said, "Huh!" and that was that. Mission accomplished.

Frank went outside and cleaned the tanks in back, running water from the hose all over the galvanized iron, making it roar like a freight train under a full head. It was a warm July evening, with the air soft as butter on the skin. When Frank turned the hose away from the tanks, the evening was quiet. It was like the whole city of Jeffersonville had been evacuated.

Then all of a sudden Frank looked up and almost jumped out of his shoes. A gray-haired old man—gaunt as death and twice as skinny—was standing there motionless in the gravel, looking at him.

Frank went over to the outside faucet and turned the water off. He dropped the hose beside him and took a good look at the old man. Finally he nodded and said, "Well kiss me, if it ain't Preacher!"

"One and the same," Preacher said. He hacked a little and then spat.

Frank shook his head. "You look like you been drug through twenty counties and mashed underfoot."

Preacher nodded. "And that's just about the way I feel. Can you help a friend from the old days?"

Frank nodded and said, "I reckon I could give you a couple eggs."

"Eggs would be lovely," Preacher said. "If you could maybe fry them and douse a little salt and pepper on them, and maybe soak some bread in the fat. I don't suppose you got any coffee, too."

"I guess I could dig you up some," Frank said. "Come on and follow me."

He went inside. Preacher followed him, paused, and said, "Well, if this ain't a city of chickens, I never seen one."

"Over twelve hundred in this building, and twice that many in the other two. Bud Wallace is a rich man by now."

"That little fat fellow who had you spitting coal?" Preacher asked.

Frank nodded. "A fair-minded man, except for drinking too much and being unfaithful to his wife."

Preacher shook his head and ruminated, while Frank put some lard in a skillet and put the skillet on a hot plate. He plugged an electric percolator in, after he'd filled it with real coffee and water. Preacher just watched, without saying a word.

Finally, Frank had a plate before him, on a little worktable covered with brown oilcloth. Before he dug in, Preacher took a good long look at Frank, who didn't look back at him.

Then Preacher ate, while Frank went in the back room and did something. Preacher could hear him whistling in there, and banging boxes around.

When he finished, he got up and went back to see what Frank was doing, but Frank wasn't taken by surprise. He had been waiting for him, and he was standing by.

The two of them were a little shy. They hardly knew what to say to each other. Preacher looked like he was seventy years old and ready to die. The skin on his face had gotten loose and was drooping all over.

"Well," Frank finally said, "things sure change."

"That is the truth," Preacher said, nodding. "You sure have gotten fat. You look like a banker."

"Where you been since I last seen you?" Frank asked.

"Oh, here and there. It gets so they all look alike."

Frank nodded. "Yes, sir! That's the exact truth. And do you know something? That's one reason I changed my ways. After while, every place got to look like Jeffersonville."

Preacher thought about that like it was a new idea, instead of something he'd just said. Frank gave him a cigarette, and then took one himself. He struck a match and lit both of them, then the two of them went back outside, where it had gotten dark and had cooled off a little.

"Frank," Preacher finally said, "what was it that come over you?"

"You mean that day right here?" Frank said.

"Yes, that's what I mean."

"I'll never be able to tell you," Frank said, sounding miserable. "It's something I'll never understand as long as I live."

Preacher nodded and the two of them stood there smoking, looking up at the evening sky.

Finally, Preacher said, "You know what I keep thinking about?"

"What?" Frank said.

"I keep thinking about McGuffey, that poor old son of a bitch. I keep thinking about how it was because of us and them dirty sardines that McGuffey died."

"It wasn't our fault, Preacher, and you know it."

"I know it," Preacher said slowly, "but the fact is, we couldn't have knocked him off any neater if we'd planned the whole business. No sir."

Frank flicked the ash off his cigarette and said, "What I figure is, a man has more important things to think about than something like that."

"Some do," Preacher said austerely, narrowing his eyes at the other man, "and some don't."

"I don't know what you're getting at, Preacher."

"Oh, it's not what you're thinking, Frank. I'm not about to preach you a sermon about how you should feel guilty, and all that. No sir. What I've got on my mind is considerably more difficult than that."

"And what might that be?" Frank asked.

"Well, it has to do with how you and me never really got

around to talking about McGuffey. We'd known him for, what, three or four years, and had passed the time of day many a time, but we'd never really stopped to think about him."

"It's that way with all them that are deceased," Frank said.

"I know what you mean, and I agree with you. But that's not the point. Here you have a man that just goes his own way, and then something happens—like he eats some poisoned sardines—and *bang!* Right away, he's dead, and everybody is wondering about him."

"I didn't," Frank said.

"Well, you should have. As for me, I haven't hardly been able to get him out of my mind. Did you know something? That poor son of a bitch was a poet."

"Big deal!"

"Well, it *is*, if you stop to think about it. Who would have thought he had the depths, Frank? I ask you. All the accidents that come together at that time and place, and *zap*, McGuffey is no more. He might as well be a tree or a building or an angel. And there you and I stand, with our mouths hanging open, and not a word to say. What was it he said?"

"Who? McGuffey?"

Preacher closed his eyes and gestured with his cigarette. "*Parlez-vous* means 'good-by'. Now you and I know that's not what it means at all. We know it means 'Do you speak?' Nevertheless, that's what McGuffey said. And that's what people say in France when they want to know do you speak French or English or something. Which is to say, that's what they say when they are just getting to know you. But do you know something?"

"What?"

"Even when you are getting to know somebody, you are already saying good-by. That's what McGuffey meant."

Frank thought a moment and said, "I don't figure he meant anything like that at all. I figure he was just confused."

Preacher raised his hands. "Don't you see, Frank? *Confusion* means something, just like everything else. *Everything* means something."

Frank narrowed his eyes in a frown. "That's deep, Preacher."

"It's true, I know that. And truth's deep enough for a man."

Frank dropped his cigarette and stepped on it. "Preacher," he said, "I hope you don't mind my saying so, but I am awful tired this evening. I've had a hard day, and what you're saying doesn't help. In fact, it's giving me a headache."

"How could that be?" Preacher asked.

"I don't know, but merely state the fact."

For a while, neither man said anything. A passenger train came into sight and roared past without even slowing down for the Jeffersonville Depot. The Pullman lights were on, showing people inside, eating their dinners and reading and gazing out into the darkness, where they would not have been able to see Frank and Preacher, although they could easily have seen the lighted windows of the hatchery on the west side.

Frank thought about what Preacher had said; then he thought about how much Preacher stank. They must have both smelled like that back in the old days, but didn't notice because it was chronic. Still, he remembered how Preacher's nose had been so sensitive, and now he wondered how he could stand himself, he smelled so bad.

Finally, he sighed and said, "Preacher, I'm a married man these days, did you know that? Her name's Louise."

"Louise," Preacher repeated. "Well, ain't that something! I guess married life must be awful nice, having you a woman and everything."

"It's nice all right," Frank said, nodding.

The distant train whistle wailed in the distance, as if calling out to them.

"Well," Preacher finally said, after the train whistle had stopped wailing and it was quiet once again, "I just thought I'd mention it. Something like that you keep thinking about a lot, you just naturally think other people are thinking about it too."

"You didn't come by here just to tell me that, did you?" Frank asked.

"Tell you what?"

"That stuff about McGuffey."

"Oh, hell no," Preacher said. "I just come by to see you, since I figured you might still be here. I was throwed off the train by a yard dick up near Lima, and come near to getting my leg broke."

For a moment Frank was silent, and then he said, "Speaking of newspapers, they wrote me up about a month ago. You'll never guess."

"You got a high school diploma," Preacher said promptly.

"Well, I'll be damned, how did you know?"

"They was some fresh newspapers stuffing the cracks in our old shack down the road," Preacher said, "Just like the old days. So I pulled them out and read them, and there was the story about you, big as life."

Frank nodded. "That's right. You always were a great reader."

"You should be proud of that, Frank."

Frank nodded. "I guess I am, sort of."

"They didn't mention you was married."

Frank nodded again. "I know. Louise was upset, and I was too. I don't know why they didn't put that in the paper."

The two men got quiet once again. A car honked over on the main street of town. It sounded far away.

Finally, Preacher held out his hand and said, "Well, I'll be moving on. So I'll say so long, Frank."

"So long, Preacher. Good luck to you." They shook hands.

Preacher thought a moment, then said, "You too, Frank. *Parlez-vous.*"

"Sure," Frank said. "Whatever you say, Preacher."

✒ *Storyhood As We Know It*

THE TERRIBLE OLD woman was obviously drunk in her blood-red satin dress, weaving back and forth like a polar bear sitting in its cage, chewing on her teeth and lisping abominations in a dense spray of gin-soaked breath upon various and sundry with liberal impartiality. Once, while making some point or other, she thrust her arm out violently, jiggling the powdery flab beneath her triceps. Her name was Theodora Bascomb, and she was known to still secretly cherish her old nickname, "Teddie"—hearing in it, perhaps, an echo of some lovely virginal slenderness she had once possessed, or thought she had possessed.

Her presence here today at the cocktail party reception on the lawn of the Coffee Hills Country Club was not to be ignored. Although Teddie Bascomb—like all the Bascombs for years before her—had contributed heavily to the club, she was nevertheless uncomfortable with its hosting regular meetings of the local chapter of the United States Libertarian Party, known by the jaunty acronym USLIP. And her voice was never entirely ignored, for three excellent reasons: first, her majestic, even tyrannical manner; second, her family's traditional influence in Coffee Hills; and, third, her personal contributions to the club over the past three decades.

Teddie Bascomb's husband, Roger (now dead for over two of those decades), had been the grandson of a charter member of the Coffee Hills Country Club, so to all of her other qualifications was added the venerable and minted prestige of old money. The Bascombs were among the oldest of the old, and the richest of the rich. The fact that in recent years Teddie sometimes got obstreperously drunk at Coffee Hills social functions was simply part of the price one had to pay for accommodating old money—which, as all Coffee Hills knew, was not simply the best kind of money, but when you thought about it, the only kind.

But even her enemies admitted that while she could be impetuously difficult, Teddie Bascomb was never downright vulgar. A few believed that at her best she could be eloquent and even impressive; and at her worst, no worse than what they insisted was merely "colorful." In the long view, in short, and by Coffee Hills standards, Teddie Bascomb was far preferable to any number of more rational, more predictable, more manageable, less wealthy vulgarians.

But nothing lasts forever, and reputations are nothing. Which is to say, the judgment expressed above was the one that prevailed before Lionel Klingaman came to Coffee Hills to lecture. He was currently the most renowned and articulate member of USLIP; he had recently been featured on national television shows and had even had his caricature on the cover of a weekly news magazine. This caricature had a certain cruel inevitability about it, for Lionel Klingaman was virtually a caricature himself—a thin, stooped clerical-looking man with a face that seemed mostly left behind by a protruding mouth and thick black mustache (some claimed that even it was dyed), giving his muzzle something of the character of an aggressively animated vacuum cleaner. Added to this were the horn-rimmed spectacles of an old-fashioned leftist theoretician, so when people first saw him, they were for a moment vindicated in their darkest, most simple-minded belief in stereotypes.

It was no wonder that Lionel Klingaman was famous and successful, for he fit the preconceptions of the world with rare felicity. But he was successful for another reason: in spite of his homeliness, he could be articulate and suave, and he had a sophistication that could easily lure the wealthiest patrons (especially affluent older women) to his leftist causes. It was almost, but not quite, as if he were mocking the very ideas he espoused—which seemed to relieve the pathologically affluent from those sinister associations which radical social programs tend to have for the rich and powerful of this world.

The incongruity between his physical appearance and his manner and voice could be almost shocking; and there were a number of wealthy matrons who, after hearing him speak, simply could not remember their first impressions upon seeing this drab little man. What he said, and the way he said it, erased forever the mere physicality of his appearance.

The evening for his reception at the club started out as mild and serene. The sunlight bathed the long fairways in its golden light, and the shadows of the trees were of a velvet darkness.

Lionel Klingaman was to speak later that evening, and the large attendance at the cocktail party reception was gratifying. Perhaps only a very small percentage of those present believed in Klingaman's USLIP principles; the rest were mostly curious. They would have shown up for anyone who had gotten as much recent publicity. Not only was it the thing to do; but who among its membership would not prefer an evening at the Coffee Hills Country Club to almost anywhere else on earth?

Lionel Klingaman emerged from the clubhouse some forty-five minutes after the first drink had been served, and there was a polite fluttering of applause from the two hundred guests already gathered on the terrace. The applause would have been more generous if so many of those present hadn't been encumbered with cocktails.

But one of those who held a cocktail would not have applauded under any circumstance. She stood in her blood-red satin dress and glared at him with her head back, so that—even though he was standing sixty yards away at the entrance of the clubhouse, which was higher than her head—she could still manage to look down upon him, in a sense . . . which is to say, glare at him contemptuously out of the bottoms of her half-closed eyes.

Yolanda Sprigg, who was somewhat active in the local USLIP chapter, as well as a lifetime member at Coffee Hills, had agreed to look after Teddie Bascomb. Yolanda was half a head taller than Teddie, and perhaps half as wide. She was wearing a shiny green dress, which showed off her handsome complexion as well; and her silver feathered hair sparkled in the late-afternoon sunlight. She was a splendidly attractive woman.

"I suppose," Teddie Bascomb muttered out of the side of her mouth, "you have already met that man."

"Mr. Klingaman?" Yolanda asked.

"You know who," Teddie growled, then tossed her drink back so hard that several shards of ice flew from her glass. Not only that, the movement jarred her sideways and she had to take a half-step to retain her balance.

Yolanda swallowed and nodded before answering in her best duchess accent. "Yes, as a matter of fact, we had lunch with him."

"We did, did we?"

Yolanda smiled. "Yes. Phyllis and Carl Bridgewater. . . ."

"Oh, the Bridgewaters!" Teddie growled.

Undeterred, Yolanda continued: "The Ackermans, and myself."

"Some lunch!"

Yolanda flicked a glance at the old woman to see if it was possible she felt neglected by not being invited. But that could hardly be, since Teddie Bascomb had no use for USLIP in the first place and, furthermore, often pointed out that social luncheons were a barbaric institution, and she preferred to eat her noonday meals in solitude, so that she could plan the evening's strategy, whatever it may be.

"Well," Yolanda said, "it was a pleasant lunch. And he seems very nice."

"Horse manure!" Teddie Bascomb growled. She tossed her glass back again; and even though it was empty, it served well as a gesture of defiance.

Yolanda Sprigg blinked rapidly and looked down at her own glass, which was half-filled with a delicate Château Coutet.

Teddie threw her arm forward in an imperious gesture. "I want to talk to him, Yolanda."

"Certainly, Teddie. I'm sure he'll be delighted."

"Delight has nothing to do with it. Now."

Yolanda looked up at the entrance. "Well, Teddie, he seems to be occupied at the moment, as you can see. Perhaps we could have the seating arrangements changed, so that you could be with him at dinner."

"I don't want to *eat* with him, I want to *talk* to him."

Nervously, Yolanda twirled her glass. "I see."

"No you don't see, and don't pretend you do. I hate the way people pretend, you know. That's one of my pet hates. Surely you knew that!"

Yolanda swallowed. "Well, yes. I suppose I did."

"I'm absolutely sure of it. And in case anybody's interested, I'm standing here practically all alone, fatigued and ginless."

"Ginless?"

"Forsaken of gin. Do you need everything spelled out for you? D-j-i-n-n. *Gin*."

"That's funny, Teddie," Yolanda admitted out of her desperation. Then she looked up and gestured to a waiter, who nodded and hurried to the nearest drink cart.

Teddie nodded and said, "I sometimes wonder why I don't resign from the club. If you ask me, Coffee Hills has deteriorated something pathetic. To think of us hosting that vulgar and brainless organization. USLIP! What a disgusting acronym! Bunch of goddamn liberal fruitcakes, is what my dead husband used to call them. He couldn't stand liberals. I'll never know how they managed to sneak them in the back doors of the club. Although, I will say we've given the club a God-awful amount of money, and sometimes I wonder why, because one way or another, it can seep into things like that. Or them. Just look at him! Cock of the walk, isn't he? My husband wouldn't have let him shine his shoes."

"I do believe," Yolanda said, "that's Diana Winthrop over there! I wonder how she's feeling?"

Teddie glared over her glass. "I tell you, we should never have let you local fuzzy-headed radicals pull the wool over our eyes. USLIP, indeed! I'm seriously thinking of dropping my Coffee Hills membership. Especially when I see somebody like that Lionel What's-His-Name who's going to talk for about three weeks this evening."

"Why I think she looks just wonderful," Yolanda said. "You remember that Diana's had a hysterectomy, don't you, Teddie?"

"I hardly know the woman. Anyway, my husband would have had him thrown out, and to hell with his politics. But that's neither here nor there. Do you know how my husband used to refer to USLIP? He'd say, 'You slip, I slip, he, she or it slips.' Sometimes I am tempted to think he was right."

Yolanda laughed and continued: "That's good. 'We slip, you slip, they slip.'"

"It's not funny," Teddie said.

The waiter appeared, holding a heavy crystal martini goblet, floating two fat olives in the ice, with a fresh napkin on his tray. Yolanda took them and handed them to Teddie Bascomb, who said, "It's about time."

Yolanda said, "Well, it's certainly a beautiful afternoon for it."

"No afternoon could be beautiful for *it*," Teddie corrected her balefully. "Just plain *beautiful*, maybe. But not *for it*. For it, you should have thunder and lightning and men on mounted steeds riding up and crying out disaster. And a fanfare of trumpets while we're at it."

Yolanda risked a laugh. "What on earth are you talking about, Teddie?"

"I want you to know," Teddie said, clutching her forearm with a heavy, cold wet hand, "that my husband never once chastised me. Oh dear me, no! Absolutely not. Or as he used to say, 'Absonotly*lute*.' Not that he wasn't capable of, you know, *yelling* at me

if he felt like it. But essentially that man was very good-natured.
Hardly anybody remembers him around here any more. All dead.
Do you know what? Sometimes I almost take it personally, think
of death as a cowardly retreat. But never mind that: He was a great
joker before he died. After he died, he wasn't much of a joker.
Are you listening to me, young woman?"

"Teddie, you shouldn't address me like that. I'm Yolanda, your
good, good, good friend."

"That's one too many 'goods'; you can't trust people who
overdo the good business, you know."

Yolanda drank her wine and smiled brightly, though somewhat
blearily, at the old woman. "I suppose you're right, so I herewith
retract one 'good.'"

"You sound like a lawyer, do you know that? Where is he?"

"Mr. Klingaman?"

"You know damned well who I'm talking about. I want to talk
to that damned anarchist. How many times do I have to tell you?
I've got something in my purse for him."

"In your purse? Really? Whatever could it be?"

"You'll see when the time comes, my girl. If you stick around,
that is, and don't go off to powder your nose. And if you can ever
get him to come down here and listen to what I have to say."

Desperately, Yolanda looked around for assistance. But everyone seemed absorbed in conversation. Or perhaps they just had
the sly good judgment to appear to be absorbed. Because who,
with any sense, would want to be caught up in the old woman's
madness, and sent on wild forays, or have to stand in one place
and listen to her drunken raving?

Eventually the fact that Lionel Klingaman was busily and justly
occupied with a large number of people seemed to penetrate even
the dark and murky understanding of Teddie Bascomb. Furthermore, she seemed to accept the fact, at least temporarily. Yolanda
managed to lure Ginny Sands, dressed in a tan dress, with a chocolate silk scarf at her neck, over to help divert the old woman; and
for a while, the two of them stood gossiping, while Teddie stood
solidly spread-legged, like a catcher about to whip the ball back
out to the pitcher, and glared past her martini. It was hard to tell
how much she was taking in . . . although Yolanda and Ginny
both saw to it that there was little of substance in what they said,
just in case she was eavesdropping. Because you could never tell;
and nobody ever said that the old woman couldn't be sharp, now
and then, as well as plain damned difficult.

So they traded inanities, with something of the relaxed self-consciousness of performing stage business in a modern melodrama pretending to be a smart and sophisticated social comedy. Finally, however, Teddie interrupted them—as if from a far distance—saying, "I'd climb up there myself, but my leg's bothering me something awful today. Don't ever laugh about arthritis."

Saying this, she suddenly flopped down in a broad black-painted strip-metal chair that seemed to have materialized behind her. With her briefly out of hearing, Ginny Sands whispered, "Trouble with her leg, spelled g-i-n."

Yolanda flicked a brief hysterical smile at her, thinking that wasn't the way Teddie Bascomb spelled it; but she was really too nervous to get any pleasure out of what Ginny had said. In fact, she thought it had been rather reckless of Ginny. Everybody knew that the old woman's hearing could prove wickedly acute, now and then; and you could never tell when this would happen. Yolanda was certain her deafness was selective, so that there were occasions when Teddie could hear things at a far distance, even after she'd just bellowed at someone right in front of her to speak louder.

"Do you suppose he's afraid of me?" Teddie asked distantly from her chair.

"Why on earth would she think that?" Ginny murmured to Yolanda. But Yolanda ignored her and assured Teddie in a loud spirited voice that there would be plenty of time for her to talk with Lionel Klingaman.

"I don't want to talk *with* him; I want to talk *to* him! There's a difference, you know."

"I certainly know," Ginny muttered to her glass, just loud enough for Yolanda to hear.

"Since nobody will bring him down here," Teddie announced, "I think I'll go up there myself. I've got something in my purse for him."

"Do you suppose it could be a gun?" Ginny whispered.

"That is," Teddie went on, "I'll go up there if you two girls will be so kind as to give me a hand. What is it they say about the mountain and Mahomet? Not that I have much use for those Arabs. Or Israelis either, for that matter. Listen, all those fellas deserve one another, it seems to me."

"Good *God!*" Ginny whispered, frowning and grinning down into her glass.

"Of course we'll help you," Yolanda said, reaching down and

plucking tentatively at one fat arm. "And you shouldn't say things like that, Teddie, because everybody knows you don't mean them."

"I mean everything I say, and lots of things I don't say. Still waters run deep, my girl."

The first part was getting her out of her chair. Yolanda was sure that Teddie was making herself heavier; but finally, after considerable effort, she and Ginny managed to get the old woman onto her feet. Her martini glass was once again empty, of course. Yolanda took it from her hand and placed it on a metal bench.

"I won't have another one right now, thank you," Teddie said, speaking clearly, loudly, politely, in the tone of one who is denying herself unnaturally for a cause that transcends momentary personal comfort.

Then the three of them started to work their way up the terrace in the direction of Lionel Klingaman, who was holding a token half-filled glass of white wine in his hand. Having watched him at lunch, Yolanda had decided that he was actually somewhat abstemious; but then that was only prudent of him, since he would be speaking this evening in the club's large auditorium. It was ludicrous to think of a member of USLIP's Central Committee being drunk, especially Lionel Klingaman.

"My leg is a source of constant distress," Teddie told them when they had proceeded some forty feet. She spoke of it as if it were a fat and disobedient child of mature years. "My husband used to joke that when you got to be old, aching limbs were the root of the problem. He certainly was a card, but people don't listen, you know."

"You must suffer terribly from it," Yolanda said, and Ginny leaned back from Teddie's other side and made a face at her.

The old woman suddenly stopped, arms akimbo. "Do I have my purse? Where's my purse? Have I lost it? Do I have it?"

"Yes, it's in your hand," Yolanda said.

"I was just checking. When I stand for a long time, my arms get numb."

Ahead of them, the object of their approach evidently said something witty, because everyone around him burst out laughing. He joined in the laughter; but before his mouth had closed, his glance drifted and fell on Teddie Bascomb, caught in her slow, painful, relentless approach; and at that instant, Yolanda fancied that his expression changed slightly. Of course, she reminded herself, she could have imagined it.

But what if the old dragon did have a gun in her purse? She was known to be subject to violent tantrums, upon occasion; and after a few drinks (which was practically any time that she hadn't had a great many) she had a way of isolating the most innocuous remark from the circumaudient noise, so that it might loom and glower like a vast thundercloud in her dark reflections.

But now, for an instant, time was suspended. Lionel Klingaman stood absolutely still and watched the three women as they approached him; and all of those surrounding him turned and watched as well. It was as if the three women had been long awaited. Perhaps Teddie Bascomb had already fixed Klingaman in her basilisk stare, so that he was paralyzed by it and could neither move nor speak.

In the midst of their approach, shaking herself out of this momentary fantasy, Yolanda called out to him. "Mr. Klingaman? Here is someone I would very much like for you to meet."

"Ah, yes!" one of the club men next to him said, nodding at Teddie Bascomb.

"I would like to introduce you to Theodora Bascomb," Yolanda blurted in the awful silence of the moment. Beside her, Teddie seemed to swell and grow taller at the sound of her name. Bravely, Yolanda continued, "When people think of Coffee Hills, Mr. Klingaman—not just the club, but the place—they have always, naturally, thought of the Bascombs. Teddie represents Coffee Hills at its . . . at its grandest. Teddie, I'm sure you know that this is our famous guest, Lionel Klingaman."

Teddie extended her hand and when Lionel took it, she swiftly fastened upon it, leaning her weight on it, so that he almost lost his balance. "Now whatever you do," she croaked, "don't try to get away until I get some answers."

Lionel Klingaman laughed nervously. "What on earth do you mean, dear lady? Why should I try to get away?"

"Because," Teddie said, "I have something for you in my purse."

Everyone looked at the old woman's purse as it was released by its strap and swung heavily from her arm. She fumbled, caught it, opened it and commenced digging in it with her free hand. Finally she pulled out a photocopied sheet. "This," she said, "is your article that was published several years ago, if I'm not mistaken, in an issue of *The Future Call*. Somebody sent it to me, Mr. Klingaman. Did you write it? It's got your name on it."

His smile lost a fraction of its geniality. "Well, if my name's on it, I suppose I must have written it."

Someone laughed half-heartedly, immediately choking off the sound.

Swaying in ponderous counterpoint to her purse, Teddie groped, finally caught her purse and started fishing in it once more. Finally, she found her reading glasses and put them on. "What it says is . . . and I will read it to you word-for-word, Mr. Klingaman . . . it says, let me see. . . . Oh, yes. Blah, blah, blah. But *then* it says: 'The time is soon coming in the history of the race when we will be forced to acknowledge that *as an institution* the family has virtually reached its term and is obsolete as a viable social structure.' *Did* you write that, or *didn't* you?"

Lionel Klingaman nodded. "Yes, I plead guilty. I wrote that several years ago."

Teddie lurched slowly, then righted herself. "I think that . . . is . . . the . . . most . . . disgusting thing I have ever read in my whole life!"

"Well. . . ."

"Well, *what?*"

"Well, did you read the rest of it? It is a perfectly reasoned theoretical statement. I admit that there would have to be transitional adaptations, as with any social change. Also, you have to take into account that I make that statement after a paragraph that begins something like: 'In view of . . .' and then I name a score of social problems that everyone agrees have absolutely no solution in today's world . . . I mean, you have to read the whole thing to get my meaning."

"I got your meaning from what I just read aloud to you, and do you know what I think? I. Think. It. Is. Absolutely. *Disgusting!*"

Lionel Klingaman frowned and nodded. "I don't suppose anybody could expect to get a popular vote by attacking the institution of the family, with all its sentimental associations. But the fact is Mrs. Burton. . . ."

"That's Bascomb!"

"Mrs. Bascomb, our institutions have to bend and change, or there's just no hope, is there?"

"Of course there is, you anarchist!"

Klingaman laughed, shrugged his shoulders, and looked over her head.

"Teddie," Yolanda said, "let's go get another drink."

"You've had enough!" Teddie snapped without moving her gaze from Lionel Klingaman.

He looked down at her, took a deep breath, and said, "I guess what you have to understand is that people have to adapt to new ideas."

"I suppose it is always hard to adjust to new ideas," Ginny agreed, trying to sound reasonable.

"Ginny, you keep out of this," Teddie muttered. "I want everybody here to know that I *hate* people who use the word 'viable'. I can't *stand* them. If they use the word 'viable' you know all you need to know about them; and there's no hope. They might just as well use the word *bourgeois*. Which I happen to notice you also used in that so-called article of yours."

"Teddie, I think these are things we can talk about after this evening's program," Yolanda said. "You know, after the speech. The question-and-answer period, perhaps."

Turning on her wrathfully, Teddie said, "Don't you play the part of a peacemaker with *me*, young woman!"

"Well, I'm truly sorry you feel the way you do, Mrs. Bascomb," Lionel Klingaman said judiciously, "but if you have strong convictions, it's inevitable that you're going to run up against disagreement, sooner or later. That goes for all of us."

"You're disagreeable, all right. You with your disgusting formula against decency."

"If I didn't know better," Lionel said lightly, smiling at those around him, "I'd think you had a Republican in your midst."

"Don't you pass *me* off with a jest, young man!"

"Sorry, I didn't mean it that way at all. No doubt some of your best friends are Republicans."

"There wasn't any other way to mean it, and they are. Just for your information, some of my best friends, not to mention most of Coffee Hills' oldest families, *are indeed* Republicans."

Looking around him, Lionel Klingaman said, "I don't doubt it for a moment."

Yolanda inhaled and smiled brightly. "Teddie, let's go get a drink, why don't we?"

"You've had enough, I told you."

"Why, I've had only a single glass of wine, and you know it!"

"Don't change the subject. The subject is the family, which is under attack, in case you haven't noticed. I wish my own daughter were here to stand up for her mother! Why, she'd tell all of you a thing or two. Not to mention my dead husband! And don't you turn away from me until you've heard me out."

Lionel Klingaman had started to edge away, but he turned back. "What the hell, I can't argue with this woman," he muttered to the man beside him.

"That's the first sensible thing you've said," the old woman cried. "You *can't* argue with me, because you're *wrong! That's* why!"

"Sure, sure."

"There are some people I want you to meet," one of the men beside Klingaman said to him, taking his arm. "Sorry, Mrs. Bascomb."

"Who's he?" Teddie asked.

"That's Don Thatcher," Yolanda said. "You know, the program chairman."

"His daddy was an utter scoundrel."

"Never mind that, Mrs. Bascomb," Ginny said.

"For two cents I'd cancel this year's pledge to the club. Not even Coffee Hills can get away with sponsoring an organization like this."

"We're not sponsoring USLIP," Don Thatcher said. "We're hosting Mr. Klingaman this evening. We brought him here because he's proved to be an important force, politically. And as you know, we've scheduled three other speakers, so there's no viewpoint lacking."

"What's lacking is brains, if you ask me. I should have known it wasn't any good from the beginning, with a name like that. USLIP. Do you know what my dead husband used to say about you people? He used to say, 'You slip, I slip, we all slip.' That was before he was dead. After he was dead, he didn't say much. Ha, ha."

"Good God," somebody whispered.

"I understand you're something of an institution at Coffee Hills," Lionel Klingaman said, "and I'd really hate to see you drop out of the country club just because of me."

"My, aren't we *selfless!* Not to mention hypocritical. I don't think it'd bother you at all, if I dropped out. I'm not even sure how much it would bother the board. Or the members. Or me, come to think of it. Or anybody else in sight, including the ducks and the geese."

Yolanda asked her to please not say such things, but it was obvious Teddie wasn't listening.

"Come on," Don Thatcher said, clutching Lionel Klingaman's arm. "There really are some people you ought to meet."

"Forget about them!" Teddie cried. "What I want to know is, how a group like USLIP ever got into Coffee Hills in the first place. I thought people around here had too much good sense! Where's morals, after all? Where's decency? I ask you, where can a person go for civilized behavior if not to Coffee Hills? Listen, you don't know what a wonderful place this was when I was a girl; but I'll tell you what it was, it was *magic*. I can remember the jazz age, but what we had mostly was waltzes and foxtrots and beautiful lanterns hanging from the trees after dark. I used to play tag under those trees when I was a little girl." She threw her arm recklessly behind her, not bothering to see what she was pointing at, but pointing in the right direction, after all.

"And the people here were wonderful. Why, I can remember Jim and Mabel Reeber and Carl and Christine Kohn; Will Goodman and Geneva Mitchell and Charlie What's-his-last-name, which I can never remember. Yes I can; it was Doans. People like that. I'd just like to have somebody answer one question: where are the likes of those wonderful handsome men and wonderful beautiful women in the world today?"

"Teddie," Yolanda said, "come on. You're going to be sorry you've said some of these things later on."

"I'm not saying them later on. I'm saying them right now. That's another joke, but I don't suppose anybody'll catch on. Nobody laughs at jokes any more, they just *giggle*. I never could stand a giggler. No, I think I'll retain my membership, because who around here these days has as much right as *I* do? It's the rest of you who are impostors, do you know that? Scanos and vulgarians! Yes, I think I'll stay in, so it's all in the family, as a matter of speaking. That's what my dead husband used to say. You know, *matter* of speaking. You think I'm drunk, don't you?"

"One can only hope," Lionel Klingaman muttered.

Two people laughed briefly, but nobody else joined in.

"Well, that's not so bad, for the likes of you," Teddie said, pointing at him. "But I'll tell you something, I've never seen such a bunch of humorless nincompoops as you people. God help us! 'You slip, I slip, we all slip.'"

"I know," Klingaman said. "We've all heard that one."

"And there's something else you should know: I'm a diehard, that's what I am. Just ask them sometime. People around here will tell you Theodora Bascomb is a real old-time diehard. All of Coffee Hills knows it. But the sad truth is, the Johnny-and-Josephine-Come-Latelys don't know what I'm talking about, anymore than you do, Mr. Lionel Know-It-All Klingaman. But I'll tell you something, if I hadn't grown up in a strong family, with a wonderful, wonderful, wonderful mother and father . . . why, I wouldn't be what I am today."

If Yolanda had been a different sort of person, she would have pointed out that that was one-too-many 'wonderfuls'; but she kept her peace. Somewhere in the silence of the crowd around them, a man did *not* keep his peace, however, for he was heard to mutter: "Jesus, what a testimonial *that* is!"

But the old woman didn't hear. She appeared to be listening to voices inaudible to others. "My family was a wonderful, wonderful family," she went on with deadly insistence. "They were filled with love and kindness. And *were they smart?* Smart as tacks, I'll tell you. No sir, they don't make people like that anymore, because I can remember, as clear as if it were yesterday. Do you know what they had? They had *tradition*, that's what they had. Why, you wouldn't *believe* how many times they sprinkled their conversation with Latin!"

"It's true that Coffee Hills does have some wonderful families," Yolanda said, trying not to sound as if she were taking sides.

Teddie swept her arm to the side in a grand gesture. "I don't suppose it's ever occurred to you why families are so important."

"Go ahead and enlighten us," Klingaman told her. "We can hardly wait to hear."

"Why, families are *interesting*, that's what! Nobody seems to understand why families are important, but that's the reason: they're interesting."

"They could have said the same thing about smallpox and diphtheria," Klingaman told her. "But most people would agree that the world is better off without them."

"You speak of the world . . . but just tell me this: whatever in the world would we have to talk about if there weren't any families?"

Klingaman smiled. "Oh, I'm sure we'd manage to find something."

Teddie shook her head. "You're sure of just about everything, aren't you? Well, don't be so sure this time, because here you just might be wrong. You think I'm crazy when I say families are important because they're so interesting to talk about, don't you? But that's just because you've never thought of them that way. But let me ask you something: how else can you tell if something is important? There's no way. It's important if people talk about it, and if they don't talk about it, it's not important."

"I'm aware of the pragmatic argument."

"You're not aware of anything! All you can do is talk about it."

"That must make it important, then."

"That doesn't follow, and you know it!" Teddie cried, shaking her purse up and down. "*Everybody* knows that families are just wonderful because they're the source of so much gossip and stories. They just don't want to say so, but it's true. Oh, yes, it may sound crazy to you, mister; but that's just because you've never looked at it in the right way."

A brief perplexity drifted over Klingaman's expression. "Families are important because they do *that?*"

Teddie blinked heavily and nodded. "I'll tell you this much: if they ever do away with families, they'll do away with storyhood as we know it."

"Good God!" Klingaman said, then looked from one side to the other as if appealing to all those present to witness the irrationality of this old woman who was attacking him.

"Think of how many stories," Teddie said ponderously, shifting her weight forward as if she were about to spill herself out upon Klingaman, "have to do with families. Why, practically *all* the good ones do!"

"In case," Klingaman said, "it's never occurred to you, I'll try to make it clear to you right now: we don't exist as a race to provide material for stories!"

"Oh, *don't* we, now! Don't you ever be so sure! The thing about families that makes for gossip and good stories is exactly what makes them important. Put that in your pipe and smoke it. There, now: I can't say it any clearer than that, can I, Yolanda?"

"Well, I guess it does seem pretty clear," Yolanda said.

Klingaman rubbed his hair down with his hand. "Well, it would be interesting to see how you'd go about convincing the voters of such a thing."

"Voters? What do *voters* know?"

"I guess I've never heard of such a fantastic idea."

"Don't be so sure," Teddie said. "And don't ever try to tell that to a gossip."

"Why should anybody listen to gossips, for God's sake?"

"Who else is there to listen to? Who has anything more interesting to tell you? What's more worth hearing than *gossip?* And how can you have gossip without families? Just explain *that* to me, and I'll polish your shoes on the ramparts at daybreak."

"I can't believe I'm hearing all this!" Klingaman cried, turning from side to side and appealing to those around him. "I honest-to-God can't believe I'm hearing what this woman is saying!"

A man's voice said, "Theodora Bascomb comes from a very old Coffee Hills family."

"What in the hell," Klingaman cried, raising his arms to the sky, "does *that* have to do with anything?"

"You'd better listen to those who know," Teddie pronounced darkly, spacing her words with unnatural emphasis.

"Teddie," Yolanda said, tugging at her doughy arm, "please!"

"All right, dammit," she said, shaking her arm loose. "We'll go get a drink, if it means so much to you. I might as well have one too. That's what my dead husband used to call the 'old one-two'. He was a great joker, that man was."

"I'm sure of it," Yolanda said, signaling Ginny with a nod of her head.

"But that was only before he was dead," Ginny whispered back.

Teddie said, "My leg's hurting me something awful. It's a constant pain, did you know that? I think that man Klingaman has made it worse. Don't ever laugh about arthritis, because it's no laughing matter. I guess you two won't be too busy to help an old lady retire from the fray, will you?"

"Sure," Ginny said. "I mean, what the hell. I'm game."

Yolanda and Ginny took Teddie's arms and they commenced their long slow descent to where they had started.

"Why were you so quiet?" Yolanda whispered over Teddie's head.

"Couldn't get a word in edgeways. And as a matter of fact, I wouldn't have interrupted, anyway. Not for the world."

"Way, way," Teddie grumbled, tentatively planting her bad leg forward on a nasty bit of sod. "And exactly what is it you two are mumbling about, anyway, back there behind my head?"

Yolanda sighed. "Isn't that sunset just too gorgeous for words?"

"Listen," Teddie said, "I wouldn't listen to that anarchist if they paid me. You two can go and listen to his dumb lecture if you want to, but I'm going to have Hiram take me home, after I join you for a drink. Say what you will, but I know when I've had enough of people like that. Have them call Hiram, will you? I'll tell you something, that Klingaman has his head screwed on wrong, that fellow does. He's exactly what my dead husband would have called half troublemaker and half damned fool. I'm surprised you girls didn't notice."

There was a long pause while they maneuvered Teddie from the sod to the stepping stones back at the level where they had started.

"Oh, I guess maybe we noticed," Ginny said. "Didn't we, Yolanda? I mean, *I* noticed. Didn't you?"

Glancing at her once over Teddie's head, Yolanda smiled and nodded. "Well you might be partly right, after all."

"And I got the best of him, didn't I?" Teddie muttered.

"You certainly did," Ginny told her, patting her arm. "And I'll tell you one thing, Teddie: what you did would make a wonderful story. For those who know you, at least."

The old woman stopped. "See? What'd I tell you? I always knew that down underneath everything we were all family here at Coffee Hills!"

"You certainly did," Yolanda said, nodding.

"Are," Ginny said, mouthing the words past Teddie's back. "We certainly are."

Yolanda nodded and said, "Yes, *are!*"

But Yolanda didn't look over or say anything, since she was concentrating so hard on trying to get the old woman started once again, and help her put her feet in the right place so she wouldn't fall and hurt herself, and find herself lying there heavy and helpless on the beautiful green lawn in her beautiful shimmering satin blood-red dress.

Fiction Titles in the Series